*To my good friend
Beryl,
best wishes always
Adair Arlen*

THE HOUSE OF
TOMORROW

Adair Arlen

D1808038

"The House of Tomorrow," by Adair Arlen. ISBN 1-58939-460-7 (softcover), 1-58939-461-5 (electronic).

Published 2003 by Virtualbookworm.com Publishing Inc., P.O. Box 9949, College Station, TX, 77842, US. ©2003 Adair Arlen.

Manufactured in the United States of America.

To my sister Adair

For their souls dwell in the house of tomorrow, which you cannot visit, not even in your dreams.

Kahlil Gibran, *The Prophet*

Chapter 1

The man known as Paul Gregory put down the phone, adjusted his expression and turned to the redhead in the green dress who had been trying to attract his attention. He placed his hands on her shoulders, looked deeply into her eyes and softly sang, "Con te partiro..." to the accompaniment of the CD playing on the sound system.

"That's lovely, Paul."

"Do you know what it means?"

She sighed rapturously. "Tell me."

"Time to say goodbye."

"Oh, you!" Realizing she'd been tricked, she frowned. "No, it doesn't!"

"Close enough."

She smiled tantalizingly and persevered. "But Paul, the night's still young!"

"And you're so beautiful, I know." He hung a fur jacket over her shoulders as he gently guided her to the double doors of his fashionable nightspot.

"Can't we have just one more drink? We've hardly had a chance to talk all night."

"The law says no, Gloria. It's after hours—they'll close me down." He pushed one of the doors open and pointed. "Look, Bill's brought the car around. He's waiting to take you home."

She directed a scowl at the driver. "Damn."

"There'll be other nights." Paul took her elbow, walked her to the car, opened the door and helped her into the seat. He spoke a few words to the driver and waved them off.

Back inside, he locked the massive doors, strode to the nearest window and watched until the headlights swung out of the parking lot and disappeared behind the trees lining the road.

"Are you really worried about being closed down, Paulie?"

He glanced in the direction of the bar and grinned. "What do you think?"

"I think you just wanted to get rid of her."

"Bingo."

He was suddenly tired and sighed heavily as he stepped behind the bar to balance the cash register receipts, a task usually performed by his hostess, Jocselyn "Jan" Janiszewski, who was now running a cloth listlessly over the gleaming mahogany bar.

He was a tall man with the kind of athletic build that wore clothes easily and well. He wore his dark hair brushed back and held a ponytail in place by tightly looping his hair around itself. His dark eyes could be mesmerizing and at times menacing under straight heavy brows. Although his smiles were frequent, they held little warmth; they either served to take the place of words or to punctuate his conversation. On the rare occasions when he truly laughed, however, he did so heartily, displaying flashing, even, white teeth. He was an extraordinarily handsome man and, to all appearances, one favored by the gods.

As he worked, he moved quickly and economically, wasting no energy on unnecessary action. Having finished tallying the receipts, he distributed the cash to his various pockets, leaving a hundred dollars in the register to begin the new day.

Jan looked up from wiping down the bar. "Finished already, Paulie?"

"Thanks to this expensive computer slash cash register. Pour us a drink, will you?"

A moment later, carrying a small brandy snifter in each hand, she set one on the bar next to him. He looked up from the stack of checks he was endorsing with a hand stamp and eyed her appreciatively. Her short, golden curls framed a lovely heart-shaped face with dimpled cheeks and a pair of large cornflower blue eyes. Her delicate appearance, however, belied surprising strength and stamina. She and Paul had grown up in the same rough south side Chicago neighborhood and, when Paul moved to Southern Illinois, she had followed him. Although they had worked together for years and were approximately the same age, she was frequently taken for a teenager and Paul spoke to her as if to someone much younger. She was careful to publicly allow him the respect due an employer, but he became "Paulie" when they were alone. It was no secret she was in love with him.

He swirled the brandy and lifted it to his nose, then raised his glass to her. "Thanks, kid." She smiled and sipped, but made no response. He swept the stack of checks off the counter and into a bank pouch, stuffed it into a safe behind the bar, closed its door and twirled the combination lock. Draining his glass, he set it back on the bar.

"Paulie?"

He raised his eyes.

"Will I see you later?"

"Not tonight, kid. That other business is getting hot and we need to be ready, just in case." She turned away. He walked over to her, bent and kissed her neck. "I'll let you know."

She twisted until she faced him, straightening and standing on tiptoe to join both arms around his neck, forcing his face down to hers while she kissed his lips hungrily. After an instant he raised his hands to release her hold as he stepped back.

"Let's not start anything now, Jan . . ."

"Paulie, sometimes I think you're just a workaholic." She pretended to frown. "You know what they say: all work and no play..."

"And they're undoubtedly right. But this dull boy is out of here." He crossed to the kitchen door, pushed it open and shouted goodnight to the dishwasher and sweeper, who would let themselves out and lock up when they were finished. He strode to the front door and turned. "Careful when you leave, kid. You aren't going to stay much longer, are you?" Before she could answer, he said more softly, "It's late, Jan. Why don't you just crash upstairs tonight? You can go home in the morning."

"Without you, lover?" At his expression, she hurried to add, "I just might." She grinned and sang out, "Don't worry 'bout me—I'll get along." She had a powerful, low-pitched, husky voice, perfect for the torch songs she sang on weekend nights while Johnny played the grand piano in the cocktail lounge. Johnny Hughes washed dishes five nights a week to help support himself while earning a music degree at the university nearby.

Paul raised his right hand to his temple in mock salute, turned and left, securing the door behind him. He crossed the lot, unlocking the midnight blue Mitsubishi Galant with his keyless entry remote as he approached it. Although he maintained an expensively furnished apartment above his night club, he only used it occasionally when circumstances didn't permit travel to his home twenty-five miles away. He enjoyed the scenic drive to and from his secluded lake house; it provided the peace and serenity his soul seemed to crave.

Tonight the club had done its usual good Sunday business, but as he headed home Paul wasn't thinking of that. His expression was bemused as he remembered the first time he'd set foot in the club. It was known as the Blue Moon Saloon then and he'd been hired as a bartender by the elderly owner, Maureen McElroy, to discover who was robbing her. The Blue Moon was busy throughout the week and did a heavy weekend business, yet the receipts didn't reflect this. Paul determined within the first hour that the head bartender was leaving the cash drawer closed but unlocked and pocketing much of the cash. At Maureen's insistence, Paul stayed on at the club as combination host, bartender and sometime bouncer. Maureen had charmed him and apparently he had in turn charmed her because she left the club to him in her will when she died two years later.

He pulled his thoughts back to the present, marveling as he always did at the sight before him as he swung round a sharp curve and the dark glassy sweep of Devil's Kitchen Lake sprang into view. Moonlight shimmered on the water, the dense woods formed a dramatic black backdrop and the silence was absolute. An abrupt twist in the road and the lake was lost to view. He slowed the car at this point; his headlights often caught an unexpected deer leaping into the road in this heavily forested section. After a few more turns, he swung off onto a narrow gravel track to the right that swept down to his isolated home at the edge of Little Grassy Lake.

Once inside, he removed his jacket, tossing it onto a sofa as he crossed to a small bar set up in a corner. He poured an inch and a half of brandy into a tall glass, walked a few steps to the kitchen and topped it from the soda siphon he kept in the refrigerator. Returning to the living room, he switched off the lights, opened the blinds and dropped into a black leather Charles Eames chair, his favorite, by the large front window. He swung his legs onto the hassock before him and leaned back with a sigh. His view to the lake was unimpeded; the utter tranquility of the water and deep woods never failed to soothe his spirit and soon, his unfinished drink on the window sill, he got up and went to his bedroom. He let his clothes lay where they dropped and when he got into bed, he quickly fell asleep and dreamed of the girl he'd seen with Sam Meredith at his club earlier the night before.

This time Meredith wasn't there. In his dream they were in an opulent ballroom and he, Pál Gregor, was dancing with her. They were performing a fantastically intricate tango in perfect unison. Others on the floor stopped dancing in order to watch Pál and the girl. People applauded. Soon a crowd had formed around them and the orchestra began to play a waltz. She looked up at him and her face was exquisite, sculpted with the high cheekbones he'd always found attractive. Her body felt so right, fitting perfectly into his arms. Her sparkling blue eyes held an exotic upward tilt and her lips smiled enchantingly as they danced faster and faster in the waltz, her dark hair glossy and flying free as they spun. The tempo accelerated. She was laughing and so was he, but suddenly he was seized by the terrible fear that he'd be unable to maintain the ever-increasing pace. He'd grown dizzy as they whirled and he began to panic, afraid he'd lead them both into a fall. He tried to tell her to save herself, but she was laughing still as he lost his balance and they crashed to the floor.

He was awake instantly, humiliation washing over him in waves. He knew it had been a dream, but his heart was pounding and his breath came in quick gasps.

———————

It was three o'clock in the morning and she lay awake in her bed with the crisp white sheets, her head cradled in the large pillow covered by the lace-trimmed case with the letters LJG embroidered in script on its hem. She'd been trying to sleep for the past two hours, but the familiar worries and fears played themselves out again and again on the screen of her memory. Vexed, she sat up and managed to discern the numbers on the square clock in the silver frame atop the lingerie chest. She was reluctant to take sleeping pills, afraid she'd develop a dependency. Sighing, she lay back.

Turning her head slightly on the pillow, she gazed at the wall where moonlight created ever-changing patterns of the moving leaves outside her window. On a breezy night they looked as though they were dancing in the moonlight. She'd learned long ago that if she concentrated her attention on the repetitively moving leaves this effort would enable her to relax and finally drift off to sleep. The ploy worked again and, as she slept, she dreamed of a man from another century, his long hair pulled back and caught at the nape of his neck—a man she was sure she'd seen before, perhaps as recently as yesterday, someone she instinctively felt was vaguely menacing. After she awoke, a feeling of unease remained. Why, she asked herself, should she dream of a stranger, someone whose name she'd never even heard?

A few hours later Liliane Greening pulled her five-year-old Chevy Corsica into her allotted parking place, entered the building, walked quickly down the hallway and opcned the door marked Research. The clock on her credenza was chiming the half-hour as she hung her coat in the closet. She performed her office-opening routine feeling somewhat bemused, the curious dream still on her mind. The insistent buzz of her desk phone broke the silence and her office day began.

Later that evening in their favorite restaurant, Le Champignon, Lili sat across the table from Sam Meredith as his gaze held hers. Looking at him, she noticed again the perfect symmetry of his features, how his straw-colored hair complemented his clear green eyes, the way he wore his obviously expensive clothes with careless elegance and she realized just how many women in this college town must envy her. Not only was Professor Sam Meredith tall and handsome, he was witty and urbane and, despite his relative youth, at age thirty-three he held the prestigious position as Chairman of the university's Department of Forestry. Although the Merediths owned the largest bank in town and Sam was a director, he had chosen a career other than banking.

Lili lifted her champagne glass by its stem and twirled it between her fingers, watching the bubbles rise. *I'm happy,* she thought, *can this person be me? Sam is looking at me as if he cares, really cares about me. I know he does, it's just so hard to believe that I'm here with him in this place at this time. Right now the hardest thing I have to do is believe that this is real, that it's actually happening to me, that it's all not just a dream.*

"Lili? Where are you? I've been saying..."

"Oh, Sam, I'm sorry. I was just thinking."

"You've nothing to be sorry for. Thinking what?"

"How lucky I am. How much I'm enjoying tonight. How much I like being with you. When all this will end." She stopped and bit her lip; she hadn't meant to verbalize that last thought.

"End? Why should it end?" He motioned the waiter to refill their glasses. "You're a paradox, you know? You're usually an up kind of person, yet at times you're fatalistic."

"Oh, I don't agree, Sam. I consider myself a pragmatist. You have to be realistic in this life or you'll get shot down every time." She fleetingly wondered how she, of all people, could be saying these things when she had some very serious dreams she had every hope of achieving.

"You're saying, 'don't expect too much for fear of being disappointed,' aren't you?"

"Sure, that's the way it is." She slanted a look at him, adding, "Of course, if your name is Meredith you can expect and demand anything."

He laughed. "I'm not going to play your little game and I'm not going to let you lead me away from the subject, the topic of which is: Why doesn't Lili Greening think enough of herself?"

She said nothing and tried to stifle a sigh.

"You're a beautiful—yes, beautiful—woman, damn it." And he smiled the lazy smile she loved as he added, "With a terrific figure. I don't care if that does embarrass you. I'm tired of hearing you disparage yourself. Or," he grinned wickedly, "is it false modesty?"

"Just because I don't fish for compliments..."

"No, of course I don't think that, you little fool," he quickly added at her look of feigned reproach. He sipped his champagne, as he seemed to weigh a decision. Apparently having reached it, he put his glass down and rested his chin on his fists. "You know, you have the loveliest lips—I'd like to kiss them right now."

Lili squirmed and sighed ostentatiously.

"Okay, let's make a list. You're—what? About five-six? You weigh..." He laughed. "Never mind—I've been around long enough to know women always lie about their weight. In your case, it doesn't matter anyway. Anyone can see you've got a great body."

"Please, Sam... ."

He disregarded her interruption. "Your hair is dark brown, very dark and very—shiny. No, that's not the word, is it? Glossy, that's it—your hair is glossy. And what style do you call it where your hair turns under at your shoulders?"

"Sam, this is embar..."

"No, don't interrupt. We're listing all your good points. I'm going to get rid of that complex of yours once and for all."

She was affronted. "I don't have a complex."

"Okay, you don't have a complex. But nevertheless, I don't think you give yourself enough credit."

"Credit for what, Sam? Just because I don't flaunt..."

"No, thank God, you don't. And I'm not saying you should. I guess I should be grateful—you'd be pretty hard to take if you strutted around like some women I know." He smiled into her eyes and she felt herself glow with pleasure. "Now, where were we? Let's see," and he sang softly, "Your lips, your eyes, your teeth, your hair are in a class beyond compare; you're the loveliest girl..." He broke off and laughed at her intense discomfort.

"No, let me finish. Let's see, we've discussed your hair—what comes next? Ah, yes, your eyes. Your eyes are blue, dark blue, and they're set so they tilt up at the outer corners. Your eyebrows kind of arch so they—what's the word? Conform, they conform to your eyes."

"Are you through yet?"

"Your eyelids give you a sultry kind of look, did you know that? I can see you don't approve—Lili Greening is not sultry and nobody should think she is, is that it? Misleading or not, it's there, that look."

"Sam, could we *please* change the subject?"

"Not yet. I've still got to talk about your—what comes next?"

"Nothing, I'm leaving."

She started to rise and he put out a hand to stop her, as he continued, "Oh, yes, your teeth."

"My teeth?" She winced, "Uh oh . . ."

"Yes, your teeth—they're . . ."

"I know. Protuberant."

"No, not protuberant—they're just a little . . ."

"Prominent?"

"Well, yes, I guess that's what they are. A little. In a charming way . . ."

She burst out laughing. "Why, Dr. Samuel C. Meredith! I've never seen you at a loss for words before. I should let you go on and give you enough rope to hang yourself." Another paroxysm of laughter shook her until finally she was able to stop, catch her breath, and wipe her eyes on the corner of her napkin. "Tell me, should I stop smiling? No more teeth; how's this?" She gave him a demure smile with closed lips.

"What I was trying to say—and obviously not doing a very good job about it—is that I love your smile. Your teeth are just off enough to be adorable."

"But you just said they're prominent."

"Well, no, that's not it—you have this cute sort of overbite. You're even more—er, provocative—because of it." He ran a finger under his collar. "How's that for a neat escape?"

"Narrow, but neat."

His eyebrows shot up. "I know who you remind me of. It's been bothering me ever since I first saw you. Have you ever seen that great film noir from the 40s, what's it called—"Laura?" That's it, Gene Tierney played Laura! She was beautiful; that's who you remind me of!"

"Oh, Sam, do you really mean it?" She stopped, her expression changing to a knowing look as she nodded, "Not so fast, buddy. You're putting me on and I almost fell for it."

"No, really, Lili. Your smile is the same."

"Talk about making a silk purse from a sow's ear. But that's a real compliment, so this time I've got to say thank you."

"You're welcome. Now, let's see—I think we need to talk about your cheeks now . . ."

"My cheeks?" She quickly glanced from side to side to be sure no one could hear and hissed, "Sam, will you stop? This is embarrassing."

"Did I ever tell you I love your high cheekbones?"

"No, of course not. Nobody has."

"Consider it said. I love the way you look and everything about you. You've got to understand you're a knockout, honey. Loosen up and live a little."

"You're right, Dr. Meredith. I'm going to obey your orders and start right now by ordering the lobster." Lili sparkled as she said it; if he wanted her to sparkle, that's what she was going to do. She took a long swallow of champagne, gave him a perfunctory smile, picked up her evening bag and excused herself from the table.

A moment later as she pushed open the ladies' room door, she almost collided with one of the loveliest women she'd ever seen. She was taller than Lili and wore an ivory sheath of a dress, her blonde hair pulled back into a classic chignon. Her face was a perfect oval, her grey eyes placid and assured under delicately arched brows. The two women smiled at one another automatically as they passed at the door.

Peering into the mirror, Lili washed and dried her hands, touched up her lipstick, then searched for the beauty Sam had just spoken of. Even if he'd been shamelessly flattering her, it was still a great ego trip. She thought her best feature was her mouth, her smile inherited from her mother. She was puzzled that the terrible events of two years ago didn't show on her face; she looked, somehow, unmarked by them and appeared younger than her twenty-nine years.

As she crossed the dining room to rejoin Sam, she passed the beautiful blonde gesturing and talking animatedly to the man Lili only knew as the mysterious stranger of her dream. Surprise made her almost stop in her tracks. She pretended to stumble and caught the back of an empty chair. She tried not to stare, but couldn't help herself as for the first time she saw him laughing and he was handsome indeed, his dark good looks no longer menacing.

As she reached their table and Sam rose to hold her chair for her, she said, "Don't look now, but in a few moments will you casually glance at the couple sitting next to the fireplace? Tell me if you know who they are."

Sam turned around immediately, at the same time the dark stranger turned to look at them. Acutely uncomfortable, Lili feigned interest elsewhere.

"Lili, my sweet, that is none other than Paul Gregory. Don't tell me you haven't heard of him?"

"Why? Is he famous?"

"Infamous is more like it. He's the owner of Pal's—you know—we were there last week, on Sunday." He turned, as if to make sure no one was eavesdropping, then leaned forward as he lowered his voice. "He's involved in some sort of underworld activities, at least that's the rumor. A while back, they say, he killed a man, something about blackmail and a woman."

"Killed a man! Why is he free and walking around?" She nodded, remembering. "I knew I'd seen him before. It must have been at Pal's." She didn't mention her dream.

He frowned. "You're certainly attracted by some odd types."

"Sam, I'm not attracted. It's just that I keep seeing him when we're out and I wondered who he is, that's all. And don't you think that girl he's with is the most exquisite creature you've ever seen?"

He looked at her and grimly shook his head. "No, I don't. But I'll admit she is good looking and she'd be the first to agree." He broke off and reflected for a few beats. "But you're right—she is physically beautiful. And rich. In case you don't know, that is Cynthia Compton, of the St. Louis Comptons, well-known patrons of the arts." He recited the words as a litany. "Your boy certainly can pick 'em." He pierced an asparagus spear with his fork.

"Don't call him my boy. I think he's scary. If the Comptons are such important people, why do you think she goes out with him? Don't her parents object?"

"Because Ms. Cynthia does as she damn well pleases. And she probably figures being seen with Paul Gregory is dangerous and exciting." Hearing the unaccustomed note of asperity in Sam's voice, Lili shot him a glance, catching his quick frown. He immediately forced a smile and changed the subject.

They'd finished their meal and were drinking coffee. She'd been laughing, telling him about the hilarious book she was reading, then noticed that, although he was observing her intently, he wasn't really listening to her. She stopped talking.

"Do you want to tell me what's on your mind, Sam?"

He smiled the lazy smile she loved, his eyes lighting his face. "You, my darling. Do you think it would be presumptuous of me to take you away from here and hope for maybe a nightcap at your place?"

"What a good idea," she responded with a mental frown. The thought of yet another downward spiral in her life frightened her. Although she'd recently begun to believe she might have a future after all, she was still picking up the pieces of her broken life.

As Sam helped her with her coat, she glanced around the crowded restaurant, nodding and waving as she recognized several acquaintances. Her glance fell on the table near the fireplace and her eyes met the dark steady gaze of Paul Gregory as he helped the blonde from her chair. Lili remembered the first time she'd seen him; she'd thought him ruggedly handsome—in a saturnine sort of way. She'd originally seen him full face, his dark hair brushed back, his sideburns cut medium length. She'd been a bit put off by the ponytail, considering it outré, somehow affected. His sardonic expression dispelled that idea, however.

Waiting by the door while Sam went for his car, she was able to observe Paul Gregory as he left the restaurant with the Compton woman on his arm. To label him handsome wasn't adequate; his exceptional good looks included something more, an indefinable magnetism. His build was muscular, yet he walked with an easy grace she found disturbingly masculine. He turned once to look back at her. She felt sure he'd known her eyes would be on him.

Lili awoke at four o'clock the following morning, just four hours after she'd fallen asleep. No moonlight this time; the sky was overcast; hence, no moonlight and no leaf-dancing to watch. Tossing from side to side, she finally admitted that on this occasion she wouldn't win, wouldn't be able to get back to sleep.

In spite of herself, her thoughts turned to the events and problems of two years ago, the outcome of which still plagued her dreams. She'd found herself in one heartbreaking predicament after another, helpless to protect her home, her marriage, unable to save her mother from the insidious cancer that claimed her. She was left feeling bereft and hopeless, totally alone.

Lili relived the pain of those days whenever she allowed herself to dwell upon the past; she normally wouldn't tolerate those bleak, black thoughts, but they enveloped her when she was tired and hadn't the mental strength to ward them off. Then the sorrow—the loss—engulfed her.

But, Lili was quick to assure herself, these bouts of despair didn't come so frequently now that Sam Meredith had befriended her.

Samuel Chasen Meredith was everything any woman would want: a wonderful companion, good looking, a witty conversationalist with an easy humor, he was welcome in any group. He was also the scion of the renowned Meredith family, one of the older, wealthy families in the area, and his home, Meredith Manor, was known far and wide as possibly the loveliest in the southern half of the state. Sam lived at the mansion with his father, an older half-sister, his younger brother and, of course, a staff of servants. The parties held at Meredith Manor were celebrated and people maneuvered to get their names on the invitation lists.

Sam's membership in the legendary Meredith family kept people frequently trying to curry favor with him. His had been a life of privilege and easy friendships, Lili had been warned, and a series of brokenhearted and disappointed females were still waiting for him to return their calls. *I'm glad Sam isn't spoiled by all the attention he gets,* Lili often thought. *He's just such a genuinely nice guy, he's almost too good to be true.*

Chapter 2

A few days later, Lili heaved a sigh, raised her arms over her head in a luxuriant stretch and pushed back from her desk. The project she was exploring promised to keep her searching the Internet for the remainder of the week and she suddenly yearned to give her eyes a rest. She'd really much rather be searching the library stacks, as she always preferred a book to a computer screen.

She swiveled her chair around and leaned back in it as she looked out the window. Although still the month of March, the approach of spring was apparent in many ways—the purple and white heads of crocus looked as if they'd just burst from the ground, massed daffodils showed up as pools of butter yellow in the distance and myriad trees were liberally covered with pink magnolia blossoms. For as far as she could see, thousands upon thousands of the flowers all faced in the same direction, toward the sun.

A large university with a sprawling campus, Southern Illinois University had been uniquely landscaped for maximum appeal, having been cleverly designed and planted with native trees, shrubs and blooming flora. Having grown up in the enormous city of Chicago, Lili never ceased to marvel that here, in the very same state, such magnificent natural beauty could be found everywhere. From the rolling hills of countless acres of fruit orchards soon to burst forth in varying shades of pink and white, to the abundance of forests and both natural and man-made lakes, the university nestled just sixty miles above the confluence of the Mississippi and Ohio Rivers. Even the weather was different; the climate was ideal for outdoor activities all year around. Lili shivered involuntarily as she recalled the many times on Chicago's North Michigan Avenue when she'd had to protect her face from the extreme cold. The weather in southern Illinois was milder, softer, kinder. And now with the advent of spring, life was getting better every day.

———————

She'd been given a pair of tickets to *Fiddler on the Roof*. It was being performed by the university's drama department and at last she could treat Sam to an evening out. He'd been a bit late picking her up and they could hear the chorus singing "Tradition" as, hand in hand, they ran up the stairs and through the large entrance doors. By the time the usher had shown them to their seats they'd gaped at one another in astonishment, their eyes wide.

"I don't know why I was so surprised," Sam said later as they faced each other across their table at Champignon. "I guess I just expected something more..."

"Amateur? I must admit, I did, too. But it wasn't, was it? I had no idea these kids were so accomplished, so professional."

Their waiter approached and filled their glasses with wine. They toasted each other silently and began to sip.

Sam set his glass down and said, "The family is planning a house party next weekend, Lili—Friday night through dinner Sunday." He touched his napkin to his lips and studied her. "I want you to be there."

"Oh, Sam, I'd love to come."

He smiled. "I think it's time you met my family, and," he added, his smile fading. "I think it's time they met you."

How can I reply to that? She kept quiet and let the silence stretch between them until she could bear it no longer. She cleared her throat nervously. "How large a party will it be?"

"Just us—Dad, Drew, Crystal and me—and two or three other couples. It'll be casual. We'll spend most of our time around the pool and patio."

"Pool?" In spite of herself, Lili shuddered.

"No, it's still too cool to swim, even with the heater on, but we hang out on the enclosed patio a lot. There's a bar out there and it's comfortable. So bring the kind of clothes for that and maybe some jeans and a sweater. And pack some walking shoes."

"When should I come? Saturday? When will the party begin?"

"Oh, my sister Crystal will give you the details. She's sort of our family hostess for parties and stuff, you know. I'll tell her to give you a call." He reached out to cover her hand with his; then he smiled and her heart turned over.

Later that night Lili lay awake well past midnight, her thoughts churning. She must do some homework on the Meredith clan. They were super achievers, she'd heard, highly motivated for success. She'd only met Drew on two short occasions and had yet to meet Stephen, Sam's father; and, of course, his sister Crystal was an unknown quantity. However, they had been a prominent family locally since Reconstruction days. There should be a wealth of information available at the university library and, after all, she was a professional researcher, wasn't she?

The week sped by and suddenly it was Friday afternoon. Lili's work was finished for the day, her dog had been given into the care of to her friend Angela Hoenig for the weekend, and Lili was waiting in her office for the receptionist to notify her that Sam had arrived. Crystal had duly phoned with assurances that the weekend would be casual. Lili had packed her best piece of luggage this morning containing clothing for the weekend.

As she waited for Sam, she went over the facts she'd learned about the Merediths. In eighteen sixty-six, a few short weeks after the end of the Civil War, thirty-three year old Logan Meredith had acquired a grand house on a fifty-five acre site, the property where Meredith Manor now stood, and he, his wife and month-old son, Richard, moved in as soon as the unfortunate previous owners could be evicted from their property. She supposed any Yankee with a large amount of cash at the end of the War Between the States looked suspicious. Although the word *carpetbagger* wasn't actually used to describe Logan Meredith, the long-ago newspaperman's meaning came through loud and clear. As the gravestones in the local cemeteries attested, allegiances from this part of the state had been divided between the North and the South.

She rehearsed the Meredith lineage—names and dates. Primogeniture reigned. At Logan's demise in eighteen ninety-nine, his thirty-three year old son, Richard, became head of the family until nineteen thirty-two when he died at age sixty-six. Richard's son, Lionel, led the family until his death in nineteen sixty-five when his son, Stephen, the present family patriarch, took over.

Sam's father, Stephen, had married twice. Before he inherited, he'd married Nora Davies and in 1962 his eldest child, Crystal, was born. The marriage didn't last and he and Pamela Chasen were married in1964. Samuel Chasen Meredith was born to Pamela in 1965, the year the thirty-three-year-old Stephen gained control of the Meredith fortune. Sam's brother, Andrew, was born in 1971. Pamela died two years later, cause of death not provided.

As the years intervened, more and more acreage was acquired so that the family now owned over two thousand acres of rolling hills, most of them forested, with wildlife and streams meandering throughout. Although they maintained a staff of indoor servants, there were also several gardeners, who kept the landscape perfectly groomed and, additionally, grew an abundance of fruit and vegetables for the family's consumption.

It was eerily coincidental, according to Lili's further calculations, that in each Meredith generation the eldest son, in his turn, took control of the family at the age of thirty-three and died when sixty-six. It occurred to her that Stephen might be understandably worried now that he was sixty-five and his eldest son had recently celebrated his thirty-third birthday.

She jumped involuntarily as her intercom suddenly buzzed, then grinned at her own foolishness. Sam had arrived and the long-anticipated weekend at Meredith Manor was about to begin.

Sam's white Jaguar XJ8 emerged from the mile-long tree-lined approach to Meredith Manor, swept up the curving drive and came to a stop at the foot of a fifty-foot-wide flight of steps. Heavy, ornate wrought iron balustrades flanked each side. Lili involuntarily caught her breath at first sight of the majestic three story mansion with its eight massive white Corinthian columns each rising two floors as they marched across the façade of the dark red brick structure.

Sam blew the car's horn and the massive front door opened. A woman in a black and white uniform came out and took Lili's suitcase from Sam, who said, "Put this in the yellow suite, please, Margaret."

Instead of taking Lili into the house, Sam led her around the far side along a gravel path, where they eventually reached a large flag-stoned patio, beyond which she saw an enormous octagonal swimming pool, still covered with its winter tarp. Two men and three women were laughing and conversing, draped in lounge chairs, each with a small table nearby to hold drinks. Another man was standing, plate in hand, at a long white-clothed table spread with fruit, cheeses, bread sticks and vegetables nestled among bowls of flavored dips and spreads. Assorted bottles of gin, vodka and tonic were placed at one end of the table, a dish of quartered limes, an ice bucket and glasses ranged alongside. Lili thought it reminiscent of a scene of the good life from a Scott Fitzgerald novel. They all turned to watch her and Sam as they approached.

Tucking her hand under his arm, Sam led Lili across the patio where he introduced Jim Evans with Cynthia Compton, both monochromatically dressed in beige—she in a beige linen pants suit, he in tan chinos and a beige cashmere pullover. Lili and Cynthia smiled at each other perfunctorily as they had when they'd met at the ladies' room door in the restaurant.

The fair-haired man standing at the food table wore a gray sweater tied around his shoulders over a long-sleeved blue polo shirt. His name was Peter something and he was married to the pretty brown-haired girl in the lavender pants and white sweater. Lili couldn't remember her name.

Sam's sister Crystal was stunning, a statuesque brown-eyed brunette wearing a long sleeved velveteen top over matching pants the color of fine old sherry. Large golden topaz jewels shone at each ear. The taller Crystal looked down for a moment into Lili's eyes, then she turned, her hand outstretched to a wiry, dark-haired man whose light eyes were emphasized by his deeply tanned skin.

"Manuel Romero, Liliane Greening." Lili held out her hand and Crystal didn't bother to hide her amusement. Lili wondered what she could have done wrong. "Manolo, you already know my brother."

"Romero."

"So good to see you again, Dr. Meredith."

His speech was heavily accented. When Sam didn't encourage the use of his first name, Lili glanced at him quickly, but he kept his expression bland and took her arm to lead her to the long table. She noted then that his lips were set in a firm line. He turned and looked away from the company for a moment and took a deep breath. When he turned toward her again, Lili was relieved to see his customary good humor had returned. He poured a drink for each of them and said, "Let's walk. I'll give you a brief tour before dinner."

As they walked, Lili asked about Manuel Romero. "Obviously, you don't like him, Sam."

"He's a polo player Crystal met somewhere. Playing polo costs money and he doesn't have any, so he mooches off her. He's a parasite. I made the mistake of letting her know I think he's a bum, so she brings him over periodically to annoy me."

"He wouldn't sponge if she didn't let him, would he?"

"You're right; Crystal will always do as she pleases and there's not a thing I can do about it."

"Are you worried that she's serious about him?"

He chuckled. "No, I guess I'm not. She gets a kick out of pushing my buttons and I always seem to oblige her." He called Lili his precious little pragmatist, put an arm around her shoulders and pulled her close.

Many hours later Lili closed her eyes and pictured again the group scene on the patio and knew she'd never forget it; it was burnt into her memory. She'd been dazzled. What beautiful, self-assured, clever people! It could be fun to join this exclusive company. They'd been welcoming and courteous, had urged her to talk about herself, and she'd enjoyed doing so. It was easy to be enthusiastic because she loved her work. When she felt she'd held center stage long enough, she'd asked Cynthia what she did for a living. A silence had fallen on the group and Sam had finally said, "Cyn does some volunteer work." *Oh, man,* Lili thought, *I've put my foot in it with this bunch. I'll bet none of them has a paying job!*

Stephen Meredith had joined them for cocktails on the terrace before dinner and, when they went inside, he took his place at the head of the table. His height was average, his light colored hair beginning to silver and thin on top, his features were regular and fairly blunt. Lili thought he looked sleek and rather smug; he seemed enormously pleased with himself. He liked talking about himself and told a series of stories about people Lili didn't know and which she found difficult to follow, so she allowed her mind to wander. She was interested to notice how Sam and his brother, Drew, an irritable, impatient edition of Sam, deferred to their father. Stephen was indeed the patriarch of Meredith Manor and, Lili observed, seemed energetic and in perfect health. Not as though, she mused, he were getting ready to pass the torch to the next in line. He laughed and joined in lively conversation with the others at the table, and treated her politely, though not effusively.

Lili had been charmed when she'd seen her rooms—as they were throughout the mansion, the ceilings here, too, were high with ornately carved moldings. The wallpaper featured alternating two-inch wide stripes of lemon yellow and white throughout the bedroom and into the adjoining bathroom. The canopy and bedspread were of white polished chintz patterned with small, green-leafed yellow flowers and the dressing table was flounced with the same fabric. Pillows splashed with a fresh green ivy print provided contrast. The gleaming hardwood floor with its yellow and white throw rugs in the bedroom gave way to large white ceramic tiles in the bathroom. Billowing white curtains more opaque than sheer covered French doors that opened onto a veranda overlooking the pool and patio a floor below.

Lili sank into an overstuffed boudoir chair upholstered in eggshell damask, her feet on a matching footstool. The sheets and pillowcases proved to be as elegant as she could have hoped. She loved to have the very best in bed linens. Her mother had always splurged when it came to sheets and towels and each year Lili found herself looking forward to the January white sales. Luxuriating in splendid bedclothes was one way she could afford to indulge herself.

The day was warm for the time of year—it was still only late March and Lili opened the French doors to permit the warm breeze. Voices carried up from the patio and she could identify Drew's loud voice in contrast to Crystal's languorous and sophisticated drawl.

"What is Sam doing with *her,* Drew?"

"My big brother doesn't keep me informed of how and why he does the things he does, Crystal dear. You, of all people, should be aware of that."

They said something Lili couldn't catch, then laughed. Their voices merged with others, as the McDonalds joined them on the patio. Lili was stunned to hear herself being discussed disparagingly by Crystal, yet at the same time mentally applauded herself for finally remembering Mimi's and Peter's surname. She had always been hopeless with names, but was making a concerted effort to improve.

She was acutely aware of the condescension in Crystal's voice as she'd spoken of her. The meaning was all too clear: what could Professor Meredith possibly see in the likes of Liliane Greening? *Indeed!,* she seethed. Although she resented and was hurt by the implication, Lili figured if having a big bankroll would make her important to people like Crystal, maybe by those terms she was right; Lili Greening was a nobody.

She called to mind her mother's admonition: *It's a good thing we don't see ourselves as others see us.* Because having overheard Crystal's words of a few moments ago, what had begun as a wonderful weekend suddenly became an ordeal. There was still today—Saturday—and tomorrow to get through somehow before she could escape. She'd had such high hopes for herself and Sam as a couple and now she ridiculed herself for being a gullible fool; she should have known things wouldn't work out the way she'd begun to hope they might.

Never mind, she'd put a good face on the situation and that would see her through; she had nothing to be ashamed of. It wasn't Sam she'd heard talking about her. He wasn't there with them on the patio. He'd whispered he loved her last night as they'd parted at her bedroom door. Incredibly, Sam Meredith had told her he loved her. She raised her chin defiantly. *So who cared what the rest of them thought?*

As she'd feared, there seemed to be a blight on the remainder of the weekend. Even the weather seemed to duplicate her mood as the day became overcast and a cold wind from the north was joined by sporadic rain. This meant no more gatherings on the patio and the party withdrew to the warmth indoors.

Lili was delighted to discover the immense game room situated in the house's lower level. It looked to be at least thirty feet in one direction and forty in the other. At one end an English billiards table commanded attention and was lit by a spectacular Tiffany lamp suspended from a heavy chain. Cynthia Compton was playing table tennis with Drew Meredith at the opposite end of the room, Drew slamming the ball on the very edge of the table so hard it careened off to one side. Cynthia laughed, dropped her paddle and held her hands up in surrender. A scowling Jim Evans, her escort for the weekend, slouched alone on the green leather bench along the wall.

Progressive jazz emanated from the speakers situated in the game room's four corners. Sam led her to a stool at the long ceramic-tiled bar and straddled the stool next to her.

"What will have to drink, honey? A Coke? Scotch, a martini? I know you like vodka and tonic. Or how about some champagne?"

Lili giggled. "It sounds like an alcoholic's dream. But it's turned cold outside, so I think I'll have some scotch to warm up."

"I think I'll join you." He got up, walked behind the bar, took two heavy square glasses off the shelf and, reaching into an icemaker, scooped a few cubes into each. Then he lifted a bottle from under the bar and poured each of them a generous amount, adding a splash of water to Lili's glass.

Positioning himself next to her again, he turned to look into her eyes, as he raised his glass to hers. "Here's to us, babe."

"Really, Sam?"

"You're supposed to drink with me while saying something like, 'I'll drink to that,' or 'to us.' What do you mean by 'really?"'

"It wasn't very appropriate, was it? Sorry."

"Lili, sweetheart, you must stop being sorry about everything. You're too apologetic. You've no need to be." He smiled to soften his words.

About to say 'sorry' again, Lili caught herself just in time and turned as she heard Crystal's low chuckle at her side.

"Maybe she does have something to apologize for, Sam. How well do you really know her?" Crystal's challenging gaze gave the lie to her teasing laughter.

Lili froze, then turned to Crystal and smiled sweetly. "I don't think I understand your meaning. Would you explain, please?"

Sam, in contrast, stopped smiling, while Lili smoldered with indignation. Crystal opened her mouth to respond, but the moment was saved by the McDonalds joining them and asking what was the drink of choice and, thanks to Lili's real effort to ignore Crystal's remark, soon everyone was at ease and laughing again.

When they were eventually called for dinner, Lili found herself dreading the impending meal, but Crystal's attention was elsewhere and everyone seemed to be on his and her good behavior. The remainder of the evening was uneventful, but Lili was grateful when the time came to say goodnight to the company. When she closed her bedroom door, she leaned against it and sighed with relief.

Sunday dawned bright and crisply cold. Lili and Sam had agreed to meet early in the breakfast room and she was relieved to see him sitting alone at a table by the door when she entered. He stood and she went to him, kissing him lightly on the cheek. Taking her hand, Sam led her to the sideboard and handed her a warm plate.

"I'll lead the way. Help yourself to anything you like. That table over there's all set up for us. If you want anything you don't see, just mention it to Alexander." He motioned to a tall smiling man looking to be in his late sixties who was standing by the door to the kitchen. He wore the black and white uniform of the Meredith staff.

After a breakfast of orange and grapefruit sections, sausages, waffles and maple syrup followed by coffee, Sam asked Lili if she would take a walk with him.

"Yes, I'd like to get some exercise after a meal like we've just had."

"Get bundled up, it's cold out there today. And I hope you brought some kind of sturdy walking shoes or boots that you won't mind getting muddy."

"I did, Sam. You told me to, remember? I always do as I'm told." She grinned. "I'll meet you on the patio in about fifteen minutes."

Sam hadn't arrived yet when Lili reached the patio. She could see part of a pond through a gateway in the high stone wall joining the side of the house and noticed several plots of earth freshly turned over. She assumed these were soon to be planted as part of the household's vegetable gardens. A wide, beautifully-kept lawn, edged with formal box hedges and gravel paths, was flanked by a professional croquet lawn on one side and by both grass and hard tennis courts on the other.

The view from the rear of the house was breathtaking. The far side of the main expanse of lawn appeared to blend into pasture land with small clusters of trees whose lower branches had been carefully trimmed at head height by a free-ranging herd of Guernseys.

"Sorry I kept you waiting, honey. I ran into Drew." Sam gave her a hug as he joined her, but didn't elaborate. He took her hand and they started walking.

She could see no sign of any fencing and was beginning to think the animals had incredibly somehow been trained to stay in their pasture away from the house. However, rounding the last corner at the bottom of the lawn, the path suddenly gave way to a narrow wooden bridge without railings over a six foot deep ditch retained by a brick wall on the garden side and sloping naturally toward the pasture on the lower side. Sam noticed her look of surprise and explained the reason for the seemingly pointless excavation and somewhat precarious means of crossing it. Apparently, in the last century the original builders of the ha-ha, which is how it curiously came to be known, wished to have an unblocked view into the distant periphery of their estate without the unattractive fencing necessary to keep the foraging animals out. The ditch couldn't be seen from the house and it acted as a fence.

Once Sam and Lili had safely negotiated the nearest crossing, the ground gradually sloped to a fast-running stream. Sam led the way across large stepping stones, extending his hand to help Lili as she leapt to the other side, avoiding the muddy areas caused by the cattle coming down to drink. From then on it was a gentle uphill grade for almost a mile to the nearest ridge still in sight of the main house. The last hundred yards to the ridge were quite steep. Breathless, Lili finally joined Sam at the top of the tree-covered hill.

"Sam, you set a brutal pace. What's the hurry?"

"I just don't feel like strolling along, do you? This is a relief after being cooped up inside yesterday."

Lili agreed, but couldn't reply, mortified that she was panting from the last climb.

"Sam," she asked when she finally caught her breath, "do you know how long we've been walking?"

"About an hour."

"Is all this land yours?"

He laughed. "All this and then some. Why?"

"I think it's beautiful. There are so many hills and streams and really gorgeous big trees. So many birds. It's heavenly."

"You haven't even seen my primary interest, the stands of walnuts. We have every variety. And," he emphasized, "you haven't seen the peach orchards in May either. People come with their cameras." His enthusiasm was evident.

"Do they! I'm not surprised. May I come in May?"

"Of course, you little fool. Do you really think you need to ask?"

Assuming the question to be rhetorical, Lili didn't answer. She was feeling better now, after the exertion of hiking. She clearly needed more exercise.

"Do you know how pretty you are now with your rosy cheeks, sparkling eyes and your hair free and blowing in the wind?"

"Oh, Sam." She despised herself for becoming tongue-tied when paid a compliment. Clearly, he enjoyed teasing her. Her face was glowing now and she tried to avert it. Taking her by the shoulders, he turned her to face him and kissed her hard on the mouth. Surprised, her mouth opened under his. When he eventually released her, his green eyes searched hers for a moment. Then, taking her by the hand, he turned towards home and started down the hill. They walked faster and faster and soon began to run, Sam's longer legs setting the pace. She tried to pull her hand away, but he wouldn't free it. When she could no longer keep up with him, Lili stumbled and fell, pulling him down with her. They rolled down the last few yards of the hill, laughing hard, covered in grass stains and mud.

Using the very real excuse of needing to bathe and change after their hike, once in the privacy of her room Lili did a little triumphant pirouette in the middle of the floor and hugged herself. She removed her shoes and clothes, pulled her hair up, secured it and took advantage of her deep bathtub to soak for a long time, giving herself a chance to think.

Settling down at the end of the tub until the sudsy water reached her chin, she recalled the way she and Sam had first met. Her boss had asked her to fill in for him at an interdepartmental meeting in the library conference room where a lecturer was propounding the virtues of stringent vegetarianism combined with meditation and yoga. She couldn't help but notice the good-looking guy with the blond hair and green eyes who sat across the table from her. He'd caught her eye and, to her mortification, she'd blushed. When she left the meeting, he'd been waiting outside the door and insisted on taking her to a fast food restaurant for hamburgers and fries as an antidote to the lecture.

She was still trying to figure Sam out. He said he was in love with her. He liked to tease her and seemed pleased that she was quick to give back as good as she got. Their relationship seemed to be one of mutual affection and warmth. The lifestyle and trappings of wealth were seductive, to be sure, but Lili was confident she had her feet planted firmly on the ground and was equally certain she could live happily without the Meredith riches. Sam Meredith was a part of this family, though, and she didn't want to consider giving him up. *But why should I have to give him up?*

She wondered if she'd ever have the self-assurance of someone like Crystal. Likely not, because hers was the kind of arrogant confidence that only inherited wealth could provide. In Crystal's case, there was probably a little cruelty there as well. She seemed to be someone who wouldn't at all mind—in fact, might enjoy—belittling people and making a scene. Lili abhorred scenes, not only because in and of themselves they proved embarrassing, but because she was too well aware she wouldn't back down from one. Her own tongue could be sharp and once said, she knew words could not be unsaid. Although she was not a shouter and rarely raised her voice, if pushed, she admitted, she could probably out-Crystal Crystal if it came to a war of words.

Crystal Meredith was perplexing. She seemed to have everything a woman could want: she was beautiful, rich, and was *to the manner born.* In researching the Meredith family, Lili learned Crystal had attended a world-renowned finishing school in Switzerland. She was sure to have had many significant offers of marriage; yet she remained at home, apparently living a life of superficial self-indulgence. Lili was puzzled, but as she couldn't imagine Crystal submitting to anyone's bidding, she was confident that Crystal was doing exactly what she wanted to do. Lili wondered idly if she occupied her time in any other way; if so, she couldn't begin to guess what it might be. She certainly couldn't picture her doing good works or devoting herself to the care of others.

Taking one of the white fluffy towels from the heated rack, Lili dried herself, smoothed some moisturizer over her face, and sauntered to the closet where Margaret had hung her few items of weekend clothing.

All three Meredith men stood in the imposing entrance hall when Lili started down the stairway. They looked up when they heard her footsteps and their jaws dropped in unison, as though they'd rehearsed it. She heard a low whistle from Sam and whispered words of appreciation from Drew and Stephen. Praying she wouldn't slip, Lili kept her head high and smiled. Then, from off to one side she heard someone singing, "There she is, Miss America... ," amidst muffled laughter. Lili froze on the bottom step, her cheeks burning. Sam came forward swiftly, taking her arm and tucking it under his while turning to glower over his shoulder.

"Don't give the juveniles among us any satisfaction, honey. They're in the minority and jealous as hell. Forget them."

He escorted her to a parlor where an impromptu bar had been set up. The McDonalds and Jim Evans joined them. A flash of revelation told Lili that Sam misunderstood her; he seemed to think she needed protection. If his declaration of love was based on that assumption, then it followed that perhaps he loved a Lili who didn't exist. Instantly banishing that notion, she turned to him with a grateful yet brave smile, aware she was continuing the deception.

A tall, stemmed martini glass in her hand, Cynthia Compton approached Lili and Sam. She was wearing a silvery cowl-necked burnt velvet dress, which clung to her body ending at her ankles. Observing her movements, Lili understood that Cynthia was well aware of her looks and enjoyed making the most of them. Her lips held a supercilious smile as she addressed Lili: "Have we met before? You look familiar."

Lili paused for only an instant. "I think we met at the ladies' room at Le Champignon. You were coming out as I was going in."

"Too right. Of course, I remember now."

"You were dining with Mr. Gregory, I believe."

"Yes. Paul." Cynthia shot a glance at Sam and smirked.

"Keeping dangerous company, weren't you, Cyn?," asked Drew as he joined them.

Lili felt Sam's arm tighten around her shoulders protectively. However, she couldn't help but feel sympathy for Jim Evans, ostensibly Cynthia's date for the weekend, as he leaned against the bar nursing a scotch. Cynthia, she felt, was making a play for Sam at Jim's expense, so she made her way over to him, keeping her back turned to the others as she spoke.

"Could I ask you to get me another drink?" She looked at him expectantly. "I seem to have been given a gin martini and I'm sure it must have been ordered by someone else."

He turned to her in relief. "Of course. What is it you'd like?" Lili spoke a few words in an undertone and he hurried away, seemingly grateful for her attention. He returned almost at once, handing her another glass. They chatted for a few minutes and soon were laughing together.

"Dinner is served." Martin's voice rose above the collective chatter and the company slowly deserted the small parlor and made their way to the dining room.

At the head of the table, Stephen Meredith held his champagne flute high in a toast. "To the homeless!" The expensively dressed, stylishly groomed company cheerfully responded in kind, their crystal glasses sparkling along with the wine.

Dinner proved to be a gala affair, everyone animated and laughing. Lili was mildly surprised to discover she was seated on Stephen's right, Sam across from her. There was watercress soup, roast lamb with garlic and rosemary, buttery fresh asparagus with lemon, and crunchy roast potatoes. The lamb gravy was superb, as were the freshly baked dinner rolls. A crisp rosé was served, along with more champagne. Stephen drew Lili out with carefully considered questions and she found herself relaxing in his company. He was full of himself and his flattery was transparent, but she enjoyed it nonetheless.

Then it was time for crème brulée and coffee. Lili toyed with her coffee spoon, thinking what a wonderful meal, what a lovely time she'd had in the past two hours, despite her earlier trepidation. Thanks to Stephen, encouraged by Sam, this had not been the uncomfortable scene she'd anticipated. Lili was not reluctant to give credit where it was due.

Catching Sam's eye, she said, "It's been so marvelous, but I do think I should run upstairs and get my things together. I hope you'll excuse me," she said, turning to Stephen. "This has been a beautiful interlude, but my real world begins again tomorrow." She smiled at everyone in turn.

"We understand, Lili, my dear. Don't feel you have to apologize." This from Stephen, who stood to excuse her. Sam, Drew, Peter and Jim followed his lead.

Lili murmured, "Please don't break up the party on my account," and quickly left the room.

"We won't." She barely heard the chorused reply from Crystal and Cynthia.

Once in the yellow bedroom, she took the suitcase from its stand and quickly gathered her belongings, running into the bathroom to collect her bath gel, tooth brush and toothpaste. Closing the lid of the case, she stood looking around the room, checking to see that she'd forgotten nothing.

Laughter and voices floated upstairs and into her room through the door, which stood ajar. She could scarcely discern Stephen's mellow baritone as he asked, "Do you mind telling us your intentions? She isn't exactly your usual type of female."

Lili stood unmoving, straining to hear the reply. Instead came Crystal's remark, heavy with sarcasm. "You're surely not serious, Sam? You could do much better than this little provincial. She's probably never even been out of the country! And I don't see any family money there." Her laughter was scornful.

Sam was responding either to the question or the remark; Lili couldn't precisely understand his words until the end of his statement as he finished with, "... and please keep your voice down." He said something else she didn't catch, then, "... she really doesn't know how gorgeous she is. She's beautiful, both her face and her mind are beautiful. Looks aren't important to her; she honestly doesn't know." He added as an afterthought. "And if she does, she doesn't care." She heard Crystal snort in derision.

Lili remained still in the middle of the room, her thoughts in turmoil. *How incredibly embarrassing.*

She could feel her cheeks burn in fury, more so because Crystal was right; she'd never been out of the country. And there was certainly no family money. She'd have to wait a few minutes, then descend the stairs and pretend she'd heard nothing. She prayed she wouldn't stumble.

───────

Fifteen minutes later, seated next to Sam in his softly purring Jaguar, Lili rode on a cloud of euphoria, as she rejoiced, "Sam loves me, he really does. In spite of his sister. And let's face it, maybe the rest of his family are against me, too. But he stood up for me!" His voice nudged her back to the present.

"Lili, how long have we been going together now?"

"Since just after Christmas, Sam. Why?"

He continued to look straight ahead, his eyes on the road. The car's headlights shone on a cluster of trees as the Jag climbed a hill in one of the highway's tight turns.

"Because I think it's time we became engaged."

Stunned, Lili couldn't reply.

"Did you hear me?"

"Yes. I'm just... engaged to be married?"

"That *was* the general idea, yes."

"I hadn't... it hasn't... I mean..."

"Let's start over. Lili, darling Lili, will you accept my ring as a token of my affection and serious intentions?" He reached across to take her hand.

"Yes, Sam." Amazed at her own instantaneous reply, she knew she sounded imbecilic, but could not think of anything else to say, except to add: "What about your family?"

"What about them?"

"Well, do you think they'd approve?"

"I'm surprised you think I need their permission." He paused, then continued: "I've got to go out of town for a few days and I'll get the ring while I'm away. We'll have a proper engagement party at the house in three weeks. Sorry it has to be postponed, honey, but Drew will be away next weekend and Dad and Crystal are doing some business entertaining the following weekend. I checked. So we're on for the third weekend. Sound good?"

"Yes, Sam, it's wonderful." Lili put some enthusiasm into her reply this time. But where was the romance? The way Sam was handling everything, it all sounded so cut and dried. He had obviously been certain she'd accept. She was sure, however, when she got home and had time to fully realize her dream coming true, she'd be so excited that she wouldn't be able to sleep.

As it happened, when Lili turned down the bedspread and crawled between the sheets, she fell asleep rapidly, only to awaken at four in the morning. The wind outside whipped the leaves so they danced in the moonlight and formed constantly changing, fascinating shapes on the wall. She tossed and turned, her thoughts chaotic, but exultant. Surely Sam's proposal was the answer to her prayers. *Wasn't he the man she'd been searching for?* She couldn't help wondering how much of his desire was genuine and how much was in defiance of his family, but at the moment she didn't care. Samuel Chasen Meredith, of Meredith Manor, wanted to marry her, Liliane Greening, of Nowhere.

––––––––

The next day she worried when Sam didn't call her at her office; then she remembered he'd said he was going to be out of town for a few days. He hadn't mentioned where he was going or for what reason. It was a bit unusual, because he didn't customarily leave town on business for more than a day; his presence was always needed at the Forestry Department. She assured herself quickly that it wasn't worth worrying about. She figured this would be a good chance to do some writing, but was reluctant to get on with it. She earnestly wanted the recognition being published would bring; at the same time she suspected she was afraid to try for fear of being rejected. But try she would.

Three days later, Lili threw down her pencil, strode to her kitchen, took the receiver from her wall phone and punched some numbers into it. Grimacing as she took a sip of cool coffee from the mug she held in her left hand, she said, "Angie? It is I. How goes it?"

Angela Hoenig's voice held surprise and warmth. "I'm so glad you called, Lili. I haven't heard much from you since Dr. Meredith started squiring you around."

"It's not as if you don't have anything to occupy your time, either, you know." She set her cup on the nearby counter. "Will your schedule allow you to meet me for dinner tomorrow?"

"Dinner sounds great. Why don't we meet at Cosmo's Café! Is six o'clock all right? We'll have time for a glass of wine before dinner and still be home by eight."

"Forgive my curiosity, but why do we have to be home by eight?" Lili pulled the curtain away from the back window and peered into her twilit backyard where her ungroomed poodle, Buffalo, barked at a gray cat perched on the fence above him.

"Of course *you* can stay out later, but PBS has scheduled a special that I need to catch. It's on my current article."

Angie was a tall, slender brunette with beautiful large gray eyes and long black lashes. She taught Freshman English at the university, Rudimentary English, she called it. She was always rushed, however, as a freelance contributor to several publications, scholarly and otherwise. Lili assumed she was currently involved in such a job with its mandatory deadline.

"Okay, I promise you can be home by eight. We'll just have to talk fast, that's all. See you there at six."

Lili had never liked talking on the phone; that is, she had no patience with small talk. She considered all the routine platitudes people bored each other with at the beginnings and endings of telephone conversations as so much wasted time. When forced into compliance, she was aware that her responses were artificial and stilted. She figured her friends knew who she was and if they hadn't been well or weren't free to talk at the moment they'd say so, just as she would. This was one way she could quickly separate her genuine friends from the artificial kind. Although conventional in most circumstances, Lili despised what she considered phoniness.

She emptied her cold coffee into the sink, then opened the door and whistled Buffalo in from the back yard.

At five fifty-five the following evening she was sipping a glass of merlot and glancing up from Cosmo's menu each time someone opened the door. She was amazed to see Paul Gregory enter, proceed to the bar, order, then turn, lean against it and casually scan the room. He was wearing faded jeans and an Aran pullover, off-white and bulky. His eyes stopped when they reached her. Flustered, she looked away, but not before the telltale blush started at her throat; she gradually felt her face begin to glow. *I'm glad I'm sitting far across this room,* she thought. *But why on earth am I blushing?*

The door opened and Angie rushed in, stopping to glance around the room in an obvious attempt to find Lili. When she spotted her, she walked briskly to their table and sank into a chair, her back to the bar.

"I'm not late, am I? It's only just six."

"No, silly, calm down. I was early. Now start telling me about your latest crisis and I'll tell you about mine."

Turning in her chair, Angie located and summoned a waiter from the other side of the room. When she faced Lili again, she leaned forward, edging closer as she whispered, "Did you see that dark-haired guy at the bar? He's looking over here. Is he gorgeous or what?"

"Yes, I saw him come in a few minutes ago. I don't know why I seem to keep running into that man. It's the strangest thing, he keeps turning up wherever I go. Do you know who he is?"

"No, but I'd like to! Do you?"

"Sam told me his name is Paul Gregory and... well, never mind. Speaking of Sam, that's who I really wanted to talk to you about. He's talking about giving me a ring."

"Engagement?"

"Well, not a telephone call!" Lili set her glass down as she gave a hoot of laughter.

"Lili! How wonderful, I'm so happy for you. Dr. Sam Meredith—what a catch! Well? I assume you've said yes. Have you set a date?"

"Yes, yes and no. Sam didn't ask me, he told me it was time we became engaged." Lili paused, her brow wrinkled in thought. "Actually, he did propose then—in so many words." She grinned. "I did say yes. And no, we haven't set a date. He's talking about an engagement party in a few weeks, so I hope you'll be able to come. It'll be at Meredith Manor."

"Honey, I'll be there with bells on. Just let me know what day and what time." Angela's face was wreathed in smiles; Lili could see she was genuinely happy for her.

"Angie, I still can't believe Sam Meredith wants to marry me! Why me? He could get anyone in town. Or out of town, for that matter." Lili sat back, a little out of breath and just a trifle surprised at her own words. She hoped she hadn't sounded disingenuous. She'd simply been stating the obvious truth.

Angela searched Lili's face. Then she said, "Well, in case you're fishing for compliments, I'm fresh out. If you don't know your own worth by now, I feel sorry for you." Trust Angie to be straight with her.

"Ange, I didn't mean... that is, I . . ." Lili sipped her wine, took a deep breath and said, "Sorry, I didn't mean to unload on you, I actually wanted you to be happy for me. I guess there's a lot I'm... uh... kind of vague about."

"I'd say so—that's the way it sounds to me. Are you avoiding the word "unsure?" Look, Lili, don't rush into anything. I mean, don't let yourself be pushed." She grinned, adding, "Even if he is the greatest catch in the world, just take your time and be certain, will you?"

"If you mean don't make the same mistake I made before, I promise I won't."

"I didn't mean..."

"Of course you didn't. Don't worry. I've learned my lesson."

The waiter approached, they ordered and talked of Angie's latest quarrels with a textbook editor.

Lili's plate was still half full when she sat back in her chair saying, "I don't know what's wrong with my appetite. I can't swallow another bite. Do you have time for another glass of wine? Or some coffee?"

Angie checked her watch. "Sure, if you don't mind if I make it quick." She began to look for their waiter. Spotting him, she held up her wine glass with one hand and two fingers with the other.

A moment later two glasses of wine were placed on the table as their waiter announced, "Courtesy of the gentleman at the bar."

Oh, no, Lili thought, as Angie said, "Thank him for us, please." She smirked at Lili, raising her eyebrows. "Been busy, have we?"

"I don't know why he did that, I promise you." Lili felt the familiar heat in her cheeks.

"Sure, I believe you. What's going on here, my dear person?"

"I honestly don't know. I think I'd better hurry so I can leave with you when you go."

"Suit yourself, but you'd be a fool. Stick around and see what's cookin.'" Angie paused, then smiled knowingly. "I would."

Lili grimaced and squirmed in her seat. "I can't, can I? I wouldn't know what to do. If you leave and I stay, it'll look like I put you up to it. And I'll feel like a fool if I just sit here alone like a pudding."

"Here's what you do. I'll run out. You check your watch and start getting yourself together slowly. Sip your wine, take your time. If he doesn't make his move, get up and walk out. You've saved face because you're not just sitting here, you've been getting ready to leave. No harm done. But he'll come over, count on it. And when he does, maybe you'll at least find out more about him and why he sent these drinks over. What can you lose?" She paused again, then added, "Besides, anyone that good looking deserves further study."

Lili laughed. "Anyone that good looking doesn't deserve anything more!"

Angela grinned in agreement. She took one more sip from her glass, grabbed her handbag, stood and leaned over to kiss Lili's cheek lightly, rushed to the door, turned, waved and winked. The door closed behind her.

The tall stranger was already on his way to their table, a beer mug in his hand. Lili's cheeks were burning and her eyes downcast. She saw a pair of faded jeans and the bottom edge of an Aran sweater stop at the side of the table. She heard a low-pitched voice ask, "Do you mind if I join you?"

She heard herself say, "Please do."

The chair scraped across the floor as he pulled it out and sat down. Her discomfort was intense; she felt she could hardly breathe. She couldn't bring herself to look at him, nor could she trust herself to speak. This reaction, so out of character, amazed her.

"You're wondering who I am and why I sent the wine to your table. I sent the wine because I wanted to meet you. My name is Pál Gregor." His tone was serious. With a tremendous effort she forced herself to look up, then realized he was amused.

Flustered, she blurted, "Did you say Gregor? I thought your name was Gregory. I mean..." She stopped in confusion. He was smiling broadly, now fully aware of her interest.

"People call me Paul Gregory. My grandfather changed it from Gregor, which is Magyar—Hungarian—to be more easily assimilated when he arrived in America. But my proper name is Pál Sandor Gregor—the Americanized version is Paul Alexander Gregory." His diction was superb, each word perfectly enunciated. She could discern no noticeable accent, and yet—yet she thought she could hear something essentially foreign in his speech.

"Oh!" She raised her brows in surprise. "So that's why the name of your club is Pal's."

"Yes, more or less. You know about Pal's?" At her nod, he continued. "The Hungarian spelling of Paul is P-a-l, with an accent mark, not an actual emphasis of sound, on the a. I simply took that away and added the apostrophe to make it a possessive." He looked at her doubtfully. "Do you follow?"

"I think so." She frowned. "Do you mean—to be perfectly correct—you'd spell it P-a-accent-l-apostrophe-s?"

"Someone who understands at last." He favored her with a flashing smile. "It's really pretty tedious, so now we can forget it."

"Okay." She hoped she'd regained her composure and grew bold enough to ask, "Why did you want to meet me, Mr. Gregor?" She noticed she was worrying a hangnail on her thumb and forced herself to stop.

"First, let me ask you a question. You've noticed me for the past few weeks when you've seen me at one place and another." As she began to demur, he added, "Don't deny it, it's a fact. Do you wonder why?"

"Why what? Why we've been to the same places at the same times or why you think I've noticed you?"

"Why we keep meeting like this."

"All right, why do we?"

"Because sometimes I've planned it that way and sometimes it's kismet."

"Kismet?"

"Kismet, serendipity, coincidence, whatever you want to call it. Luck. My luck is always good because

I make it that way. I wanted to meet you, talk to you."

"Me? But why?"

"I know your name is Liliane Julia Greening and that you are a researcher-cum-secretary for C.J. Rankin in Graphics and Pubs. Excuse me, I believe secretaries are now called administrative assistants."

"I suppose they are the same thing, aren't they?"

"I digress." He raised an eyebrow and continued. "You are frequently seen in the company of Sam Meredith. Excuse me once again; I should say Dr. Sam Meredith."

She caught his sarcasm and suddenly wondered if he coveted Sam's title. But then the thought vanished.

He had paused and was looking deeply into her eyes, allowing her to notice his weren't black, as she'd thought. Even in the dim light she could tell they were a deep brown with golden flecks at their centers. She imagined those eyes could flash with temper as well as they could beguile. He put his elbows on the table and rested his chin on his laced fingers. "Other than that, I don't know you. Yet."

What self-assurance, what nerve the man had. In spite of herself, she was intrigued.

Lili betrayed her agitation by clearing her throat. "You didn't answer my question. Why do you want to talk to me?"

He shifted position to lean his back against the chair and let his heavy forearms rest on the table. He was very still. "I think it's a little premature to tell you the reason. Instead, why don't we relax and enjoy each other's company." It was a statement— almost a command—not a question. Then he added, "Let's have another drink. Will you have the same?"

She paused for only an instant. "Yes, please." *I'm ready to do anything he asks,* she thought wildly. *What's come over me?*

For the next half hour he entertained her with stories and anecdotes about local townspeople, friends from the university and some people she'd never met at all, but felt she now knew. At one point she laughed so hard she had to rummage in her handbag for a handkerchief to wipe her streaming eyes. Before she could find one, Paul handed her a folded square of white linen and she was grateful. When he laughed, she noticed he had beautifully even white teeth. Everything about him seemed perfect. He asked her if she'd like another drink and she reluctantly shook her head, murmuring something about having to work the next morning. To her surprise, she found she was unwilling to end this encounter with the mysterious stranger who made her laugh.

Paul signaled the waiter, left money on the table, took her arm and led her to the door. They walked to her Corsica. He asked for the key and opened the door for her.

Feeling like a teenager, she said the only thing she could think of. "Thank you for a lovely evening, Mr. Gregor."

Placing his hands on her shoulders, he turned her to face him and looked into her eyes. For a moment she thought he was about to kiss her, but then the moment passed and he said, "It's been my pleasure, Ms. Greening," as he released her.

Before she turned the key in the ignition, she rolled down her window and looked up at him. "Good night, and thanks again."

His only reply was, "Be careful." Then he turned and walked away.

Wow!, she thought as she drove home. *What a night! What was that all about? I don't think I've ever*

*met a more exciting, a more enigmatic man in my life.
But he didn't say anything about calling me or seeing
me again.*

She suddenly felt curiously deflated. She gave
herself a mental shake. *"What am I thinking? Dr. Sam
Meredith has asked me to be his wife and he's my
dream, everything I've ever wanted. How can I even
think of another man?"*

Chapter 3

I t was Thursday afternoon and Sam phoned to say he was being held over for another day, but he'd pick her up the next night at seven and they'd go to Champignon for dinner. He said goodbye and rang off. Well, Lili thought, since Sam's not coming back tonight, Buff will keep me company again as I make further headway with my novel. At long last she was beginning to feel optimistic about her writing project.

Lili had tried hard to put Paul Gregory out of her mind. She told herself he was an intriguing fantasy, nothing more, and she would probably not see him again, at least not alone. It was just as well—the man spelled trouble. She couldn't help but wonder, though, why he'd sought her company and had taken the trouble to learn her name and where she worked. She'd probably never know, but so what? She had other things on her mind, such as becoming engaged to the man of her dreams, the man who would keep her safe, who would take care of her for the rest of her life and they would have wonderful times together. Sam was so attractive, so distinguished, so eligible—the catch of the decade, at the very least. She still couldn't believe her good luck in attracting such a remarkable man.

That night Lili microwaved a TV dinner, bathed early and got into her pajamas and robe. She spent four hours in the spare bedroom where her computer and printer were set up, but found she couldn't keep her mind on her heroine's troubles. She glanced at the clock on the wall, sighed, saved and exited her document.

Draping her coat around her shoulders, she took Buff for his evening walk. She was in her nightclothes and didn't want to be seen, so she called to him each time he strayed and they kept to the shadows of her own property. No whisper of wind moved the trees; the night was strangely silent. As she strolled around the boundaries of the side yard, a movement from an automobile parked across the street caught her eye. The driver's window was silently being raised. The reflection of a streetlight on the glass prevented her seeing who was inside. Remaining in the shadow, she strained to see the driver, but couldn't discern the make of the car, a dark colored late model something expensive. She stood in the shadows for a few more moments, then, as there was no further movement from the car, she retraced her steps and re-entered the house through the kitchen door.

At four in the morning she woke, her eyes searching for the pattern of leafy moonlight working its way across the wall and onto the ceiling. She could no longer be sure that it was not her imagination that seemed to perceive the fluttering leaves as patterning the profile of the mysterious stranger. He's no longer a stranger; his name is Paul Gregory, she reminded herself. But he is mysterious. It occurred to her that this might be a contrivance of her own active imagination and—to be completely honest—possibly wishful thinking. She didn't fall asleep again until much later.

"What a beautiful ring, Sam! I don't think I've ever seen anything so magnificent." Lili gazed at the ring in its velvet box and knew it was, indeed, one of a kind. Its central stone, as Sam had explained, was a dazzling two carat gem quality blue-white diamond, marquise cut. Twin single carat marquise diamonds glittered on each side. The setting was platinum. The ring was exquisite, breath-taking. They were sitting at their usual table at Le Champignon, a bottle of *Möet et Chandon* chilling in the silver ice bucket in its stand next to the table. There was a hollow-stemmed saucer champagne glass before each of them.

"Put it on, honey. Let's see how it looks on your hand."

Lily felt somewhat foolish; why wasn't he putting the ring on her finger? Sam might be a great catch on the marriage market, but he didn't seem to be a bit romantic. Well, she reminded herself, that's not what's really important in a marriage.

Her thoughts flew back to the night her ex-husband, Steve, had proposed to her. They had been dining at a popular supper club in Chicago. He'd ordered champagne and, as he toasted her and they drank, he'd asked her to marry him in a speech sublimely ardent and amorous. She'd been careful not to accept, as she wanted time to think of a way to refuse without hurting his feelings. After their meal she'd excused herself from the table and, as she returned from the ladies' room, found a famous celebrity, the headliner at the club that night, at their table joining them in a champagne toast as he congratulated them on their engagement. A true showman, that evening had been vintage Steve and typical of his controlling, I-get-whatever-I-want-and-don't-take-no-for-an-answer personality. She'd known even then it would be a mistake to marry him and was ashamed to admit she'd allowed him to steamroll her into accepting. But at least his proposal had been supremely flattering and certainly a romantically baroque event. *Perhaps I'm just a romantic fool, doomed to repeat my mistakes over and over again. No, I've grown up!,* she assured herself.

Sam was a different man altogether. He certainly wasn't reckless or out-of-control and he didn't destroy the people around him along with himself as Steve did. Sam was much safer, and she no longer needed the trappings of romance, no longer needed to be courted. Sam would make her happy and she was sure she could make him happy, too. He must think so, or he wouldn't have asked her to marry him, would he? *Of course not,* her inner voice replied. *Just look at this spectacular ring. It's certainly a tangible expression of his regard for me.* She forced herself back to the present.

"Sam, why don't you just keep the ring until the night of our engagement party and put it on my finger then?"

"What? Do you mean you don't want it?"

"Of course that's not what I mean. I guess I'm what you'd call silly and sentimental, but... ," here Lili groped for words. "But I really would like you to put it on my finger." She looked at Sam, willing him to understand.

"You mean you want me to get down on one knee?"

"Sam, for a man who has been around as many women as I think you have, you've never paid much attention to their feelings, have you? What I mean is, I should have thought everyone would know that a woman wants a man to say he loves her and wants her to be his wife. That is what I mean to you, isn't it?"

"Lili, my darling, you're really something." Sam stopped as the waiter advanced, asking permission to pour. He nodded.

Lili was at a loss to understand Sam. Sometimes he could be so smooth, worldly and, yes, courtly. But lately he'd been behaving as if he had other things on his mind, things that were more important than she was. Sam's right, she thought, I guess I'm being silly. Any woman in her right mind would be thrilled to wear this fantastic ring, become Mrs. Samuel Chasen Meredith and live a life of secure luxury forever after.

Sam lifted his glass and extended it to her. She raised hers to meet it as he said, "Here's to us, sweetheart."

She smiled, responding, "To us." They drank.

"You want me to be more romantic, is that it? Okay, you got it: Darling, will you marry me?"

"Oh, I don't know, Sam." She laughed and continued, "This is so sudden."

He removed the ring from the velvet box and, taking her left hand, gently slipped the ring on her finger, where it glittered in the candlelight. She guessed that Sam Meredith could easily have afforded to buy an even more expensive ring, but she thought his choice suited her perfectly and was privately glad he hadn't. Anything larger would have been ostentatious.

They dined on fillet of sole, fluffy rice and fresh asparagus with lemon-butter sauce and proclaimed everything to be excellent. They ordered coffee and Martel brandy. Lili's ring sparkled in the candlelight every time she moved her hand. Finally, they stood and Sam helped her with her coat. They walked to the door and almost bumped into Paul Gregory, who had just entered. Paul said, "Good evening, Ms. Greening," to Lili, ignoring Sam.

Lili, surprised, murmured, "Mr. Gregory." She could feel Sam's questioning presence next to her. Should she introduce them? Surely not, that would lead to too many questions she didn't want to answer.

Outside, Sam helped Lili into the passenger seat. He didn't speak until they'd pulled out of the parking lot, and then only asked, "Well?"

Lili decided it was best to plead ignorance. "I have no idea, Sam."

"Why did he speak to you and how does he know who you are?"

"I really can't imagine. Don't let this ruin our lovely evening, please, darling."

Miffed, Sam dropped her off at her house with a perfunctory kiss and a promise to call the next day. Lili was left feeling somewhat dismayed; Sam could be possessive and spoiled, but he'd always redeemed himself later by being adorable and charming. It seemed he could also be childish. *Well, why not?,* she thought. He'd been reared among riches, with the knowledge that he could invariably have whatever he wanted. It would be very strange, indeed, if his habitual behavior had been that of an ordinary man.

———

It was Thursday afternoon and Lili and Sam's engagement was two weeks old, yet it seemed to her that they'd been closer before he'd given her the ring. He didn't phone her as often as he used to do, nor did they see each other every day. As a matter of fact, she thought, we only meet a few times a week now and almost half of those few times we run into each other accidentally.

Paul Gregory was another matter. He was on her mind almost constantly. She'd seen him at least three times incidentally and once at a convenience store where she'd stopped for coffee on her way to the office early one morning. He'd spoken only to wish her good morning and she'd responded in kind. Last night as she walked Buff she observed what she believed to be the same dark car parked closer to her house this time. When she turned out her bedroom light before getting into bed, she looked out the window and saw it quietly pull away from the curb, its headlights not coming on until it was a block away.

There was no reason to think it was Paul Gregory's car, yet she suspected it was. Was he watching her? And if so, why? As she pondered this very strange behavior on his part–if indeed the watcher in the car *was* Paul–the more she felt herself being relentlessly carried into a seeming maelstrom of unknown danger, a whirlpool whose depths she couldn't fathom until it might be too late.

Danger signals were going off in her brain. Why was this inscrutable man so interested in her? Surely his interest couldn't be romantic; he was behaving far too strangely for that. And surely, too, a man of his level of sophistication and appearance needn't resort to following and spying on her. She had no doubt he was sufficiently self-assured to pick up the telephone or walk up to her door with an invitation, if that was what he had in mind. No, what he was doing could be described as stalking. She told herself she should be terrified, should perhaps notify the authorities of her fear. Perversely, however, Lili pushed those thoughts to the back of her mind and, in spite of herself, she shivered, not with fright, but with mounting excitement as she became increasingly intrigued by the puzzle as it unfolded and each revelation itself created a new perplexity.

Then came a time at her office when she wondered if she could ever catch up with her backlog of research. It seemed everyone had a demanding project that required her full attention and she found herself wishing she had at least one clone of herself. Lili worked at top speed, trying to please everyone, yet falling further behind as each day passed.

One such morning she rushed into her office for a notebook and found C.J. Rankin sitting in the visitor's chair at her desk. He stood at once, motioning her to come inside.

"Sorry, C. J., I didn't know you were waiting for me." Her arms full of books, she tossed her hair out of her eyes. "Do you need me, boss?"

"Not for anything that can't wait until after lunch. I just wanted to let you know I'll be at the Dean's Office for a meeting. Call me a taxi, would you?"

"You're a taxi."

"I've always wanted someone to take me up on that," he chuckled. "Tell the driver I'll be waiting out in front. *Ciao.*"

With a campus the size of Southern Illinois University's, an on-campus taxi service was provided for departmental staff. She picked up the phone and ordered a cab.

Lunch was, as usual, a sandwich eaten at her desk, nibbled between phone calls and sips of coffee. The afternoon hours rushed by; it didn't seem possible when the clock on the credenza chimed five o'clock. Lili was in no hurry, however, as she rarely left before five-thirty or six to avoid the day's-end campus traffic.

Stacks of work remained on her desk, but she pushed some of it aside, leaned forward and rested her head on her arms. She recalled the day C.J. had interviewed her. It had been a dreary morning, the rain streaming down, when she'd raced across campus trying to locate the building. When she'd finally found it, she'd dashed inside drenched to the skin, her hair dripping, umbrella blown inside-out and floundered directly into C.J. Rankin, the very man she'd intended to impress with her poise, maturity and intelligence.

Her change in fortune seemed to have begun that stormy day. Not only had C. J., as he was known on campus, hired her, but best of all, in her estimation, there was no discernable departmental unrest, backbiting or scheming. Lili liked her co-workers—from the designers and artists in Graphics to the editors and writers in Publications. She thought them a diverse and interesting group and welcomed the research assignments they heaped upon her. But it was, she had to admit, now beginning to be a bit much for one person. She pushed herself out of her chair, took her coat from the closet and, exhausted, left for the day.

The next morning C. J., aware of her predicament, offered to hire a student worker to help her and her eyes shone with gratitude and relief. "You've read my mind, boss."

Kevin had arrived that same day. Lili gave him the smallest job on her list, a brief explanation of what he was to do, plunged back into her other work and forgot about him. He returned to her office at five o'clock and placed a neat stack of typed notes on her desk and asked what she wanted him to do next. His studies only allowed him to work for her twelve hours a week, but he was Lili's right hand for seven hours on Tuesdays and five on Thursdays. From the first day Lili considered him irreplaceable.

Thanks to Kevin's timely help, deadlines had been met and at last she could relax and begin to gather material for an early morning meeting. She was deep in thought and the phone's insistent buzz irritated her. She grabbed the receiver with an impatient, "Yes?"

"Ms. Greening, will you meet me tonight at the Rosewood Inn, say six-thirty? I'll buy you dinner." The deep voice asking a straight question with no frills. It could only be Paul Gregory. She caught her breath.

"Is this Mr. Gregory?"

"It is."

"I think you should know I'm engaged to be married."

"I'm aware of that."

She was flustered. "Well, why do you want to see me?"

"I give you my word, your honor is perfectly safe with me. I want to talk to you. And," he added, a smile in his voice, "I enjoy your company. Will you be there?"

"Yes." She'd known she would from the beginning. *What could he want?* Her hand was cold as she put down the receiver.

It was a thirty minute drive to the Rosewood Inn from her office and Lili had worked up to the last minute getting everything ready for the next morning's eight-thirty meeting. She knew she'd be lucky to get to the inn by their agreed-upon time, but traffic in town was light and the inn was located on an empty stretch of road at least twenty miles away, so she was able to make good time. She was happily aware that, although it was six o'clock, she hadn't needed her headlights, tangible proof that the days were growing longer.

As she pulled into the parking lot and drew to a stop, her door was opened and Paul Gregory stood waiting to help her out. She took his hand; it felt warm and strong.

Pulling her to her feet, he drew her to him so that they stood facing each other, only inches separating them. With her left hand still in his, Lili felt him rub his thumb over her ring, which he then raised and scrutinized.

"Very nice," he murmured.

She said nothing, and he led her to the restaurant's entrance, still holding her hand, only releasing it as he opened the door and stood back to allow her to enter. The room was half-filled with early diners and there was standing room only at the bar. The floor was bare wood, though the tables were covered with cloths and set up with napkins, glasses and cutlery. Despite the fact that management wasted no expense on elegant window treatments, sumptuous carpeting or crystal chandeliers, the Rosewood Inn's reputation for fine dining and excellent service was widespread.

A hostess, smiling at Paul as if she knew him well, showed them to a table in the most remote booth on the far side of the room, saying, "I'll send Peggy over, Mr. Gregory."

A waitress appeared and Paul said, "I'll have a Stoli martini on the rocks—very dry—and," turning to Lili, he asked, "one for you?"

"I'll just have a glass of white wine... no, I'll have a martini, too." *Why not?,* she thought. *I've never had one.* Looking at him, she asked, "Do we still have to be Mr. Gregory and Ms. Greening? Can't we be Paul and Lili?"

"I was keeping up the formalities for your benefit." His dark eyes never left hers. She was at a loss for words.

Their drinks arrived along with a basket of breadsticks. Peggy asked if they wanted to order, and Paul, his eyes remaining on Lili, only said, "Not yet."

At the first sip of her martini, Lili tried not to grimace. Quick tears sprang to her eyes. Then, through the icy crispness of the vodka, she could feel the heat descending to her stomach, not an altogether disagreeable sensation, she decided. For some reason she was reluctant to mention it, however; she didn't want to make known the fact that she'd never had a martini before.

Paul pushed the breadsticks closer to her, saying, "Have one. It'll help." He looked away, then back at her. "You're twenty-nine, aren't you?" At Lili's expression of alarm, he burst into laughter, then said, "Sorry, I usually try not to be so blunt. That was rude of me. It's just that…"

Lili broke in with, "I know, you're wondering if this was my first martini and if it was, where I've been all my life. How I could reach this advanced age and not have lived, so to speak. The answer is I truly don't know." She took another sip.

He studied her unabashedly. "When I telephoned to ask you to meet me here, I told you the truth. I really want to talk to you. More to the point, I want you to talk to me."

Again she became aware of the slightly foreign aspect of his language. Maybe that was putting it too strongly, however; she should describe it, rather, as an absence of the local American inflection. Perhaps it was the way he strung words together; perhaps it was his careful enunciation of each sound that caused her to feel there was something exotic about his speech. She regarded him, in turn, as he sat across the table from her. He was completely at ease, as if this were his habitual pose, leaning back comfortably, his hands very still on the table. He didn't seem to have to fidget with things, the way most people would. She noticed he wore a gold signet ring on his right hand.

"Talk about what, Paul?" Another sip. *Martinis might not be so bad after all.*

"You. I want to know about you." As she opened her mouth to speak, he went on, "No, don't ask me why. I'll tell you later."

"Well, my life has been pretty dull, you know." She raised her glass to her lips. "I'm sure we can find many more interesting subjects."

"Talk to me about your childhood. I know you've been married and divorced. Tell me about that. I want to know about your work, how you like it, where you expect to go with it, if you do. Tell me about your life now, what you hope for. Your dreams." As the waitress walked toward them, he raised two fingers and she hurried away.

"How did you know... ?

"Forgive me for being inquisitive. I do have a reason. I already know all about you; that is, I know the facts of your life. Now I want to hear about the real you. Tell me."

And she found herself telling him about her happy childhood and her much-loved parents. About not wanting to go to college, but being sent anyway— for her own good, as she later realized. She'd never been away from home before, new friends had to be made and apron strings had to be cut. She told him about being miserably lonely at first, but growing to love her new life on campus until it was cut abruptly short by her father's sudden death. She briefly told him about her marriage to Steve, then the divorce, her mother's dying and about feeling so desolate and alone, close to despair.

Paul listened without interrupting. All the while she talked his eyes never left her face. They held an expression she couldn't read.

At his prompting, she divulged her secret ambition: her dream, impossible though it seemed, to become a novelist, to have her efforts legitimized by being published.

She confessed, "I've never told this to anyone."

"I'm flattered you told me. Thank you. But why have you kept it secret?"

"I didn't like the idea of being laughed at, I suppose."

He regarded her solemnly. "No one is laughing."

Taking a deep breath and forcing a smile, she said, "That about brings us up-to-date. Well, you asked for it. Are you sufficiently bored?"

Before he could answer, she looked down, noticed her empty glass, and added, "I think I'm feeling slightly odd, Mr. Paul Gregory, or whatever I'm supposed to call you. Did I really drink two martinis?"

"You did and it's my fault. I wanted to hear everything. Now I'm going to order dinner for you, but first I want you to get up and walk to the ladies' room. It's important to walk around when you're drinking."

Lili excused herself and left. When she returned to their booth she found bowls of tossed salad at their places and a basket with bread warm from the oven. It was wrapped in a white linen napkin.

"You know, I think I'm hungry," she remarked, sliding into the booth. "And if you're lucky I won't embarrass you by passing out."

He smiled a charmingly crooked smile. "You'll be all right, especially after you've eaten the steak that's coming."

After they'd eaten, she sighed, saying, "I feel better now. That was delicious. Thank you. And martinis are a good idea before a steak."

"I've always thought so."

Their waitress removed their plates and brought coffee. Lili leaned forward, her chin propped on her fists. "And you, Paul? Don't you think it's your turn to tell me about yourself? Or do you intend to remain a man of mystery?"

"What do you want to know about me that you don't already know?" Again that fascinating half-accent.

She gave a soft hoot of laughter. "I can only know what you choose to tell me. So far that's been nothing."

He maintained an impassive façade. "My life is an open book; I am, after all, a public man, if only because of my involvement with Pal's." He spread his hands. "With me what you see is what you get." He started to speak again, but Lili forestalled him.

"Tell me, are you a reader, Paul? Do you like books?" At his nod, she continued. "Do you prefer prose or poetry?"

"Prose, of course. Can you see me reading poetry?"

"I'm not sure. Perhaps."

"Can we change the subject? I don't like to talk about myself."

Lili was intrigued. "That's a very revealing statement. Most people wouldn't admit that; it's too honest. And most people do like to talk about themselves." She twisted a strand of hair and slanted a look at him. "Now I'm curious—I think you may be a bit of a philosopher, Paul, aren't you?"

"Hardly. I'm a pretty boring guy."

"Oh, come on, Paul. That tells me you're just the opposite."

He laughed. "You're trying so hard to make me interesting, I guess I'll have to try to help." He ran his finger around the top of his coffee cup as he seemed to study it. "There is something somebody wrote... it's always bothered me."

"And that is?" Lili raised her brows.

"I'll paraphrase. In "The Prophet," Gibran wrote about the future—he calls it the house of tomorrow. He says we can't live there; only our children can. We can't even visit it, not even in our dreams."

"This troubles you?"

He continued to frown. "Well, yes, I guess it does." He brightened in an effort to lighten the atmosphere. "I think we should go now. Are you ready to leave? Unless you want something more, of course."

"No, nothing more. Is it late? I feel so relaxed." She resolved to get out her *Bartlett's Familiar Quotations* as soon as she reached home and read any excerpts from "The Prophet." Tomorrow she'd research it in its entirety at the university library.

When Peggy came with the bill, Paul paid with cash. They rose from the table and, tucking her arm under his and holding it next to his body, he walked her to her car, opened the door and helped her in. She lowered the window. Leaning down, he said, "Lili, I apologize for being obscure, for not explaining things to you. Will you see me if I call you again?"

In a heartbeat. Aloud, she said, "Am I to consider this a date, Paul? What if I said, 'Yes, I'll meet you again?' I'm engaged to be married. What would that make me?"

"It makes us special friends, with the accent on the us. I told you your honor was safe with me and I mean it."

"Yes, Paul, please call me." She couldn't explain it to herself, but she did trust him.

Feeling quite sober now, Lili, nevertheless, drove home very carefully. She was aware that a midnight blue Mitsubishi followed her from the time she left the Rosewood Inn until she drove into her carport, then double-parked in the street until she entered the house and turned on the lights. She felt happy, as though she'd acquired a newly-discovered guardian angel.

Chapter 4

Sam nosed the Jaguar into the curb under the trees in front of Lili's house. She was seated half-facing him, her back angled against the bucket seat and the door. He cut the ignition and turned to her, reaching to take her into his arms. She sank against him, a vague feeling of guilt washing over her, as she remembered that just the night before she might have fallen into Paul's arms. If he'd offered.

Sam kissed her mouth. "Lili, my love, I've missed you," he whispered into her hair.

"Where have you been, Sam? What have you been doing?" She pulled away from his embrace and frowned. "Why haven't we seen each other more often lately?"

He leaned forward and kissed her lips again. "Business, my darling, always business, some damn fool forever screwing up." He drew her to him. His hands reached inside her open jacket and moved over her silk covered breasts. "Let's get rid of your blouse and that piece of lace beneath it."

She squirmed and, taking one of his wrists in each hand, held them away from her. "Sam, darling, I've got to go in now."

"Yeah, that's a great idea. Let's go in."

"I mean, I have to go in to go to bed."

"That's what I mean, too." Though it was dark, she knew he was grinning.

"Sam, please. I have to get up early in the morning to go to work. I need sleep..."

He cut her off with, "Tomorrow's Saturday. Your office isn't even open tomorrow." He stopped and moved back. "What's wrong with you, Lili? Why do you always play the startled fawn? I turn you on, I know I do. Come on, baby, let's..."

"Sam, I..."

"Damn it, Lili! We're engaged to be married! What does a guy have to do to..." He closed his eyes and sat back, sighing extravagantly. "Okay, you win for now. I guess I'm lucky my girl isn't easy. More to look forward to, right?" He laughed, but there was no humor in it. He turned to grasp the top of the steering wheel with both hands, then bent to rest his head against it, heaving a great sigh. "I just wish you'd be easier with me." He turned to look at her. "I want you so much." She didn't reply. He banged the steering wheel with his right hand, then sat back as if to collect himself.

"Okay," he said again. "Don't worry, I'll be a good boy."

"I'm sorry, Sam, I..."

"No more sorries, remember?"

"It's just that..."

He interrupted her with a brusque, "Forget it." He fell silent, then added more gently, "Remember, honey, our engagement party is next Saturday. You'll spend the weekend, of course, so bring enough changes."

"Yes, Sam. I've been meaning to ask you, what sort of dress should I wear? Will it be very formal?"

"Crystal loves to dress for public admiration, so the more formal it is, the better she'll like it. Get something classy and long." He paused and reached into his pocket. "Do you need some money?"

"Of course not." She was abrupt, then softened it, adding, "But thank you."

"It's just that I know you're on a budget, honey. I don't want you to run out of cash."

"Don't worry, Sam, I'll be fine." *Is he worried I'll embarrass him?*

"If you're sure..."

"Sam, honestly, I can manage." She hurried to change the subject. "Oh, and may I bring Buffalo?"

"Sure, Buff can sleep in your room. Remember we have dogs, though. Be careful they don't eat him."

Pulling her to him once more, he gave her a peck on the forehead. "There, does that suit you better? That's the only kind of kiss I can afford to give you at the moment or you'll have to fear for your virtue all over again." His green eyes smiled into hers. "I'll call you, honey. I may have to leave town again, but I'll let you know."

Standing in her nightgown in her small bathroom, toothbrush in hand, Lili searched her mirrored reflection as if to discover her true self. *How can I look so calm, so serene, while it seems I'm so duplicitous. Sam doesn't deserve to be betrayed and I certainly don't mean to betray him. I haven't yet and I won't.* "I think there are two Lilianes," she said aloud. "One is presumably in love with Sam Meredith—the other is fascinated by Pál Gregor."

———

Lili didn't hear from Sam at all over the weekend, so on Monday she first called his office, then tried calling him that evening at Meredith Manor. Martin picked up on the sixth ring, when Lili had been about to hang up. Now she felt guilty, afraid that the ringing telephone had probably brought him up from the wine cellar at the very least. She greeted him and asked for Sam.

"Who is calling, please?"

"Sorry. This is Lili." When he didn't respond, she explained, "Liliane Greening. I was there for a weekend a few weeks ago."

"Oh, of course, Miss Greening. I do apologize for not recognizing your voice. Mr. Sam is not at home at the moment. Would you care to leave a message?"

Now there's an efficient well-trained butler; there's no reason on earth why he should recognize my voice. We only met once. "No, Martin, there's no message except to tell him I called, please."

Puzzled, she sat on the edge of the ivory velvet chair in her bedroom. Where could Sam be all weekend when he wasn't with her? It was evident there were still quite a few things she didn't know about him.

Sam Meredith was sitting at a table in the golf course restaurant belonging to one of the most luxurious hotels in Georgetown, Grand Cayman Island. The air was oppressively humid and he sprawled in his chair. He drew a design on the tablecloth with a swizzle stick, while his other hand dangled listlessly off the arm of the chair. Although the overhead fans helped somewhat, he had removed his suit jacket and loosened his tie. He'd tired of trying to explain the intricacies of captive insurance companies purchased with offshore funds to the man and woman seated at the table with him. At the moment they were engaged in their own conversation, so he allowed himself a mental intermission as he observed his companions. The man wore a brightly colored sport shirt, no doubt his idea of tropical *de rigueur*. Sam had tried to advise him that Caymanian consulting and banking business was conducted like other international banking business; it was not only professional, but courteous, to wear a suit and tie, even if the coat did come off when one stepped outside. He'd been perversely pleased that Tropical Shirt had looked self-conscious and out of place amidst the bustling, well-dressed staff in the agent's lavishly appointed offices. Sam watched him nervously sipping a bourbon and water, looking dazed, as though he couldn't quite believe he'd actually committed himself to the gray world of offshore investing.

Both Sam and the woman were drinking gin and tonics. Although suitably attired, she wore her voluminous golden hair in an intricate arrangement of curls around her face and her fingernails were very long, squared at the tips and painted white. Probably false, he figured. The inappropriate, artificial structure of her hair style was beginning to wilt in the humidity. Sam eyed her with distaste and let his mind race ahead to his afternoon meeting with another fledgling investor. He hoped he could break it off soon so he could get back to the comfort of his family's opulent condo on Seven Mile Beach. He yearned to stretch his muscles in the pool before dinner. Or perhaps instead he'd choose the sea.

The American couple eventually fell silent. The man in the bright shirt cleared his throat, leaned forward and asked conspiratorially, "What do we do next? I mean, what's next on the agenda?"

Sam was amused. What did he think everyone was doing here on Grand Cayman? Vacationing? He fought a sigh of exasperation; he'd explained all this to them at least ten times, five of which while they were still in the States.

"Today we met with your agent and hopefully you acquired at least a superficial knowledge of each other. I saw you taking notes, so presumably you understand his fee structure and what he is expected to do in your behalf. If you talk on the phone, you should be able to recognize each other's voices, but try to keep phone calls and faxes to a minimum."

They nodded.

"Tomorrow morning at nine-thirty we have a meeting with your banker. Remember I told you to come up with a name for your company?" He didn't wait for their reply and continued. "Your agent is setting up a Caymanian corporation for you and tomorrow your banker will open an account in its name. I'll get your gold Visa card to you as soon as it's available."

They nodded again and the woman said, "Ah," as if this were new to her.

Sam signaled a waiter to bring the bill. He turned back to his companions, smiled and waved an arm in the direction of a couple on the eighteenth green just yards away on the far side of the small lake next to them. "Since you're staying in this hotel, you might want to take in a round of golf this afternoon. It's a short course, land being at a premium on the island. The fairways might not look long enough to accommodate a full swing drive, but you can—Jack Nicklaus has designed a special short-distance ball for this particular course." He paused before wickedly making a suggestion he felt sure would horrify them. "You'd still have time to do something else before dinner. The island is famous for its world-class diving. Why not go to Stingray City and arrange a dive with the stingrays?" He hurried to add, "They call them stingrays, but they won't really sting. It's fun!"

"Oh, no," the woman said. "We'll just sit around the pool."

How did I guess you'd say that?, thought Sam. When Stephen had told him about the people he'd shepherded around for their initial Caymanian investing, he'd said they were mostly alike. Of course, during Stephen's recent trip here, he'd been with the Comptons, who were familiar with the region and its operations. This couple was different from the usual people Sam brought here; they seemed a paradox: timid and predictable in the conventions, but risk-takers in going offshore with their funds.

Sam permitted himself a sigh as he made a motion with his hand drawing them closer to the table. "Let's go over our schedule for tomorrow once more. I just have time before I have to leave for my afternoon appointment."

The couple sitting at the table by the railing seemed engrossed in each other as they sipped punch from tall glasses sprouting mint leaves. The woman sighed ostentatiously. "This is almost too easy, boss."

The man cocked his head slightly. "You feel guilty? You think we're not working hard enough to earn our fee, kid?"

"Don't get me wrong—I'm not complaining. All jobs should be like this." She sipped her drink. "But this Meredith chap doesn't even try to be hard to get."

"Why should he? What he's doing here is perfectly legal. And I don't suppose he's doing anything that a great number of others haven't already done—and aren't still doing, if it comes to that."

"And what's that?"

"He's getting paid to lead them by the hand."

"Then why does that fellow in the States want us to watch him?"

"He wants to be sure of his man. He wants to be sure his suspicions are correct."

She sighed again. "If it's all legal, then why does he care?"

"Ah," he leaned forward and said softly, "The illegal part is where the money comes from and how they get it here. You see, they bypass the tax man." He made a small gesture toward Sam Meredith. "He teaches them how to get away with it and the Internal Revenue Service in the United States doesn't approve. They want every penny they can get from their citizens—that's why they have laws against operations like this."

Chapter 5

"Lili, can we get together tonight?," Paul asked. "Just for an hour or so."

She had picked up her desk phone on its first ring and he could hear her sharp intake of breath as she recognized his voice.

Recalling how he'd asked to see her again after their last meeting, Lili was nevertheless puzzled. "Do you want to come to my house? I'll be home after six."

"I'd rather meet you somewhere else. Do you know that little coffeehouse off campus on Jackson? It's called Hava Java. Can you meet me there around six?"

"Yes, all right."

"Good. And, Lili? Park on one of the side streets, not on Jackson itself."

She agreed, mystified, as she put down the receiver.

He was waiting for her in a dark booth with a cup of coffee in front of him when she tugged the door open and peered around the dimly lit, crowded coffeehouse. Spotting him, she crossed the room and slid into the seat opposite him. He admired the way she instinctively kept her voice down, not greeting him effusively as many women would have done.

Although she had no clue, she seemed to know this meeting was clandestine and was conducting herself accordingly. She said, "I parked around the corner where there was no streetlight."

He nodded approval. "I'll get you a cup of coffee." He hesitated. "Regular?"

"Did you think I was a latte drinker?"

"I hoped not." He grinned and left the booth. He was wearing a natural crew neck sweater and soft, dark brown, full cut trousers. From her various observations of him, it was obvious that Paul Gregory was a man who did not want to be conspicuous, who always dressed well enough to go unnoticed. But he was conspicuous in spite of himself, she was amused to note. Accustomed now to the dim light, she could see how all the women turned to look at him as he walked by. And a college town was one of the few places he wouldn't be remarkable by the length of his hair, even though he always wore it neatly brushed back, caught at his neck in a self-styled ponytail.

He returned to the table, setting a coffee cup in front of her and resumed his seat. "Why did you come?"

Color rose in her cheeks. "You apparently want something from me. You said we were friends. I assume I can I help you in some way?" She raised her brows.

"Yes, I think you can."

She giggled nervously. "This is all so weird, Paul. What are you talking about? How can I help you? Help you do what?"

"How serious are you about your friend Meredith?"

"About Sam? I told you, we're engaged to be married. In fact, our engagement party is planned for next weekend. I'd say that's pretty serious." Her eyes looked enormous in the semi-darkness. "Why are you asking me this?"

"Maybe I was hoping..." He seemed to search for a word, then shrugged. "Never mind. Have you set a date yet?"

"No, we haven't. Actually, we haven't even discussed any wedding details at all," she responded somewhat ruefully.

"How well do you know Meredith?"

"What exactly do you mean? We've been dating for several months now, and we see each other every day or so." She stopped, then sighed. "At least, we used to. Come to think of it, we've seen each other much less often since we've become engaged. He's been out of town a lot and..." Her voice trailed off as she realized how feeble the excuse sounded. She looked away, then back again as she asked, "Why do you want to know? I mean . . ."

He broke into laughter. "What business is it of mine, you mean."

"Well... ?" She widened her eyes at him.

"I guess I can't blame you. The obvious answer is it isn't any of my business. But as your friend—I know, we've only just met—but I do know you and I consider myself your friend. And so I want to know more about the man you intend to marry. How much do you know about him?" He picked up his coffee cup, adding, almost as an afterthought: "And his family." He drank and set the cup down.

Lili looked earnestly into his eyes. "Paul, I've got to tell you I know a lot more about Sam than I do about you, yet you expect me to bare my soul to you. Sam and his family?" she asked incredulously, not expecting a reply. "It's a matter of public record. The Merediths have been here forever, since the Civil War." She paused and compressed her lips. "Even if I take you at your word when you imply you only have my good at heart, still..."

"I know, it's asking a lot. And, believe me," he searched her face, "I do have your good at heart. Just humor me, will you?"

Lili sniffed to express doubt. She sat for a moment, unmoving, then exhaled deeply and said, "Okay, I'll tell you what I can, as long as it's not too personal." He nodded and looked at her expectantly.

Absently wondering why she trusted this peculiar man, she filled her lungs and began, "As you know, the Merediths own the First Mercantile Bank, but Sam doesn't work there. He's on the Board of Directors, but he chairs the Department of Forestry at the university."

He nodded again and she continued, but after two minutes she stopped her narrative, realizing she had nothing more to say. For the next half-hour Paul asked carefully worded questions, the answers to most of which Lili had to admit she didn't know.

Finally, she said, "Sam never talks much about the bank, but I think I know enough about him and his family to know they're perfectly respectable people, if that's what you're getting at."

He hesitated and suppressed a sigh. "Right." Then he glanced at his watch and said, "I've kept you here longer than I promised. There's something more that I want you to do for me; give me your hand." He reached across the table, took her left hand and pressed a scrap of paper into her palm. "That's my beeper number on top. The other one is my home number; it's private, unlisted. I want you to call me if, at any time or for any reason, you feel you need a friend." He added, "Or if you think you need help." At her look of bewilderment, he changed the subject. "Let's go."

He watched her as she slowly put the paper scrap into her wallet. He had satisfied himself that she had no knowledge of Sam's actual whereabouts and seemed genuinely ignorant of his activities. For her part, Lili thought Paul altogether perplexing.

He walked her to her car and, as he opened the door for her, he said something so softly she couldn't be sure of his words, something about souls dwelling in the house of tomorrow. It made no sense, but when her glance questioned him and his expression gave away nothing, she decided she was mistaken. Paul said goodnight and stood at the curb looking after her as she pulled away from the curb.

Reaching the corner, she turned left, planning to go straight home, but changed her mind as she remembered she needed to stop to buy milk and bread. She made a U-turn at the next corner and drove back past the coffeehouse. She was two car lengths behind Paul's Galant as it pulled away from the curb and merged with the Jackson Street traffic. The streetlight shone into his car and Lili's mouth dropped open in surprise as she watched the blonde woman in the passenger seat reach over to kiss him.

Chapter 6

Saturday morning dawned clear and bright, one of those warm, spectacular days that can occur in early spring. The redbud trees were in full bloom, their delicate flowers ranging from light pink to deep violet, their still leafless branches darkly graceful and ethereal against the more dramatic splashes of wild crabapple blossoms massed along the roadsides.

Lili drove to Meredith Manor in her own car, having explained to Sam the many things she had to do before she could leave home. She felt mildly presumptuous as she pulled to a stop at the base of the stairs leading to the mansion's imposing entrance. She grabbed Buff with one arm and got out of her car, ran up the steps and, grasping the massive brass knocker, let it fall once. Martin opened the double doors immediately, saying, "Everyone is on the patio, Miss Greening. I'll show you the way."

"Please don't bother about me," Lili protested. "I know I'm late, so I'll just go upstairs and get settled. Am I in the same room, the yellow room?"

"Yes, Miss Greening. I'll bring your things upstairs now, then I'll go out and tell them you're here."

"Thanks, Martin."

Her suitcase open on the bed, Lili carefully unpacked her things for the weekend at Meredith

Manor. Hands on her hips, she lovingly examined the long dress and hooked its hanger from the top of her closet door. It was the color—or non-color—of champagne. The high necked tightly fitted bodice was made of intricately woven ribbon lace, deepening to a point in both the front and the back a few inches below the narrow waistline. The lace cuffs of the long sleeves were also tapered to appear as graceful points atop each hand. Its silk chiffon skirt, neither narrow nor full, would sway gracefully as she moved. The whole effect was one of understated elegance. The magnificent diamond ring would be the only piece of jewelry she would wear that night.

An hour later she had bathed and dressed, applied her makeup, and was seated at the dressing table, having finished pinning her hair into a gleaming French twist. Buff had contentedly curled himself up in the chintz covered chair and Lili was holding her much loved and carefully preserved bottle of Raphael's Réplique perfume in her hand when she heard a knock at the door.

"Come in!" It was probably Sam checking to see if she was ready. The door opened and, to her surprise, Stephen entered the room.

He stood for a moment in silent appreciation. "My dear Lili, you look beautiful," he said as he approached her. He had the sure instincts of a consummate actor, she thought. He didn't just enter a room—he made an entrance. She began to rise from the flounced dressing table stool, but he motioned her to remain seated, saying, "Stay just as you are. I've brought you a small engagement gift which I hope you'll wear tonight." He held a velvet box toward her.

Looking a question, she slowly reached for the box and opened it. Inside were a pair of glittering diamond stud earrings, about half a carat each, she judged.

"They belonged to my wife, Sam's mother. I bought them for her in Montparnasse many years ago. I can't think of anyone I'd rather have them than you, my dear. I'd like you to wear them tonight if you will."

"But surely Crystal... ?"

"Crystal has plenty of her own jewelry."

"Mr. Meredith, I hardly know what to say," Lili murmured.

"Say thank you and put them on." Stephen smiled, smug in the knowledge he'd made a grand gesture and she was now in his debt.

Laughing, she said, "With pleasure. Thank you." And she did so.

"You're more than welcome." He smiled. " Now, if you're ready, may I escort you downstairs? I think guests are beginning to arrive." He offered her his arm and they descended the stairs together. In her high-heeled evening slippers, Lili observed that her eyes were on a level with his. Although she still couldn't quite feel comfortable in his presence, Lili was touched by his generosity and courtly manners.

As Stephen and Lili took their places next to Sam and Crystal, the large foyer was quickly becoming packed with people arriving faster than they could disperse down the wide hallway. Martin could be seen directing the crowd through to an anteroom where a long bar was arranged and where many already had gathered. A wide doorway led into a connecting room where row upon row of coat racks had been assembled and three young ladies were busily hanging various coats and wraps. The spacious hallway was crowded with guests on their way to the ballroom ablaze with light. A combo was tuning up in a near corner. Just before Sam and Lili entered, the lights were lowered and she was mildly surprised to recognize Johnny Hughes, the sometime-piano player from Pal's, at the keyboard of the concert grand in the corner. A pretty blonde vocalist began singing "At Last" as a spotlight singled her out, turning her short curls into a shining halo. She was wearing a strapless sapphire blue satin gown and long blue gloves extended just above her elbows. She stood on a carpeted platform before a hanging mike, her arms relaxed and at her sides as she continued, "... my love has come along..." Her voice was lovely, Lili thought, almost husky in timbre, true and straight from the heart. She was beautiful.

"What do you think of her, honey?" Sam put an arm around her waist, drawing her close.

"She's wonderful, Sam. And so is the piano player. Who are they?"

"When we talked about entertainment for tonight, I asked around. These two perform at Pal's and everybody raves about them, so I called there."

"You called Pal's?"

"Sure. She's the hostess, but she sings there, usually on weekends—and he's the dishwasher and piano player." Sam laughed and added: "He's working his way through as a music major."

"What are their names, do you know?"

"Johnny Hughes, I think it is." He turned to the singer as she bowed to the applause. "And her name is Jan something."

A passing waiter holding a tray of champagne glasses interrupted them. Sam took two and handed one to her. What appeared to be a squadron of servants passed trays of canapés and kept glasses filled.

At that moment Stephen stepped up to the microphone and asked for attention. He motioned the waiters to fill everyone's champagne glasses. When this was accomplished, he called for silence. There was an immediate hush as he announced, "I'm pleased to see so many of our old friends here tonight—and newer friends as well." Lili spotted everyone from Graphics and Pubs standing in a group. Angie was there, too, talking with C.J.

Sam whispered, "Dad's in his element playing to a crowd," to Lili's delighted agreement.

Stephen, smiling, lifted his glass in a toast. "I am happy to announce the betrothal of my son, Samuel Meredith, to Miss Liliane Greening." He turned to locate them in the crowd, held his glass high and raised his voice. "Welcome, Lili." He looked down at her and continued. "I consider myself fortunate to be gaining such a lovely and charming daughter-in-law. And I'm equally lucky to have such a discerning son; Sam has chosen well. To Lili and Sam!" He drank.

"To Lili and Sam," the crowd chorused.

Sam turned to Lili, saying, "To us, blue eyes. You look terrific; you're the most gorgeous woman here."

As she looked up into his green eyes, her own eyes misted and her heart filled. "I can hardly believe this is happening to me, Sam," she breathed. "I'm so happy."

"I do love you, Lili." To the delight of the crowd, he pulled her to him and kissed her. "I'll always love you."

He released her before she could reply, grinned and said, "You're a knockout in that dress and I like your hair that way, too. I'm glad I didn't let Crystal take over for you."

At Lili's questioning look, he went on, "Yes, she wanted to, but I told her you'd do all right on your own." He smiled down at her, "Come on, honey. I want to dance with the future Mrs. Meredith."

He swept her away to the open dance floor. An enormous chandelier sparkled overhead and myriad crystal sconces shone brightly on the walls. A male vocalist, one of the combo, began to sing "The Girl

That I Marry" and Sam led her into the first dance of the evening. The diamond ring on her left hand resting on his shoulder flashed brilliantly as they moved to the music.

Placing his cheek on her hair as he held her, Sam murmured, "You not only look terrific, you smell terrific, too. What perfume are you wearing? I want to get you a big supply of it."

"I'm glad you like it, Sam; it's my favorite, too, but I rarely wear it. It's called 'Réplique' and it's made by Raphael. I'm afraid you can't buy any more, though. Lately I can't find it anywhere, short of going to Paris and I'm not sure they even have it there. I'm afraid they've discontinued making it. Since this is my last bottle, I treasure it and save it for very special occasions." Lili smiled up at him. "Like tonight."

"We'll go to Paris and if it still exists, we'll find it for you."

"Find what?" Crystal whirled by in the arms of Manuel Romero. Sam grimaced when he recognized Crystal's partner.

Lili poked a finger into his side and hissed, "Behave, Sam." The four of them came to a breathless halt in front of one of the small cocktail bars in each of the room's four corners. Champagne flutes were arranged at one end and Sam motioned the barman to fill two of them. Crystal and Manuel took two more before she repeated, "Find what?"

"Lili seems to have the last remaining bottle on earth of her favorite perfume," Sam explained. "So I told her we'd buy more when we go to Paris." He grinned down at Lili and hugged her.

Crystal raised her eyebrows. "Oh? What's it called? Did you bring it with you, Lili?"

"Réplique. Yes, and I'm being ever-so-careful with it. Making sure its stopper is in tightly, you know, keeping it in its box in a dark drawer and all."

Lili laughed. "I guess I'm being paranoid, but it was my mother's favorite, too. She introduced me to it and I'm afraid when this is gone I'll have one less thing to remember her by."

The orchestra started playing a waltz and Sam swung Lili into it. He spun her around and around until she became quite lightheaded. Which was only to be expected, she later reflected. Because she would remember this party and this night as marking the beginning of the end of her dream.

———————

Lili woke abruptly to the faraway high-pitched yelping of a dog. She turned over, restless in the large canopied bed, but the pained yelping continued. Buff. She was instantly awake. He was hurt, she knew at once. Abruptly, she sat up, threw her legs over the side of the bed and punched her arms into the sleeves of her dressing gown. As she opened her bedroom door, the dog's pain-filled cries became much louder and seemed to be coming from downstairs. She raced down the staircase, her bare feet pounding each tread, then along the hall to the dining room. She came to an abrupt halt in the doorway, tears springing to her eyes as she ran forward and knelt before the body of the little dog whose fur was soaked with blood. Unable to rise, but sensing Lili's presence, he pathetically tried to wag his tail.

She was dimly aware of someone standing by the wall where the portraits hung and, bewildered, she looked up. "What happened?"

"I kicked him and I'll keep kicking him until he stops that insane squealing," a furious Crystal spat the words.

"You what? You kicked him?" Lili was incredulous. She looked at the hard points of the toes of Crystal's high-heeled satin slippers. The slipper on her right foot was deeply stained with blood.

Crystal's face was white with rage and she was out of breath. "The little bastard jumped on me and tore my silk negligée. Of course I kicked him." The cook was now standing in the room, along with a serving girl and one of the maids. Martin, the butler, joined them as Lili, holding the bleeding dog in her arms, rose slowly to her knees, then got to her feet, her eyes never leaving Crystal's.

"You must be mad." Lili's face was burning as her anger grew, but her eyes were blue and icy as she went on, "Don't you ever dare touch my dog again, or..."

"Or you'll what, you little tramp?," Crystal cut in. "What are you and your stupid dog doing here anyway?" She swept her arm about in a gesture encompassing the opulence of their surroundings. "You've tricked Sam with your phony shy and demure act, but you don't fool me, you conniving little fortune hunter." Here she lowered her voice to a hiss. "He can do so much better than the likes of you, Little Miss Nothing." Her words dripping scorn, she said, "Look at you, bare-footed, your hair untidy—you don't even know how to behave in a proper house." Then, turning to the servants standing aghast in the kitchen doorway, she shouted, "Don't you have anything else to do? Perhaps you don't like your jobs anymore?" Gathering her negligée around her, she stormed past Lili and out of the door into the hallway.

Lili was astounded at this unwarranted attack, not only on Buff, but also on herself. It was so unfair. Tears again started in her eyes and she glanced around in pained embarrassment. Crystal was right; she didn't belong at Meredith Manor. She had never been welcome here and the future loomed menacingly. At the same time, she was aware that her own behavior was somehow out of synch and not appropriate for the situation, but she couldn't seem to comprehend the reason why.

Suddenly she no longer held Buff; her arms were empty and she cried out in despair. Then she felt a sudden thump as a small furry body jumped on the bed and she opened her eyes to see Buffalo standing on the pillow next to her face and looking down at her curiously, his head cocked to one side in earnest entreaty.

"You precious little dog," she exclaimed as, overcome with relief, she held him to her tightly. "You're safe, you're all right, aren't you? It was only a dream—a bad dream." *And what an ugly dream it was.* She shuddered.

Sometimes it takes a dream, she considered a little later, to bring certain truths to our conscious minds. She wondered why she hadn't realized before how perfectly obvious Crystal was in her implacable opposition to her marriage to Sam. Then she understood that of course she had realized it, but deliberately and resolutely refused to confront it. When Sam had entered her life it had been as though the sun had at last come out from behind endless clouds. When Sam had asked her to marry him, she'd felt like a storybook princess. Sam represented all that was bright and safe and—be honest, she reminded herself—the Meredith family represented security, wealth and power. She'd believed that if only she could be part of this immensely confident, influential family she could leave behind those dismal years of poverty, unhappiness and futility.

So, having come to this new state of awareness, what do I do now?, she asked herself. *You must win over the opposition,* came the immediate reply.

She sat up and peered at the clock on the dressing table. Time to get up, dress and get downstairs. She vowed to hold her head high, paste her best smile on her face and keep it there. *Everyone will like me—I'll make them like me—even Crystal—and we'll all live happily ever after.*

An hour later as she sat with Crystal and Sam in the sunny breakfast room, Lili was very close to screaming with frustration, but forced herself to smile as she responded with civility to Crystal's incessant conversational barbs. Sam, on the other hand, had clearly had enough.

"What's your problem, Crystal? Are you going to blame one of your famous headaches for your bad manners? Or is it your stomach this time?" He sighed in exasperation. "Why are you continually trying to provoke Lili?"

"I don't know what you mean, Sam." The bold expression in Crystal's eyes told him she understood perfectly, however. "Let Lili speak for herself."

He rose abruptly, taking Lili's wrist and drawing her up with him. "Her good manners prevent her from responding the way you deserve, Crystal. I think we've had enough of your filthy disposition for one morning." He walked to the door, his arm around Lili's waist. *So much for my good intentions,* thought Lili. *Crystal's going to prove much more difficult than I'd anticipated.*

Crystal's scornful laughter followed them and he turned, exasperated. "When are you going to grow up? You're nothing but a spoiled brat, an embarrassment to the family." He led Lili from the room, slamming the door.

His arm still around her, he drew her closer to him. "I apologize for my sister's bad behavior. Sometimes I can't understand her. No, make that most of the time." Without waiting for a reply, he brightened, saying, "We still have all day before you have to go back. What would you like to do? Feel like a hike? I'll show you the walnut trees!" Whistling for Buff, they ran from the house hand in hand.

Hours later they returned breathless, but laughing and happy, Buff scampering after them. Running into the house ahead of Sam, Lili came to an abrupt halt as his arms encircled her from behind. He turned her to him and kissed her lengthily.

"I can't seem to let you go even for a few minutes," he said as he finally freed her.

She matched his solemn expression with one of her own. "And I don't want you to, Sam." But then she laughed. "But I'm only going upstairs to get my things."

"If you're away for more than five minutes I'm coming up after you."

"Time me!" And she and Buff ran up to the yellow room.

When she opened the door, Lili and Buff looked at each other in astonishment. The scent of Réplique was everywhere; it permeated the air. Incredulous, Lili stood perfectly still in the middle of the room as she surveyed the destruction. Her carefully preserved perfume bottle had been thrown with sufficient force to smash the mirror of the dressing table. Shards of glass were scattered on the table and some had fallen to the floor. There were some damp and sticky spots on the table top where the perfume had eaten the wood's finish, but what remained of her precious supply had been spilled and had entirely evaporated. Lili stood in the bright and cheery yellow bedroom slowly shaking her head as she took in the extent of the damage. Crystal had indeed declared open warfare.

"Sam, I mean it. I'm not going back into the house. No, please don't hold me." This last was added as Lili struggled away from Sam, who was trying to stop her flight down the front steps of the mansion.

"Wait a minute, Lili!" Catching up and passing her, Sam stood on the step below and faced her, holding her by each shoulder. "You little fool, you're going to fall. Let me help you." He took her suitcase away from her; she carried the dress she'd worn the night before folded over one arm. He opened her car's door for her, then walked around it and got in the other side. He turned and faced her, his back resting against the door.

"Do you mind telling me what's going on? What's your big rush?"

"Couldn't you smell it?" Lili was still breathing heavily. As she'd stood in the yellow room, after the first moment of disbelief and shock, she'd grabbed Buffalo and run out to her car with him under her arm. After she'd stowed him safely inside the car, she'd gone back up to the room where she'd thrown all her things into her suitcase, pulled her dress down from the door where it was hanging, and run out of the house. She'd had no further plan than to get into the car and drive away.

"Smell what?" Sam's was baffled.

"My perfume. She's smashed it on the dressing table and it's all gone now. The room reeks of it." Lili thought it was just as well she couldn't get any more

Réplique. She could never again experience its scent without associating it with Crystal's implacable hatred. Almost as an afterthought, she added, "She broke the dressing table mirror, too."

"Come on, let's go back inside. I want to see this." Sam began to get out of the car.

"I mean it, Sam. I'm not going back in there." Lili was unrelenting.

"What? Honey, please come in. Don't worry, I'll take care of Crystal. I don't understand what this whole thing is about, but I'll let her know she's to leave your things alone..."

"It's about much more than ruining my things, Sam. She hates me, it's as simple as that. She doesn't want me at Meredith Manor." As she spoke, Lili had been looking at the house, but now she turned and looked directly at Sam as she added defiantly: "And that's fine with me. I don't want to be in the same house with her ever again. And I won't be."

"We've got to face her now, honey," Sam entreated. "When we're married we're going to live here, and..."

"I can't do it, Sam. I cannot live in the same house with your sister. Surely you can see that? How can you expect me to?"

"Not live at Meredith Manor? Lili, I'm..."

"I know, Sam; you're the eldest son. But... look, can't we get our own place, just a little house? Or we can live in mine."

Appalled, Sam said, "When you think about it, that's pretty funny. Can you see *us* living in your little rented house? Like poor relations, banished from the family home. Get real, Lili."

"It's so real to me right now that I know I'm not setting foot in that house again." She gestured to the mansion as if to make sure he understood which house she meant.

He sighed deeply. "Okay, you win for now. I can't even take you home because you drove over in your own car. And I'm going away again tomorrow, but I'll call you when I get back."

He looked so disconsolate she relented a little. "When you see your father, Sam, tell him it was a wonderful party. And tell him I'm sorry. When he learns what happened, I'm sure he'll understand why I can't go back there."

A few minutes later as she pulled away from the house, Lili turned to wave at Sam. He was standing on the steps waving to her and above him Crystal stood framed in a brightly lit window. Lili couldn't see it, but she was sure she was smiling in triumph.

———————

Just before she fell asleep that night, Lili thought it puzzling that, although it was perfectly clear to her why she wouldn't return to Meredith Manor, Sam couldn't seem to comprehend the enormity of Crystal's hatred. And as far as Crystal was concerned, she'd proven herself to be vindictive and amazingly reckless, an adult who used the tactics of a spoiled child. She only played the game according to her own outrageous rules. How could she, Lili, hope to win without lowering herself to Crystal's level? She asked herself if she really wanted to win Crystal over and knew she no longer cared to try. Crystal was hateful, thoroughly wicked. Surely Sam wouldn't blame her for not setting foot in Meredith Manor while Crystal was there.

She eventually dozed, but her sleep was fitful and, when she woke sometime around midnight, she instinctively turned to see if the leaves were dancing in the moonlight. There was no wind, however, and the leaves were still. Lili found herself watching the pattern of moonlight as it worked its way across the wall and onto the ceiling into the wee hours of the morning before sleep finally overcame her.

Chapter 7

Sam didn't call her on Wednesday and by Thursday Lili, at her desk with Mendelssohn's First Symphony playing on her office radio, wondered if he was neglecting her purposely. Could he think she'd change her mind? *No, Sam's not like that,* she decided. *He isn't juvenile; he wouldn't pout if he didn't get his way. Or would he?* On the other hand, was she being childish and stubborn about not returning to Meredith Manor? Maybe so, but she didn't care; she was never going back, not as long as Crystal still lived there. Crystal would like nothing better than to break them up, and it looked as if she might get her way if Sam insisted on their living in that house. She didn't understand why he couldn't share her point of view.

Conversely, she thought, to be completely fair, maybe he wondered why she couldn't see it from his angle; it was, after all, his home; it was beautiful and luxurious and in the Meredith family the eldest son traditionally lived in the family home.

She got up and paced back and forth in time with the tumultuous music. As she walked, she tossed a small paperweight from hand to hand, then exclaimed aloud, "Oh, why can't Crystal run off and get married or just disappear?" A passing student worker glanced curiously at her through the open office door, so she returned to her desk and sat down before resuming her dialogue with herself, this time in silence. *More to the point, why does she hate me so much? Why doesn't she want Sam to marry me? What's her real reason for hating me?"* Lili shook her head in bewilderment. As the music ended, she sank into her chair, crossed her arms on her desk and rested her head for a moment. The clock on the credenza chimed the hour before she raised her head again and as she did so her face revealed she'd reached a decision.

As he hadn't telephoned her, Lili called Sam and, learning he was out of the office, she left a message with his administrative assistant, Diane Newsome. Diane had worked for Sam for the past five years. According to Sam, Diane was the perfect admin—dependable and unobtrusive. She was quietly efficient and managed his departmental offices smoothly. Sam didn't seem to know much about her private life and probably didn't particularly care. Diane never spoke of herself, was never ill and, most important, bothered him with no personal problems.

"I'll tell Mr. Meredith you called, Ms. Greening. He wasn't clear about whether he'd be back to the office today or not. Would you like to leave a message?"

"No, thanks, Diane. It's nothing important. I'll talk to him later. Incidentally, please call me Lili."

"Thank you, but I wouldn't want Mr. Meredith to think I was being over-familiar. He's still 'Mr. Meredith,' you see. He likes to keep the status quo." Diane's voice held no objection, was non-judgmental and Lili found herself concluding that Ms. Newsome did indeed seem to be the perfect secretary for a busy administrator.

After she put the receiver down, Lili sat looking at it for a few moments. She hadn't appreciated the fact that Sam seemed to have such a highly developed sense of self-importance. Or, in all honesty, was it really that? It wasn't only that he wasn't interested. Understanding Sam as she was beginning to, Lili reflected that he simply liked everything in his working life, as well as in his personal life, to run smoothly without undue effort on his part. As he'd said more than once, that's what he hired others to do. Therefore, she concluded, if that were true, it would explain his neglecting her. He wouldn't see it as neglect; he'd be unaware that his continued absence was causing her anxiety or distress. He had courted her, had proposed to her, their formal engagement had been celebrated, and they would be married in due course. He would feel that, to all intents and purposes, he had won her; she was now safely under his control, and he could turn his attention elsewhere, attend to other matters.

To Lili's surprise, Sam stepped into her office Friday morning, just as she was leaving her desk, her arms filled with notebooks for the weekly staff meeting. He took them from her and set them on her desk, then drew her into his arms and kissed her. "I've missed you, honey," he whispered softly. "Where've you been?"

"Where have *I* been, Sam? I've been right here every day and at home every night. Where have *you* been?"

He ignored her question. "Let's have dinner tonight. I'll take you someplace you've never been before."

"Really, Sam? Shall I dress up?"

"Not tonight, darlin.' Wear your jeans. I'll pick you up at six." Turning at her office door, he grinned and then he was gone.

Lili's eyes were sparkling as she gathered up the notebooks again and hurried to the meeting room.

———

"Sam, I don't think I've ever eaten anything so good. This is delicious." Lili placed her knife and fork together on her plate and leaned her back against the cane chair. She took a long drink of beer from her frosted mug and wiped her lips on a paper napkin. "What's the name of this place again? And where are we?"

"Catfish Charlie's and we're right across the river in Kentucky. This is channel cat we're eating, along with hushpuppies and cole slaw on the side." Sam took another forkful of catfish and finished off the last hushpuppy. "Glad we came here?"

"Oh, yes. How did you find this place anyway? We're a little off the beaten track, aren't we?"

He swallowed the last of his beer and set his mug down. "I've been doing some business at this side of the state for a while now and thought I might start introducing you to it. It's a completely different aspect of Illinois, isn't it?"

"I suppose so. Remember, I haven't seen much of it in the daylight." Lili smiled at him, thinking: *I was right when I told Paul that Sam was often out of town on business. He's been lecturing and consulting about trees all along. I just knew it!* Sam was so good, so right for her. Everything was going to be fine after all.

Later that night as she stretched out in her bed, luxuriating in the smooth Egyptian cotton sheets and pillowcase, Lili relived all the wonderful things Sam had said to her. He'd told her how much he loved her and how he couldn't live much longer without her. Then he'd gone on to say that he hoped she'd reconsidered the position she'd taken about living with him in his family home. He told her how he had talked with Crystal, who denied breaking the perfume bottle. He hoped there would be no lingering hard feelings between them.

Lili realized just how much it had cost Sam Meredith to make this concession—as he must consider it a concession. She was mollified—he'd taken the first step—so she'd smiled and said it was something to think about. In reality, she had no intention of living at Meredith Manor while Crystal held sway there. But she hadn't wanted to ruin their happy time together and so allowed Sam to think she might consider changing her mind. She'd find a way to talk him around to her side later. She was sure Crystal didn't want her living in Meredith Manor any more than she wanted to live there.

As she lay there waiting for sleep, the shadowy leaves danced, forming fantastic patterns on the wall, but Lili eventually turned away from them and closed her eyes in slumber.

Chapter 8

A t ten o'clock the next morning Sam braked the Jag to a stop in front of Lili's house and ran up to the door. Lili opened it at once and handed a large picnic basket to him, which he took and placed in the car's small back seat. Buff trotted outside, lifted his leg at a nearby bush, then jumped into the passenger seat. Lili went back inside for a moment and emerged wearing a light-weight poplin jacket with the university logo displayed on the left shoulder. Turning, she locked the door, then followed Sam to the car, got inside and they pulled away.

As they passed the next intersection, a midnight blue Mitsubishi Galant turned from a side street to follow at a safe distance. After turning east on Highway 13, the Galant stopped at a service station and parked next to the building; its driver then got into the passenger side of a nondescript older model grey Toyota, which pulled onto Highway 13 heading east.

Once inside the Toyota, Paul Gregory relaxed and stretched both arms over his head, his feet pressing against the floorboard in front of him. He was wearing faded jeans, a dark T-shirt and over it a black and grey plaid flannel shirt hung open. He turned, craning to examine the VSS® equipment in the back, then grunted to indicate satisfaction.

Rummaging in the back seat, he found a black baseball cap and put it on his head, pulling its bill down in front. Adjusting his position so he could sit sideways, he bent his gaze on the driver. She was casually dressed in jeans, short brown leather boots and a bulky light blue sweater.

Aware of his scrutiny she turned her face to him and smiled, displaying two perfect dimples. "Okay, lover, do you have another informant? Exactly how did you know what time he'd be coming through?"

"It figured. Remember, I've been watching him for a while now. His new habits are now more or less routine. I think he's familiarizing himself with his hothead brother's area." He stretched a hand over to tousle her short blonde curls. "Don't tell me you were waiting long."

"No, Paulie. Actually, I just got there. Lucky for you," she laughed.

"Lucky for you," he said and did not smile.

They continued driving for roughly three-quarters of an hour, conversing desultorily. She reached over and switched on the radio, tuning in to a light rock station and singing with the music. He leaned back against the seat and closed his eyes. "Let me know if they do anything unexpected. My idea is he'll drive straight to Cave-in-Rock."

She said, "Mmm hmm," and they drove on.

Mile followed mile of rural landscape, which became less hilly as they progressed eastward. Although peach and apple orchards continued to be seen, many small farms were already planted with vegetables, due to this part of the state's long frost-free period. The Shawnee National Forest, nevertheless, covered much of the area, and it was apparent that forests comprised a highly important agricultural resource—nearly two million acres— more than one-fourth of the land was forested.

"Wake up, lover. Our man has turned on his signal—he's leaving the highway."

"I'm awake." He eased himself upright and glanced at the map he held. "Follow him off the ramp, but turn in the opposite direction at the bottom. You know—whatever way he goes, you go the other way. Then stop at the first place you can and make a U-turn, like we've made a mistake. We can keep him in sight then and follow at discretionary speed."

The XJ8 turned onto a narrow road leading into a forested picnic area and came to a stop under some trees near a table with attached benches.

"Damn," Paul groaned. "Keep going. We'll have to park farther up the road and double back on foot."

"Right, chief." They drove on for another mile before she said, "I haven't seen any turn-offs, have you? I think we're out of luck."

"It's okay. I don't think much is going to happen back there anyhow. They're probably just going to sit around and have lunch *al fresco*." He paused, wondering if he sounded affected. Sometimes foreign phrases were more succinct. "But we need to pick them up when they leave." Sighting a slender track twisting off to the left, he said, "Pull off here, then turn it around the first chance you get." He rolled his window down and inhaled deeply. "There's water down there, I can smell it. Let's get out and stretch our legs."

The path widened and divided to accommodate a tree in its center and, with much maneuvering, she turned the Toyota so they were facing the way they'd come in. As Paul reached over and switched off the ignition, she grabbed his wrist, drawing his hand to her cheek. She searched his dark eyes as she turned

113

his hand and kissed his palm. He looked away. She dropped his hand.

"Right," she said.

"Jan..."

"Don't worry, Paul." Her tone was chilly. "I won't take you by force."

"It's just that—I don't want to miss this cat Meredith. I've been after him too long to screw up now."

"Screw up? No pun intended, Paulie? I seem to remember a time in the not-too-distant past when you weren't averse to a quickie and the more dangerous the circumstances the better you liked it. Nothing ever got in your way." She paused. "Or should I say, nothing ever got in the way of you and what you wanted at the time."

They sat in silence until he broke it with, "Let's go down to the water and walk in their direction, make sure they're still there." As they started walking, Paul took the lead and reached up to adjust his cap, tucking his length of hair under it.

Reaching the water, he stepped back to let her precede him as they walked along the shoreline, their feet snapping twigs and rustling last season's dry leaves as they progressed. When they came upon a section of underbrush growing wildly over the edge of the shoreline, they were forced to hold it back with their hands while they bent low in order to crawl beneath the thicket. The small dry branches snapped and cracked alarmingly and as Jan, in the lead, stood upright, she came into a clearing where Lili and Sam were sitting on a blanket under a large oak tree. They were holding stemmed glasses and Sam was pouring wine from the bottle he held in his other hand. A picnic basket was on the blanket, its lid open. The dog was lying next to Lili; he growled and started to rise at sight of the two intruders. Lili put her hand out protectively to hold him back.

Paul pulled Jan around to face him and kissed her lengthily. Then, with his arm over her shoulder, carefully keeping her between him and the others, they continued walking along the shoreline, stopped once more to kiss while they were still under possible observation.

When they'd passed safely out of sight of the clearing, Paul led Jan in an upward climb, leaving the lake behind, as he held branches aside for her. When they reached the road they trekked along it until they recognized the turn-off where they'd left the Toyota. Paul opened the car's trunk, stripped off his plaid flannel shirt, removed his baseball cap and pulled a black turtleneck sweater over his head. He reached back into the trunk and threw a soft fabric zippered bag to Jan.

"You better change. Looks like we've got some time to spare. They hadn't even started eating yet," Paul remarked.

Jan gave Paul a sideways look and dimpled at him mischievously. "Got anything good to read, boss?"

———————

After their picnic in the clearing by the lake, Sam and Lili drove back through a small town with an old-fashioned town square. He parked in a little side street just off the square.

Lili looked at him questioningly. "Are we getting out of the car now? What are we doing here, Sam?"

"No, honey, you just sit still for a few minutes. I won't be long, just..." He halted as he saw Drew's white Ford Taurus came to a standstill behind them. His hand on the door, Sam turned to Lili. "I'll be right back, darlin,' I just have to say something to Drew."

115

He got out of the car and walked to the Taurus, standing with his hands on its roof, bending down to talk through the open window. At one point Lili could hear Drew's voice raised in anger as she heard him speak her name. Sam's tone became conciliatory in another low exchange. Then there was a loud curse from Drew and Sam's voice grew harsh. "You'll damn well do as I say! Get out of town and stay away until you hear from me!" He slammed his palm on the roof of the Taurus. He turned and strode back to his car as Drew sped away, tires squealing.

Lili sat mystified. "What was that all about?"

"I'll tell you about it sometime." Tight-lipped, Sam drove with barely restrained fury.

"I heard my name. Was it about me, Sam?"

"Don't worry about it. I'll handle him." Sam drew a deep breath, turning his face to Lili momentarily. "Honest, honey, everything's under control." He forced a smile. "Now, I promised to show you some really pretty country, didn't I? Let's get on with the tour."

They drove through many miles of beautiful countryside as they neared the Ohio River. Lili was pleasantly surprised to see the extent of the picturesque landscape and when Sam told her about Cave-in-Rock's river bandits she was frankly fascinated.

"Do you mean there were actually pirates on the Ohio River, Sam?"

"Indeed there were, sweetheart. And they murdered and plundered the riverboaters they were able to lure into the cave."

Lili's lips twitched. "I've never heard that story before. You're putting me on." She sobered when she saw he was serious. "It is true, isn't it? How terrible, Sam."

In reply, he pulled her to him with his right arm, murmuring into her hair, "That's one of the things I love about you—you're so cute, so..." here he searched for a word and, finding it, finished with "unsophisticated."

Lili pretended to pout. "That's not much of a compliment. Is that the best you can do?"

"Will 'naive' do?"

"No! Sam..."

"How about 'genuine' then? And that *is* a compliment, believe me." He gave her a quick hug.

She sighed and leaned against him contentedly, the hum of the tires on the highway gradually lulling her to sleep.

"Wake up, honey, we're there." Sam slowly removed his arm, which had fallen asleep, from under Lili's head. She sat upright and looked around.

"Why, it's grown dark. Have I been asleep long, Sam? And where are we?"

"Cosmo's—it's all we're dressed for. Thought we could use a bite to eat before I take you home." He opened his door and got out, walking around the car to open Lili's door. She tried to smooth her hair with one hand while she rummaged in her handbag for a lipstick.

Sam held her door open. "You're beautiful enough." Then, as she turned to Buff in the back seat, "He'll be fine where he is, it's a cool night. We'll crack the window. Don't worry about him, he just wants to go back to sleep." Knowing he was right, Lili allowed herself to be drawn out of her seat.

Although the lighting was dim inside the café, Lili stood blinking uncertainly for a moment before Sam took her arm and led her to a booth. She couldn't be sure, but as they were walking to their table, Lili thought she recognized Paul Gregory sitting with a light haired woman. She remembered her as Paul's hostess, the singer at her engagement party. A few minutes later, however, when Lili excused herself and crossed the floor to the ladies' room, the table where Paul and the blonde had been sitting was empty.

Sam's car slid neatly into the space in front of Lili's house an hour later and Sam switched off the engine. Before he could take her into his arms, Lili asked, "Sam, why were you and Drew arguing this afternoon? I heard my name mentioned. It was about me, wasn't it?"

"Honey, I told you not to worry about it. Drew was just being asinine, as usual. Don't give it another thought."

"You and he were having a fierce argument. It's very hard to ignore something like that, especially when I'm afraid it might concern me." She looked at him solemnly. "Is there anything I can do to help?"

His eyes and his smile were warm. "Just bear with me, Lili. Everything will be all right, I promise." For another moment he looked at her tenderly. Then he said, "Tomorrow's the beginning of another busy week. I don't know my exact schedule yet, but I'll be away for two, maybe three days." He kissed her forehead, the tip of her nose, then her lips. "It won't always be like this, I promise, Lili. In a few weeks this schedule will slack off and I'll be able to do more work around town... the university, I mean." He gazed into her eyes for a long moment.

"That'll be a welcome change. And Sam..."

He looked at her inquiringly.

"Today was wonderful. Our picnic, I mean, not your fight with Drew. That clearing by the water was a perfect setting, wasn't it? I'll always remember today."

"You made it perfect, darling." He drew her to him once again and kissed her, then gently pushed her away. "Now, let's get you and your pup inside the house before I get carried away. You've had a long day and I don't want you getting too tired and then coming down with something."

Although she'd heard the platitude before, Lili found herself appreciating the sentiment; it was very comforting having someone concerned about her well-being.

Crystal Meredith restlessly paced up and down the pool decking. The day was overcast and cool with a light wind from the north. She was wearing a woolen sweater under a blazer and slacks, but even so the chill was penetrating and she wanted to go inside. She exhaled audibly, demonstrating her impatience as she saw Drew approach, looking warm enough in his leather jacket and corduroys. He took a chair at the far side of the pool and motioned her to join him, saying, "Don't give me a hard time, Crystal. If I'm late, I apologize. I got here as soon as I could."

"Oh, it doesn't matter."

Drew sighed. 'It doesn't matter" was one of her favorite expressions, indicating long-suffering; this was not going to be easy. So he forestalled her, saying, "If you have any other bright ideas about how to break Sam and Lili up, let's discuss them first. You really alienated yourself after that fiasco with her perfume and you only made it worse when you denied knowing anything about it. Everybody knows you did it."

Crystal, surprisingly, looked abashed. "Yes, I guess you're right. Actually, I didn't intend that to happen. Something came over me when I saw it on her dressing table." Her eyes demanded his understanding. "It was as if it represented Lili herself—it obviously meant so much to her that I wanted to smash it to let her know we want her out of our lives..."

"And out of our business," Drew cut her off. "Let's not waste time blaming each other. As it stands now, Sam is determined to marry her—says they're in love and all that." He stared into space for a moment, frowning.

"Can you believe it." It was not a question. "We've come this far—this far! And he's screwing everything up because he's in love." Crystal dragged out the last three words, her voice dripping scorn. Her piercing gaze fell on Drew. "He acts like he doesn't care about the business any longer. If we let her, she's going to ruin everything, Drew, you know she will."

"Yeah, I know. I met Sam yesterday like we agreed, and she was in his car. He'd brought her with him, can you believe it? They're still together. He can't leave her alone!" He made a sound of exasperation. "So of course we couldn't talk with her there. I tried to point this out and he orders me out of town!"

"I notice you're still here."

"Well, naturally I'm not going to let him order me around." Drew stood, took a few steps and frowned at the grass under his feet. "He's taking some unnecessary risks. It's like he's playing Russian roulette," he said, turning back to look at her.

"With our lives," Crystal agreed, thinking it ironic that Drew should be complaining about anyone else taking unnecessary risks. Why, he himself was probably the most brash, reckless person in the world!

Brother and sister looked at each other for a moment in silence, each intent on personal considerations. Then he said, "Sam's so cocksure of himself. It's almost like he knows he's going to inherit this year, so he doesn't have to be careful or worry about anything."

Crystal said, "Yes, I've been thinking that too. It's as if there's some unwritten law that says Meredith fathers have to retire at age sixty-six and eldest Meredith sons take over at age thirty-three." She twisted her scarlet lips to one side in thought. Then she said, "It doesn't have to be that way, though, does it? Daddy won't be sixty-six until August, but he seems perfectly healthy now, doesn't he?"

Drew turned to look at her, narrowing his eyes. "And if the eldest son is incapable, why can't the younger son take over?"

"Or the daughter?"

"Crystal!" Drew was alarmed. "You've got to back me!"

"If it comes to that." She smiled slyly. "Not that I don't think I could do a better job. But I know you only want this for yourself, you'd never help me out. That being the case, I think we've got to stick together."

He sighed in relief.

She rose. "But remember, brother dear, I think Sam can run the family business better than you, so I'm still going to try to make him see the light."

Drew's patience clearly came to an end and he stalked off, kicking a wrought iron patio chair out of his way. The sound it made as it hit the flagstones resonated in the suddenly still air.

"I rest my case," Crystal murmured.

Chapter 9

Paul Gregory's Galant wove through evening rush hour traffic, heavy for a small town, but not surprising considering the large university population, most of whom had wheels. The area was still in the clutches of a cold snap, so he wore a heavy dark woolen turtleneck sweater, jeans and short leather boots. He parked on a tree-lined street across from the building where Lili worked, checked his watch, and let the engine idle.

Ten minutes later he saw her leave the building, walk briskly to her Chevy Corsica, start it up and pull out of the lot. He let three cars pass before he swung into line behind them on the one-way street. He had followed her only for a few blocks when she turned into a supermarket parking lot. Paul sighed and parked nearby. This kind of thing was always the most boring part of surveillance. You couldn't go get a beer or a cup of coffee, you couldn't read, you couldn't lean back and shut your eyes because you might miss something. So you just had to sit there in the cold or the heat and try not to let your mind slip into neutral.

After about fifteen minutes Lili came out, loaded some grocery bags into her trunk, then resumed driving. Paul followed at a discreet distance. Satisfied that she was going directly home, he took an alternate route, parked around a corner on a nearby street and began walking. When she pulled to a stop and got out of her car, he caught up with her, asking, "May I help you carry some of those bags into the house?"

Lili caught her breath and spun around to face him. "Why, Paul, what are you doing here?" He was relieved she didn't jump or scream in surprise. Many women would have.

He bent at the hips in a mock bow. "I'm here to serve, ma'am."

"All right and thanks, but that doesn't answer my question. Why *are* you here?"

Taking a bag in each arm, he motioned her to close the trunk lid, then followed her up the steps to her porch and into the house. Hitting the switch just inside the door with her elbow, she led the way into the kitchen where they put the bags of food on the table in the middle of the room. As he followed her to the kitchen, he'd been able to glimpse an old upright piano against a wall with a bench in front of it, a long tan sofa under the front window, a coffee table aligned before it, and a pair of off-white club chairs angled at each end of the table.

Lili pulled the chain on the light hanging above the kitchen table and stooped down to say hello to Buffalo, who had come to greet her, his tail moving back and forth so fiercely it seemed to wag his entire body. She went to the back door and opened it so he could go outside. Then, turning to face Paul, she raised her eyebrows.

He shrugged. "I happened to see you coming out of the grocery store and thought you could use some help unloading."

"You don't have anything better to do?"

"Not really." He kept his expression bland.

"Well, should I offer you a cup of coffee or something?"

"How about a beer?"

"Sorry." She looked crestfallen, then brightened. "I know! How about a martini? I bought some vodka and olives." She was pleased with herself.

"Planning to practice?" Before she could reply, he asked, "Do you also have some dry vermouth?"

"No. What's that for?"

"Then we can't have martinis. But there's no reason we can't have vodka on the rocks with an olive thrown in." He peered at her. "You do have ice, don't you?"

She laughed and pointed to the refrigerator's freezer compartment as she opened a cupboard door and took out two short tumblers. "Are these okay?"

"Perfect."

Paul prepared the drinks while Lili put the food away. Then he followed her to the living room, where they sat in the club chairs, arranging them so they faced each other with the length of the low table between them. Lili kicked off her shoes and sat with her feet tucked under her; Paul sprawled comfortably, slumping low in his chair, his head resting against its cushioned back. He raised his glass in a silent salute, his eyes never leaving hers. She did the same. They drank.

"Wow," she exclaimed, her eyes shining with sudden tears.

Paul laughed. "Remember, it's a martini. You're supposed to sip, not gulp."

"I'll remember next time, that's for sure." She shook her head. "Now, tell me—to what do I owe the honor?"

"I saw you coming out of the store, I followed you home because I wanted to help, and that's the truth."

"You wanted to help me carry groceries?" She narrowed her eyes at him. "Come on, Paul, give me credit for a little intelligence."

"The truth of the matter is exactly what I told you: I wanted to help you." He paused, then went on. "More specifically, I want to help you, present tense."

"I don't get it. You're being pretty obscure. Help me how?"

"Let's leave the subject for now, all right? Suffice it to say I wanted to see you again."

"Okay, we'll drop it. But you must admit, you're being oh-so-mysterious." A tall, dark, handsome mysterious stranger—all the clichés rolled up in one hunk, she added to herself.

He sipped his drink, his eyes on his glass. "Have you set a wedding date yet?"

"No, not yet." Lili's expression was serious as she added, "But Paul, you do know I'm going to marry Sam. You and I—we've talked about it."

"As my grandmother used to say, 'Many a slip twixt the cup and the lip.' Of course, this is the English translation."

Lili fidgeted in her chair. "What game are we playing here?" She was uncomfortable asking such questions, but they had to be asked.

"Ms. Greening, this is no game." Paul sighed. Then he said in a voice so low Lili couldn't be sure she heard him correctly: "Should I take a chance on you?" Louder, he said, "Where's your boyfriend tonight?"

Surprised, Lili replied, "Why, I'm not sure. He said he'd be away on business for a few days, that's all."

"Business where? Doing what? Aren't you curious?"

"I imagine it's something to do with his trees, the silviculture industry, his walnut trees. He often gives seminars on the subject and he consults with other out-of-town growers." That sounded rehearsed, even to her. She was a little nervous now, aware that her knowledge of Sam's job was sketchy at best, yet she was reluctant to admit her ignorance. The truth was, she'd always been hesitant about asking too many questions and being thought too inquisitive. She hoped Paul wouldn't probe too deeply, that he'd let the matter drop.

"Doesn't he confide in you? Is it that you're simply not interested in your future husband's business affairs?" He frowned and continued, his gaze direct, "Or are you—believe me, I really don't want to hurt your feelings—are you as artless as you pretend to be?"

Lili was stung. "What do you mean?" She could feel her face begin to burn. "I honestly don't know what you mean."

"How can I be more specific?"

"Well Paul, I think you're being a little rude. And while we're speaking of business: this is none of yours." She took another breath and added, "And I don't mean to hurt your feelings. Really."

"Touché." He looked at her admiringly. "I deserved that—and more, if I take you at face value." He raised an eyebrow and continued, "You're either remarkably innocent or you're one of the best actresses I've come up against." He looked at her closely. "Which is it, I wonder."

To her extreme annoyance, Lili's composure was beginning to desert her. "And while we're on the subject, Mr. Paul Gregory, people who live in glass houses, you know, shouldn't stow thrones." She paused for a beat. "I mean, throw stones."

"Block that metaphor!" He was laughing at her. "Does that mean you've heard terrible things about me? Should I take offense?"

How infuriating, she thought, her cheeks flaming *I'm becoming incoherent. What next?* "You know what I mean," she added lamely.

"I'm sorry, Lili, but you're so cute when you're angry. Your face gets red and you become tongue-tied." He was still laughing.

"Tell me something I don't know." She looked so pathetic, he abruptly sobered and that made her laugh.

"Well, really, Paul, how would you like it if your face turned red and gave everything away? And not only my face, look at my neck." She pulled her hair behind her ears so he could see the red blotches that had appeared on each side of her neck, spreading to her throat. She held her arms out. "And my wrists." The insides of her wrists looked rosy as well.

"You *are* a mess, aren't you?" She obviously wasn't amused, so he assumed an air of concern. "How long do these episodes last?"

"About twenty minutes if I try to think of something else. And my wrists itch like mad."

"I don't want to irritate you again, so I guess we'd better drop the subject."

"Actually, my becoming irritated isn't the whole of it; I think it's a symptom. I have a skin disorder called rosacea." She darted a glance at him to see if he was laughing at her. Satisfied he wasn't, she continued. "Some light-eyed people like me with a fair complexion and sensitive skin are prone to it. It also doesn't help that I'm of Irish descent...."

"I thought you looked like you might have some Irish blood."

"Did you? Yes, my grandmother was an O'Donnell."

"Was she now?"

She couldn't help laughing. "Yes, her family were O'Donnells from Country Armagh, even though she herself was born in England. And her daughter, my mother, had auburn hair, green eyes and freckles." She took a sip of her drink. "Anyhow, this rosacea business must have been with me a long time. Ever since I was a little girl my face would turn red whether I was outside playing in the snow or playing tennis in the hot sun. I just thought it was normal for me. But the rosacea acted up quite seriously about a year or so ago, so I finally went to a dermatologist. She informed me I have a classic case." She grinned wryly. "My good luck. Leave it to me to get some exotic disease I'd never even heard of before. They say it's exacerbated by stress."

"And I'm stressful?"

"Obviously."

"When will it go away?"

"Never, from what I'm told; there's no cure for it. It's not life-threatening, you see, so I guess nobody gets too excited about finding a cure. And it can be controlled to an extent by antibiotics, which, I might add, I don't wish to rely on for the rest of my life. I use a topical gel on my cheeks every morning and night. I'm thankful that it's been keeping it under control for the most part."

"I'd say so."

She wondered if he meant his remark as a compliment. He didn't seem the effusive type.

"So I'd better behave myself or you'll give it to me."

"It's not contagious!" She giggled. "But I wish I could give it to you because you're making fun of me!"

He found himself liking her, enjoying being with her. He was already aware he was physically attracted to her, but now he felt at ease in her company.

He stood and looked down at her. "May I make myself another drink? How's yours?"

"Of course, go ahead. Mine's okay, thanks. Oh, and Paul? Buff's been outside long enough. Let him in, would you?"

Lili could hear him open the kitchen door, heard Buff's nails clicking on the vinyl floor, heard Paul rattling ice cubes and dropping them into his glass. *The man is an enigma,* she decided, *and I wish I knew what he's after. Why is he so curious about Sam? He seems so kind, I don't believe he's as bad as they say. And—I wish he weren't so attractive; I find myself staring. But,* she reminded herself in a rush of loyalty, *Sam's good looking, too. They're such opposites, it's almost allegorical. Sam's the guy in the white hat representing goodness and Paul—Paul is….how am I to know?*

Paul came back into the room and sat down. Careful not to look at him, Lili took a deep breath and asked, "Paul, I've been told something about you and …. ."

He raised his eyebrows.

"Is it true that you killed a man?"

The question hung in the air for a moment before he replied. "What makes you ask such a question?"

She was watching him closely. "Is it true?"

"Do you want an excuse or do you want a one word answer?"

"Both."

"First, tell me where you heard this."

"Sam told me."

"Under what circumstances? How did the subject come up?"

"I asked him if he knew who you were, that's all. This was weeks ago."

"And he just volunteered this information about me?"

Lili was looking at him intently, as if willing him to deny the rumors. Then she frowned in sudden memory and said thoughtfully. "Oh, I remember when I asked him. It was the night you were at Champignon with that tall blonde, I think Sam said her name was Cynthia Compton. She and I ran into each other, literally, in the ladies' room; she was sitting with you that night." Lili picked up her drink and held it between her palms as if to cool them. "I asked Sam if he knew who you were. You, plural."

"He also knew the Compton woman, didn't he?"

"Yes. How did you know that?"

Paul, having resumed his comfortable sprawl, was again the picture of relaxed masculinity. "Because she's the one his family picked out for him to marry and Cynthia and her family were in favor of it, too. It would have been the perfect match for all of them—an alliance of wealth and power." He spread his hands, then turned one palm up. "In addition to that, Cynthia Compton and Crystal Meredith are the best of friends." He raised his glass to his lips, drank, and lowered it before adding, "But our Sam chose you instead."

Lili's eyes widened and her mouth fell open in astonishment. That explained a lot. She remembered the first weekend she'd spent at Meredith Manor. Cynthia had been there then. How could she ever forget the mockery and malice behind the singing of "Miss America" as she'd descended the stairs to join Sam and the others waiting in the entranceway. Crystal and Cynthia had had their heads together then and hadn't even bothered to deny it when Sam questioned them. Yes, now everything was becoming clear—she almost said *Crystal clear.* No wonder Crystal and Drew had been so unfriendly, so cold to her. She'd felt at the time that Stephen sincerely liked her, but now she knew he'd successfully charmed her. Acting was one of the things he did best—he'd probably just been using her to stay in practice. And from what Paul had just divulged, Stephen had a better reason to prefer Cynthia as a daughter-in-law.

Paul waited a moment to let her regain her composure. "To state the obvious, this is news to you, isn't it?"

"Yes." She was looking into her glass, slowly shaking her head.

"You know, you really are transparent." He chuckled. "I hope you'll never try to get into the spy racket. You'd be lousy."

Still dazed, she smiled in self-deprecation. "I know. And it's lucky I don't try to earn my living playing poker. Not only would I look amazed when I shouldn't, but I'd probably turn red, too." She burst into laughter and he joined her, but her laughter slowly trailed away and stopped. She put her drink down, stood, then walked slowly to the piano bench and sat facing him, her back to the piano. "Paul," she said slowly, "now it's your turn to answer my question."

"I suppose it is." His expression was now solemn, too. He hesitated and suppressed a sigh. He opened his mouth to speak, then closed it again, his lips firm. Finally, he said in a husky voice, "I won't lie to you, Lili. If I said 'yes, I've killed a man,' what would you think of me?"

"I'd want to know why. I'd want to know the circumstances."

"Sorry, but I don't think I want to answer your question now."

"Then I'd have to wonder why not." Her voice was low, her eyes fixed on him, trying to read him.

For an instant she saw him as dangerous, arrogant, a ruthless killer; then he was her friend Paul again, as he asked, "What do you think of me now?"

"Honestly?"

He leaned forward, his elbows resting on his knees, his hands clasped as if in supplication. Furrows appeared on his forehead as he said earnestly, "I told you I won't lie to you, but I can't explain these things to you, not now." His expression fleetingly begged her to understand, then, at her continued silence, became cynical as he stood and raised his chin. "I don't want to outstay my welcome. I'll go now."

"No, really... ," she protested, without putting much effort into it. She left the piano bench, crossed the room and sank into the club chair again.

He walked to the door, opened it and turned to face her. "No, really... ," he mocked her and laughed. There was a certain brutality in his laugh that did not encourage her to join in. Then he left, closing the door softly behind him, and she was alone.

She remained in her chair for a few moments, her drink forgotten on the table before her. This man had an obsession with secrecy. She knew some men liked to cloak everything they did in mystery. Her ex-husband did, for example. And Sam seemed to be inclined that way, too. Maybe it was simply their nature; perhaps all men were like that when you wanted to know more about them.

She got up and wandered listlessly around the room, eventually collapsing on the sofa, her eyes open but unseeing. She dropped her arm and patted her hand on the floor. Buff came over, circled the spot a few times, then curled up and fell asleep while she stroked him.

"I must get up and feed Buffy," she decided. "And I haven't eaten yet either." Yet she remained where she was.

She thought of Sam and the miracle of his choosing her rather than the wealthy and stunning Cynthia Compton. She thought of the Meredith family and how they must resent her for dashing their expectations. And the hopes of the Compton family as well, whoever and wherever they may be.

Then she thought of Paul, who, by his own admission, might be a killer. Suddenly, her own small world, ordinary and routine as she'd found it, seemed comfortable and safe. She heaved a great sigh. What a night for revelations this had been.

Hours later, just as she was falling asleep, a series of questions occurred to her, jarring her awake. What was Paul doing with Cynthia Compton that night at Le Champignon? Was that just one of the many times they'd been together? Was Paul in love with Cynthia? And even if he were, why should that matter to Liliane Greening?

———

After leaving Lili's house, Paul walked swiftly to his car and drove out of the area. He glanced at the Galant's green digital clock display and accelerated onto Highway 13, heading west into Murphysboro. Then minutes later he turned off a rural road into the entrance of a small trailer park. He slowed, carefully drove to the far corner lot under some trees and parked in the space next to a tan and white mobile home. It was well-maintained and roses had been planted on either side of the steps. He had his hand raised to knock when the door opened and Jan, backlit, stood framed in the doorway, her light curls a halo.

"I heard your car." She motioned him in. A Gary Hirstius song was playing softly in the background; he could hear Gary singing the hauntingly beautiful 'Heartbeat Away.'

"Yes, in answer to your unspoken question, everything's ready." She stood with her elbows bent and her hands pushed down into the back pockets of her rolled-up jeans. She wore a soft pink cotton shirt, its collar turned up in back. Her feet were bare.

"Did you have any trouble?"

"Nope." She chuckled. "I don't think anyone saw me, but just to be safe I managed to drop an armful of books and papers by his front bumper as I was stepping off the curb. I had to reach way under the car to get some of my notes. Slippery little devils really slid under there." She grinned and raised her right hand, thumb up. "Piece of cake."

"Great. Explain to me how this is supposed to work."

"What do you mean, explain? Either it does or it doesn't. Don't expect me to understand the theory."

"You're much more apt to be successful if you know how it works."

"Okay, Mr. Smartie. You tell me."

He dropped into a black vinyl armchair, the vinyl torn in several places, and motioned her to the sofa across from him. "A bug basically works by measuring signal strength. It's a small radio transmitter with its own power pack and integrated circuits. As you know, the one we use is about the size of a pack of cigarettes, although smaller ones are available now. The antenna is determined by the frequency—the higher the frequency, the shorter the antenna. It affixes to a metal frame of a car and the antenna must be clear of metal obstructions. The newer units have Doppler components. The new stuff uses a combination of GPI, global positioning from satellites and..."

"What's Doppler?"

"Radar."

"All right, Paulie, that's enough. I understand now."

"You don't, do you?"

"Not really, but I probably never will, so save your breath."

He shrugged and cleared his throat. "Sam's apparently going to be away at least for another day, maybe two. In the meantime, we'll stick to Drew starting tomorrow morning at six. I'll take that shift; you relieve me around noon—I'll let you know when and where as soon as I know." He fingered a place where the vinyl was torn on one of the arms of the chair. "We'll have to meet to switch the VSS® to your car. We probably won't need it yet, but I don't want to be caught without it, just in case. If Drew's on his own without big brother overseeing him, he may take some risks. More likely, he'll lose that lousy temper of his and do something stupid." He twisted in his seat and looked toward the kitchen. "Got a beer?"

"Sure, Paulie. And I've got a minute, too. Why don't you ask me?" She looked at him for a moment, then, as he didn't reply, opened the refrigerator door. "Bud or Miller?"

"Bud."

She opened two bottles and hung glasses over the tops. Returning to the dim living room, she handed one to him and kept the other. She sat again on the darkly patterned sofa, one knee bent under her, and rummaged between the cushions, eventually coming up with a crumpled half pack of cigarettes. She put one between her lips, then started searching between the cushions again.

He swallowed beer and sighed with satisfaction, then eyed her, saying, "I thought you quit."

"All this sexual tension is getting to me." She pulled out a blue plastic lighter, lit her cigarette and leaned back, inhaling deeply.

"Jan, I thought we..."

"Paulie, Paulie, I'm just teasing. Can't you take a joke?" She raised her eyebrows at him. "I'm just trying to get a rise out of you." She grinned. "That's pretty good, isn't it? Trying to get a rise, get it?" Her expression changed to one of coy flirtation and she batted her eyelashes. "If this old couch could talk, huh?" At his look of exasperation, she continued, "Oh, what stories it could tell."

Unsmiling, he drank deeply, then said, "Jan, we both decided to lay off."

"You decided, Paulie."

"We had a serious talk, remember?" He enunciated every work carefully. "You want to nest-build. I am not a nest-builder." He paused for her reply, but she said nothing. He went on, "What, do you need me to tell you again" You're a wonderful, beautiful, talented, desirable girl—you're fantastic. We're a great team. We work together well. But in our business romance is not a good idea; in fact, it can be fatal."

"It never bothered you before."

He stood. "We've gone through all this time and time again, but I'll say it once more. "We need to stay cool and not be distracted by raging hormones at the wrong time." He crossed to the kitchen, rinsed his glass in the sink and put the empty bottle in the trash container under it.

"Sounds good, Paulie. But what really turned you off?"

"Nest-building." Gary was now singing "I'm a Fool." *How appropriate. I wonder if she's playing that CD for me.* He came back, sat down again and gave her a rueful half-grin. "Sorry, kid. I must be nuts."

"Yeah." Her eyes held the sheen of tears. She was silent as she dragged on her cigarette. Then she shifted her position, sighed deeply, and re-arranged her expression.

Well," she said brightly, "can we talk about the VSS® before you go? I know what it does and I think I know how to work it, but I haven't used it on my own yet. Can we go over it? And I keep forgetting what VSS® stands for."

"Video Surveillance System. I've got it in the car now." He motioned her outside and then into the passenger seat of the Galant. He climbed into the back seat where he pulled a cardboard box off a small television monitor. The box was closed on all sides, with its bottom cut out. He cleared away a nylon sports bag, a tennis racquet and other sports paraphernalia that had served as disguise for the apparatus.

"Okay, you understand the premise, don't you, Jan? The VSS® is a remote controlled camouflaged video camera, and here's the important part." He paused for emphasis. "It can be operated from an unmanned vehicle, which means you don't have to be sitting in the car. You can be shopping, having your hair done, taking a walk, anything. Once the camera is situated at a target area, you can point it anywhere you want, turn it on and leave."

"But what about the technical part, Paul?" She wrinkled her forehead. "You know that's going to be my weak point."

"You'll be able to handle it before I leave tonight, buddy. It's no big deal to operate, just pay attention." He showed her how he had hidden the camera in a pair of stuffed dice hanging from the rear view mirror.

"When I switch the equipment to your car tomorrow we can disguise the camera as a speaker in your rear window if you want to give the dice a rest."

"To avoid repetition and similarity, right?"

"Exactly, to avoid compromise. We never want to sabotage our own effort. And you don't have to worry about running out of tape because I'll put a new one in for you. Besides, it has an extended long-play feature." He crawled out of the back seat and walked around to her door, opening it. "Now let's trade places; you get it situated and start it running."

Twenty minutes later he was satisfied she could handle it on her own. "Now that you see how easy it is, you're not going to worry, are you?"

"No problem, boss." She opened her door, got out, leaned back inside the open window and said, "See you tomorrow."

"I'm off then."

She began to walk to the trailer. "And Jan?"

She turned.

"You're okay, kid."

She gave him a twisted smile, sketched a mocking salute, and went inside.

Chapter 10

It had been a bright and brilliantly sunny day and now, as evening approached and the breeze dropped, the air remained balmy. Drew, Crystal and Stephen were sitting at a glass-topped table on the patio at Meredith Manor. Stephen sat on one side, Drew and Crystal together across from him. Tension could be seen in their various positions and was apparent in their voices, which they were trying to keep low.

Stephen's expression was troubled as he faced them. "We've tried persuasion with Sam and it hasn't worked." He rubbed the back of his neck. "Let's be honest, we even tried coercion. He's set on marrying Lili." He looked away, then back again, adding, as he confronted them, "And I can't say I blame him. She's a lovely, unspoiled girl, who will make him a good wife."

Crystal put in, "Cynthia is lovely, too. Her family and ours see eye to eye; we're alike; we all understand each other. Cyn would be a definite asset. And she wants to marry Sam."

"Well, it isn't mutual. Sam doesn't want to marry her, on that point he's adamant." Stephen beheld the two of them ranged against him and viewed them with disfavor.

"It seems to me that when a family has achieved our status, we owe it to each other to marry intelligently." Drew's tone was sanctimonious. "And I think Sam's letting the family down. You should force him to see reason." He thrust out his lower lip stubbornly.

"Love shouldn't enter into it?," Stephen asked mildly. His question was academic, but their answers would be revealing.

"Love," Crystal spat the word as if Stephen had uttered an obscenity. "Daddy, get real."

"Yeah, it's time you ordered Sam to stop thinking of himself and to think of us for a change, Dad." Drew's voice was growing strident, his temper barely controlled. He stood and gestured wildly. "I've tried. He's so bullheaded, he won't listen to me, but at least I tried."

Stephen said, "Keep your voice down." He asked himself how he could have produced such a short-tempered fool.

Crystal tossed her hair away from her face. "Well, as you both know, I've tried too." She regarded Stephen earnestly. "There's real danger here. You know, Daddy, Sam just might get some silly idea about coming clean with her and he'll ruin everything, including us."

"I think we know Sam better than that." Stephen's voice was firm as he added, "You two had better get one thing through your heads. I won't be badgered and neither will Sam." He stood, put his hands in his pockets and rocked back on his heels, looking down at them. His voice grew soft, reassuring. "Look, maybe it's all for the best. The Merediths have always been lucky, but good luck can't last forever. There's another kind of luck, you know. Maybe it's time we retired the family business." He continued in spite of Crystal's quick intake of breath. "We need to think seriously about the future generation and the good name of Meredith." He ran a hand through his hair and struck a pose from long habit. "I, for one, would like to consider us as civilized human beings. And," he paused for emphasis, "here's something else to think about: we have wealth enough; surely with what we already have we can increase our fortunes in a respectable manner." Then he went inside.

Drew and Crystal looked at each other aghast, their eyes large. "Do you think he means it?," Crystal asked.

"He can't be serious, he's just in a snit." Drew put a hand in his pocket, brought out a ring of keys and sat down again jiggling them in his hand. "If he thinks I'm going to stand for this, he's crazy." He glowered at Crystal. "And so is Sam!" Able to contain himself no longer, he flung out of his chair, toppling it to the ground behind him. He stomped through the open door to the house and slammed it with force.

Crystal remained sitting in her place, eyes narrowed as she gazed at the surface of the wind-rippled pool, not seeing it. "Daddy," she said softly, "could it be that you've finally begun to worry about your upcoming birthday?" Several minutes passed and still she didn't move. She said simply, "I wonder..."

The wind dropped and the pool's shimmer reflected the last of the daylight. The nesting song of birds and the scent of lilacs filled the suddenly still air.

In his study, settled in a favorite leather armchair, Stephen closed the slim gilt-edged book he had been reading and placed it on the lamp table next to him. He raised his feet to the burgundy leather ottoman, stretched his legs, leaned back and sighed. The heavy curtains had been pulled together and the lamp light glowed golden around him. He fancied himself somewhat of a philosopher and recited aloud the words of Donald Perry Marquis in his poem, "what the ants are saying." He appreciated how apt these lines were and had unintentionally committed them to memory:

"… each generation wastes a little more
of the future with greed and lust for riches."

He made a steeple of his fingers and gazed at them in frowning meditation. He felt sorry for himself, sorry that two of his offspring were excessively greedy. This hampered their thinking. *How could they be so credulous? As if he'd ever want to dissolve the family business…*

His thoughts turned to Sam, who had always been his favorite, whose talent for deception matched and sometimes exceeded his own. But even Sam seemed incapable of coherent thought since he'd fallen for the Greening woman. He, Stephen, had thrown out a new idea, hoping that between them Drew and Crystal might come up with a workable plan of their own to change Sam's mind about marrying an outsider. Let them earn their very comfortable living for a change. He didn't even care to know what they'd decide to do; he was only interested in a positive outcome.

He sighed audibly. He felt himself settle more deeply into gloom as he considered these things.

———————

"I spent the entire morning waiting for Drew to make a move and he didn't even go outside the house. He's still at home. I'm calling from a box at the Valu-Serv station—you know, on Highway 51 on the right coming from town—so if he goes past I won't miss him. Meet me here and I'll take you to the only feasible vantage point where you won't be seen." Paul listened for a moment, then said, "Of course, if I'm not here when you arrive, that means he's moving and I'm tailing. Then just wait for my call." He hung up the receiver and got back into his car.

Fifteen minutes later Jan's elderly Toyota pulled in, turned and backed into the space beside the Galant. She rolled her window down and Paul passed a small piece of equipment to her, which she affixed by a magnet under the dashboard. Then he brought the VSS® , placing it on her back seat. He looped the camera disguised as the pair of stuffed dice over her rear view mirror, explaining, "Nobody's seen them yet, so you might as well use them as they are." He quickly scanned the Valu-Serv lot and said, "Follow me out and I'll lead you to the location."

The sun was still high overhead when Paul, satisfied that Jan's car could not be seen from its position behind the trees, quietly withdrew and walked back to the Galant in its hiding place a quarter mile away. He slowly backed out of the leafy shelter, headed for town, then turned off and drove to his secluded house by the lake. In his opinion, one of its best features was its situation at the rim of an isolated arm of a large lake at the edge of the vast and sprawling Shawnee National Forest. In the early morning Paul enjoyed watching deer and other forest animals drinking at the shoreline and he maintained he did some of his best thinking during the beautiful drive to and from his home.

Martin answered the telephone at its first ring. "Meredith Manor."

"Sam, please. This is Mel Becker." Paul had never been comfortable with lying, even though he knew that subterfuge was necessary in his line of work.

"Sorry, sir, Mr. Sam is away. Would you care to leave a message?" Martin, as ever, was properly solicitous.

"Do you know when he's expected back?"

"I believe he'll return Thursday, sir. But I'll be glad to give him a message if he calls."

"I'll be away myself. Thanks anyway." Paul's expression was unreadable as he hung up. He punched another series of numbers into the phone, spoke cryptically for a moment, then replaced the instrument in its cradle and sat back staring into space, a smile playing around his lips. "Good old Jan," he said aloud. "She's earning herself a bonus for this."

Chapter 11

After having struggled with an idea he knew his family would consider bizarre and having reached the most difficult decision he'd had to face so far, Sam had cut short his Caribbean itinerary, got an early flight to Miami, a good connection to St. Louis, picked up his car from airport parking and was speeding toward Carbondale. He'd felt heavily burdened for a long time, but now his heart was lighter and he breathed more easily. Although he knew the consequences of his decision would plague him indefinitely, he was convinced it had been the only way open to him and the sole conclusion he could reach—that is, if he intended to marry Liliane Greening. He was amused to realize he'd actually been fighting his increasingly warm feelings for her, seeing love as a weakness he couldn't afford and didn't want. He'd surprised himself when he'd asked her to marry him knowing the family would think her unsuitable. They were pushing for an alliance with the Compton family. Cynthia Compton, however, was the antithesis of what he wanted in a wife.

The simple truth was—he was in love with his angel Lili. Although he recognized the irony in the situation, he couldn't help but see her as his lifeline to humanity; she meant everything to him. Her beauty, her goodness, her honesty were beyond price. He longed to take her in his arms, confess everything and ask for her absolution. Of course he couldn't do that, couldn't indulge himself in such a way; it would be too self-serving; he had a responsibility to protect his family, so he didn't dare. But, oh, he thought, it would be such a relief to unburden himself.

It seemed to him he'd been deluding himself for years and had finally found his true nature. He, who had beaten everyone running on the fast track, he who had broken female hearts by the dozen, he who had gloated that he fooled everyone as he lived his double life now saw his past as a shameful waste. Since he'd finally admitted to himself that he'd fallen in love with Lili, the only thing he longed for was a calm, uneventful life—the everyday sort of life normal men led—a tranquil existence. A wife and family, a successful career that didn't interfere with his home life, that's what he now hungered for. He was only thirty-three, but for as far back as he could remember it seemed he'd always been an adult, a responsible adult. Surely he must have had a happy childhood, but the truth was he couldn't recall much of it. His childhood had come to an end when his mother died. His college years had been pleasant enough, but his carefree life had been terminated the day he graduated from the university and his father had revealed that banking was only a part of the real family business. Oddly enough, his younger brother Drew had not only known about it but also had already been included in a few projects. Crystal, older than he by three years, had been in on the planning since she was in high school. She and Drew were fascinated by it, but in fact Sam had been shocked to learn the truth. Then, as Stephen had involved him more and more deeply in the machinations of the family's various interests, he had displayed certain devious talents and introduced innovative ideas of his own. Stephen had been delighted at his initiative and had increasingly relied on his judgment.

His recent decision, therefore, was a two-edged sword: he looked forward to getting out of this association he had come to loathe, while he dreaded the moment when he must announce that he, the heir apparent to Meredith Manor and all it entailed, intended to abdicate. He winced as he considered how Stephen would react when he learned of it.

Instead of taking the turnoff to go to his campus office, as he'd planned, Sam drove straight on to Meredith Manor. He wanted to shower, change, and see Lili as soon as possible. She'd been right all along, he concluded—the two of them would be much better off living on their own away from the family.

He pulled to a stop behind Drew's Taurus, which was parked at the base of the staircase leading to the double-doored entrance, ran up the steps and into the house.

From her vantage point in the woods across the way, Jan slowly lowered her field glasses in surprise. So Sam was home now and, according to Paul's information, he'd arrived three days early. Picking up her cellular phone, she tried Paul's number and was about to give up when he answered on the ninth ring. Mindful of his instructions, she was brief and used no names.

"He's home," was all she said.

A pause. Then, "I'm on my way."

She settled back to watch and wait, grateful that her elevated view of the mansion was unobstructed by the avenue of trees leading up to the main entrance.

Half an hour later the double doors opened and both Drew and Sam emerged, talking together as they descended the steps. They parted, Drew driving off in his Taurus, while Sam followed in the XJ8. When they arrived at an intersection, the Taurus turned to the right. Jan's gray Toyota followed at a distance, while Paul's Galant trailed Sam into town and directly to Lili's house. Paul circled the block before parking at a far corner, a position that still provided a clear view of her front door.

Inside, Sam and Lili were in a tight embrace, his left hand cradling her head while his right pressed the small of her back, holding her to him. When they finally separated, he led her to the sofa and they sank onto it together.

He took both her hands in his and looked into her eyes. "Lili, I want us to get married now. How soon can you manage it?"

Her eyes widened in surprise. "Why the rush, Sam? What's happened?"

"What's happened is I'm in love with you and— for want of a better phrase—'I want to make you mine.' I couldn't stand to lose you." His eyes implored her. "I want us to be together forever, sooner rather than later. Is that so hard to understand?"

Her heart melted at his evident anxiety. "Why should you lose me? I'll talk to C.J. tomorrow. At the moment I don't know exactly what vacation time I have coming."

"Even if you don't have any vacation time, why can't we get married over a weekend? You won't have to keep on working unless you want to, you know, honey. But if necessary, we can honeymoon later."

"Do you mean not have a big wedding? I thought you were looking for the social event of the season. That would take months to plan." Lili looked away, not meeting his gaze. "And where would we live?"

"In some wonderful house where we could be happy, entertain our friends and," he paused for dramatic effect, "where we could be alone."

Lili swung around in surprise. "Sam! Not live at Meredith Manor?" She was incredulous.

He looked at her sheepishly. "I've given it a lot of thought, sweetheart. And I've decided you've been right all along. We shouldn't live with the family."

"Oh, Sam!" Lili threw her arms around his neck and hugged him. "Any place I live with you will be wonderful. Except one, of course," she added parenthetically. "I'll make you happy. You'll see."

He loved her so much, he ached with it. He felt foolish, but he couldn't keep his eyes from misting over.

———————

Slumped in the driver's seat of the Galant, Paul was also having trouble with his eyes—he was trying to keep them open. He yawned hugely, stretched and forced himself to sit bolt upright in his continuing battle to stay awake.

Sam and Lili eventually emerged from her house an hour later, he helped her into his car and they drove off, the Galant following at a safe distance. Seeing the direction they were taking, Paul played a hunch and passed them in traffic, pulled into the parking lot of Le Champignon and went inside, where he took a place at the bar. He saw Lili and Sam enter and observed the host lead them to their usual table. He saw the waiter bring the ice bucket holding champagne, saw him open it, fill their glasses, and he saw them toast each other and drink.

He watched them while they ate, laughing and whispering together. He observed them as they had coffee and brandy and his eyes followed them as they left holding hands. Still he remained at the bar, knowing he should eat, but for once food didn't interest him. Eventually, he dropped some money on the bar and drove home.

His answering machine message light was blinking as he entered. Jan had left word at ten-thirty that there was nothing noteworthy to report, that she'd followed Drew home and she was going home, too.

What a washout the day had been. He knew he should eat and sleep, but didn't care. He turned out the lights, opened the blinds, slumped low in his Eames chair by the window and stared out at the subtle gleam of dark water a hundred yards from his house. There was little light from the moon and the water looked black. He sighed. *Black as my thoughts.*

―――――――

Lili was sitting at the round table in the staff meeting room, basking in the pleasure of the beaming faces about her. *They are genuinely happy for me,* she thought. *I'm so lucky to be here, to have this great job and these wonderful friends.*

"What marvelous news! We're so thrilled for you," Dorothy, one of the publications editors, exclaimed. "It's just that when you got your engagement ring, you said the wedding probably wouldn't take place for a year or so."

"I know. I thought it would take that long to make all the arrangements."

"So when exactly is the wedding to be?" Joanna Bartlett looked up from a note she'd been adding to a manuscript draft and dropped her pen in distraction as she did so.

"Sam wants us to be married the Saturday after next, I guess that would be May sixteenth." Lili frowned at the calendar she held. "And it'll be here before I know it." She paused and bit her lip as another question was fired at her. "I thought we were going to have a big wedding, too, but frankly, I'm relieved we're not. I'm just sorry it will be so private that my friends can't be there with me. Sam suddenly wants to keep it small," she explained with an apologetic shrug.

Stan, one of the junior designers, asked: "Will you take time off for a honeymoon?"

"I've talked it over with C.J. and he said to take time now if I want; I can make it up later." Lili's fingers were busily tearing off the little ragged edges of paper along the wire spiral binding of her notebook. "But I think maybe I'll just take a long weekend for now and that's because we have to get settled in our new home."

"Oh, right—Meredith Manor. That wouldn't be too hard to get used to. Get the servants to do it." There was light laughter all round the table.

Lili didn't correct their mistaken impression. She didn't want to go into the reasons why she and Sam weren't going to live at the manor house. Not now, anyway.

"Thank you, Angie, I knew I could count on you," Lili said gratefully. "I don't have an exact time or place to give you yet, but it will be the sixteenth of May, the Saturday after next. We'll go somewhere rather elegant afterwards for a champagne supper, I think, so wear a street-length something chic." She listened to the voice at the other end of the line, then laughed. "Yes, my dear, you have my permission to go after Paul, 'The Hunk,' as you call him. As if you needed my permission—he was never *my* hunk. Actually, I think he's 'his own hunk,' but good luck to you." After she hung up, Lili's smile faded rapidly as she sat back in her chair and sighed. Things were happening so quickly, she was beginning to feel as if she were on an out-of-control roller coaster ride.

At Meredith Manor, Sam and Stephen were seated in Stephen's study in the familiar burgundy leather chairs, which had been there, positioned in the same familiar manner, for as long as Sam could remember. He'd chosen to reveal his plans to Stephen in this room because he'd always felt close to his father here; this was where they'd had father-son discussions before and after events large and small. He felt it to be a haven now, impregnable from the forces outside. *How imaginative I've become,* he reflected. *What could I have to be afraid of?*

Stephen, on the other hand, appeared to be unperturbed. "I can't say I'm surprised, Samuel; I feared I could see this coming." He stifled a sigh of exasperation, then forced a half-smile. "But still I can't blame you. Lili will be a lovely bride and I imagine she'll make you a good wife. But as far as your leaving your family position is concerned, are you absolutely sure this is what you want? Remember, once you announce your decision, it can't be changed."

"Yes, Dad. I can see now that I've wrestled with this for a long time without actually realizing what a struggle I was having with myself." Sam sipped amber liquid from a beautifully cut sherry glass. "The other day it simply dawned on me that this was the only decision I could come to and be happy. I should say, 'and not be unhappy.' As hard as I've tried, my heart's never been in the business. In fact even though I seem to have some talent for it—I'm sorry, Dad—but I guess I've hated it ever since I found out about it. And I can see that it would be beyond me to continue to keep Lili in the dark, what with my unexplained absences and odd hours." Sam walked over to the tantalus of crystal decanters on a side table and, selecting one, refilled Stephen's glass, then his own. His father cleared his throat and suggested mildly, "Cynthia's definitely out of the running then? Are you positive about Lili?"

"Dad! I should have thought it was obvious. I love Lili; more than that, I need her in my life." Sam's smile twisted. "And I think you and Crystal and Drew would all agree that she would never fit in with the family's agenda."

"Hardly. Yes, yes, of course you're right." Stephen thought for a moment and said, "Samuel, I don't think it would be wise to announce your early retirement, as it were, to your sister and brother. Not yet. Let's leave that for a later conversation. It's going to be tough enough informing them of your rapidly approaching wedding date."

Sam, who had wanted to get it all over at once, said only, "I was hoping to cut myself loose now, Dad, but we'll do whatever you think best. When do you think they should be told, then?"

"Let's wait until after the wedding. If you're sure this is the direction you want to go, we don't want any nasty shocks until the deed is done, so to speak." He didn't elaborate, but gazed into the bronze depths of his sherry.

Sam fingered a decorative brass nail head on the arm of his chair and studied his father through half-closed eyes. "You know, Dad, I've often thought that you'd like to get out of this business, too. Maybe I'm way off base, but all this subterfuge doesn't suit you, does it? Ever since I've known about it, I've had the feeling you'd rather be doing something else, too."

Stephen wondered how his favorite son could so thoroughly have misread him. Then he congratulated himself on his continued success at veiling his true character. He met Sam's eyes and said steadily, "Strictly between us, Sam, I won't deny it. To tell you the truth," he lied, "I've been looking forward to my sixty-sixth birthday this year because it will mean I could step down and pass the torch to you." He drew his shoulders up in an elaborate shrug and tilted his head. "But now you say you don't want any part of it." He sighed and his posture relaxed. "I suppose that means Drew will take over and that worries me, doesn't it you?"

"You mean because he's such a loose cannon?"

Stephen nodded. "He could land all of us in a lot of trouble with that temper of his. And he doesn't think things through to their logical conclusions. He can't seem to see further than his own interests and as far as long-range planning is concerned, I'm afraid he hasn't a clue." He looked at Sam. *Nor do you, you love-struck fool. Have you any idea what you're throwing away?*

Sam brought him back to the present. "Dad, could you see Crystal in charge?"

"Yes, I think I could." It was obvious that this idea was not new to Stephen. His lips formed a mirthless smile. "I think she'd be damned good at it, perhaps as good as you, in fact. Certainly better than Drew."

"She has the stomach for it, Dad."

"You're right. My only daughter and, after observing her all her life, I can't help but conclude that she has the traits necessary to head this particular enterprise." He set his empty sherry glass on the table next to him and made a steeple of his fingers. "Here's her résumé as I see it. She has a good head for planning, organizing and following through. She is conniving, manipulative and she isn't hampered by sentiment. She can be a hard-headed businesswoman and I think she'd be very successful. Primarily, she has the temperament to rule this bunch of jackals." He paused briefly before going on. "The question is, how would Drew take it?" He took a deep breath and exhaled audibly.

Sam shifted in his chair. "Crystal is the eldest. Why not use that as our logic? Drew can be her second-in-command. I think she'd go for it; let her figure out how to handle Drew." He drained his sherry. "Those two have always thought along the same lines. I don't think there'd be too much trouble getting him to agree when she explains how she's going to change things around here, which would be welcome news to him. You know how he considers me too conservative." Sam cleared his throat nervously as he broached what he knew would be a difficult subject. "Ideally, Dad, we should close down the whole operation, you know we should. Why can't we just do that?"

"Can you imagine the hue and cry if we tried?" Stephen shuddered. *As if I'd close down this gold mine.* "And not only from Crystal and Drew."

Sam leaned forward earnestly. "But think, Dad. What's to prevent us from doing just that? It's time, it's more than time to pull out."

"Do you really think so, son? I admit, the thought isn't new to me. In fact, I'd welcome it." *Has Sam lost his mind?*

"If we want to terminate, what could they do about it?"

"Don't let's go too fast. We've got to consider all possible ramifications. And the family, Samuel, we must consider what such a move would mean."

"Dad, the family would be infinitely better off if we close down the whole operation. You know it's true." At Stephen's pained expression, he rushed on.

"Drew's been dealing with that drug lord Gates for too long now. Dad, that's black money! Drew is unstable and he's headed for a fall. Can you begin to imagine what could happen to us then? God knows we have enough money now—have had for a long time. Even if we didn't have, so what? Is it worth it? We'll all be dragged down if we don't pull out soon. I've felt it for so long; I'm certain of it."

"All right, Samuel, I'll think seriously about it." Sam glanced at him speculatively, so he added, "I promise I'll give it some thought."

"I'm getting out, Dad; I mean it. I hope you will, too, before it's too late."

Stephen sat in silence for a long moment, his head bowed. Then with an effort he brightened and looked at Sam as he changed the tone of the conversation. "So you're going to put all your time into the forestry business." It was a statement as well as a question.

"Yes, I'd like to. After all, that's what my degree is in. I think I should be able to make a living." He smiled to show he meant it as an understatement. Then he sobered. "If you're willing to let me continue with the family's walnut trees, that is."

"Of course; I don't see why not." A cloud crossed Stephen's features as he considered the very real battle he and Sam would shortly wage with Crystal and Drew.

Stephen loved harmony within his home almost as much as he loved control. He wasn't fool enough to think his daughter and second son wouldn't have plenty to say in argument and he licked his lips in anticipation. He felt certain those two would make it clear to Sam that he couldn't desert them in order to marry the Greening woman. Crystal was right: Cynthia Compton would be the logical, sensible and inevitable choice for Sam, even if he couldn't see it now. He hoped that after the coming battle things could settle back to normal at Meredith Manor. He did miss the peace and quiet.

"You're what? You're getting married in less than two weeks? Are you crazy?" Crystal was shocked. Stephen turned away to hide a secret smile as his daughter's expected response proved him right once again.

Drew rose from his chair on the patio and joined in. "You selfish bastard! Don't you ever think of anyone but yourself?"

"How can we plan any sort of decent wedding? There's no time." Then Crystal's outrage changed to a cynical sneer. "Oh, I get it. Your girlfriend's preggers, little miss goody-goody has made sure she'll become Mrs. Meredith, and you're letting her force you into it. You fool!" Crystal's voice threatened to rise out of control. She made an effort to hold the volume down, but she couldn't keep the venom from her words.

Sam reacted as if she'd slapped him. He took a step toward her, but Stephen intervened with a muttered, "Let me handle this," in Sam's direction as he played the role of peacemaker.

"You're way off base, Crystal," he said. "As it happens, Sam is the one who wants an early wedding date."

Drew chimed in with, "What are you using for brains, your..."

Stephen cut him off. "It's their private business, Andrew." He looked at each of them, adding, "And Crystal." His expression was benevolent. "Sam and Lili simply want to be together." Seeing Crystal's sneer, he added, "I know how you feel about love, Crystal, so I won't mention it. Suffice it say they don't want a big splashy wedding." He and Sam had been standing and now he pulled a patio chair away from the table and sat down. "And I fail to see why they can't do as they please." Stephen fixed his gaze on a frowning Crystal, who had compressed her lips to a thin line. "When you finally get around to marrying, your wedding can be as grand and ostentatious as you like." He turned to Drew. "The same goes for you, Andrew. And it won't be any of Sam's business whether he approves or not, although I can't imagine Sam interfering. So do him the courtesy of leaving him alone even if you can't wish him well."

Drew sat down again, but couldn't resist an aside: "The heir apparent can do no wrong."

Sam sat silent and unmoving, slumped down in his chair, his chin on his chest. He'd rather get all the shouting over with now, announce his refusal to have anything further to do with the family or its business and tell Drew to stuff it. But he'd agreed to let Stephen run this show, so he would keep his mouth shut. One more spiteful, snide remark from Crystal, though, would be all it would take to make him forget his promise.

An hour later, as Sam was stepping out of his shower, Drew opened the bedroom door and entered the room. He sat down on Sam's bed as if intending to stay for the interim. Sam tucked the end of a towel in around his waist and looked at Drew inquiringly.

Drew leaned back, his elbows sinking into the bed. "You might as well get dressed, because Crystal's coming in too."

"Do you mind telling me what this is about?"

"I think you know."

Sam began dressing and didn't reply. He removed a white shirt from a hanger and thrust his arms into the sleeves, buttoning each at the wrist, then buttoned the front, leaving the neck open. He topped it with a beige cashmere pullover and pulled on a pair of dark brown corduroys. He yanked on a pair of socks and was stepping into his shoes as Crystal opened the door and peered in.

"Come on in, Sis," Drew said.

Crystal sank onto the bed alongside Drew. She lay on her right side, her right arm and hand supporting her head. Cringing inwardly, Sam knew he was doomed to an argument and hoped it wouldn't take long. He pulled the chair out from his desk, turned it around, straddled it and faced them.

"Lili isn't right for you, Sam," Crystal began. "You know Cynthia would suit you much better, and she'd fit in with the family too."

"You might as well turn right around and leave because my mind is made up and I won't hear anything against Lili." Sam glared at her. "And forget Cynthia; she's not in the cards. Never was; I told you that a long time ago."

Drew sputtered in anger. "You self-centered cretin…"

Crystal held a hand up to stop him. "Lay off, Drew. You see the way the land lies." She was sitting up now. "Sam," she said reasonably, "Say you marry Lili. With your itinerary, she's going to become suspicious and eventually you're going to have to confide in her. Then what?"

Once more regretting his promise to be discreet about his plan to quit the business, Sam forced himself to remain silent, as he ran a comb through his hair and straightened his collar.

Crystal repeated, "Will you confide in this woman?"

"How would I be able to avoid it?"

Drew exclaimed to Crystal, "There! You see?" He turned to Sam. "How can we trust her? You're asking us to put ourselves in jeopardy because you've got some insane crush on this piece."

Crystal fixed Sam with an earnest intent look. "She'll talk, Sam. Sooner or later the Feds or somebody will squeeze her and she'll tell them everything she knows."

Sam could easily understand why they were worried. Lili was an unknown quantity as far as they were concerned. But he said only, "You've got to believe me. She won't." *Because I'm getting out and she'll never have to know.*

"Oh, well, that's all right then. If Sam says she won't, she won't. So why are we worried?" Drew got up and paced, hands in his pockets.

"Is there nothing we can say or do to make you change your mind?" Crystal continued to maintain a calm veneer.

"Look, Crystal, I know you don't like Lili. And I know you don't either," Sam said, turning to Drew. "And because of you two, she doesn't feel comfortable in this house. So we're not going to live here; we won't be in your face every day and none of us will have to pretend we're fond of each other." Sam eyed them boldly, again wishing he hadn't agreed to keep silent about his plans. He wanted to reassure them that they didn't have to worry about any possible indiscretion on Lili's part. He only added, lamely, "Now if you'll excuse me, I have a date." As he reached the door, he flung over his shoulder, "If Cynthia Compton is so right for our family, why doesn't Drew marry her?" He left the room, clattered down the staircase and they heard him slam the front door.

Brother and sister remained in Sam's room for another hour, whispering together.

Chapter 12

S tephen and Lili were sitting at a small table at the University Club on Main Street, each sipping a gin and tonic. Lili pretended to study the menu as she waited for him to explain this impromptu meeting.

"Hope you'll forgive the short notice, my dear, but I suddenly had this compulsion to ask you to dine." He smiled and she automatically returned the smile. *Sam must have inherited his height from his mother,* she thought irrelevantly. Stephen's hairline had begun to recede, the remaining hair had thinned and silvered, yet he was not unattractive. He was extremely well-groomed and his perfectly tailored clothes were well chosen. The expression in his large gray eyes was self-assured and determined. He spoke again, recalling her wandering attention.

"After all, if you're marrying my son in little more than a week, I feel you're family already."

Could this be a prelude to an attempt to delay the wedding? Wary, Lili picked up a bread stick and nibbled it. "What a nice thing to say."

"Not at all, my dear. I know you'll be a fine addition." He drank. "Sam tells me you two don't plan to live at Meredith Manor."

"No, sir." *The man really had a wonderful speaking voice.*

"Please. Call me Dad, can't you?"

Lili bit her lip. "I'm sorry, it's very kind of you and I'm honored. But it's going to take some getting used to." She cleared her throat. "Anyway, we thought probably it would be better for us to live by ourselves. I mean, alone." Here she took a deep breath. "I'm not saying this very well, am I? What I mean is..."

Stephen laughed and said, "I know what you mean, and I don't blame you a bit. In your place I'd feel the same." Then his face grew serious. "One of the reasons I asked you here, Lili, was to get to know you better, of course, but also to offer some advice. Please don't be upset at what I'm about to suggest. I've given it long and careful consideration and I feel it best for all concerned—and that includes you as well as all the Merediths. We hope you'll consent to a prenuptial agreement."

Lili's throat constricted and two red spots appeared on her cheeks. "Did Sam... ?"

He fingered his tie. "No, indeed. We haven't spoken of this. In fact, I'm sure he'd be annoyed if he thought I'd broached the subject, so I'll appreciate your not mentioning this to him."

He wants me to keep this between us. Next he'll want me to quietly leave town without telling Sam the reason why.

Stephen adopted an avuncular air. His smile was kindly, but Lili thought the expression in his eyes cold as he continued.

"Sam is in love, my dear. And men in love don't always take all contingencies into account. Sam has, when all's said and done, many family obligations and responsibilities that most young men never encounter."

She said nothing, waiting for him to continue.

"You and Sam will probably be together for the next fifty years, but I'd be negligent if I didn't propose an agreement between you," and here he paused for emphasis, *before* marriage, so others will feel secure."

Their waiter approached, but Stephen waved him away. Lili opened her mouth to speak, but he hurried on. "Not that we don't all think you'll be the perfect wife for Sam, Lili. But circumstances can arise unexpectedly where lawyers run rampant and..."

"I assure you, I have no intention..."

"Of course you don't, my dear. Not now. But who can say what the future holds?"

He has a beautifully mellifluous voice, Lili concluded, *and a sincere and reasonable manner, which must have served him well in the family bank. No doubt he is speaking good sense—from the standpoint of a Meredith. But his soul is devoid of romance and he hasn't a vestige of sensitivity.* Realizing he was still talking, she frowned in an effort to follow.

"... . so I know I can rely on you to do the right thing, Lili dear."

Lili knew she had to get away from Stephen before she told him precisely what she thought of him and his prenuptial agreement. Even the few minutes it would take her to walk to and from the ladies' room would work to her advantage. She was seething, but knew she couldn't let him know, wouldn't give him the satisfaction of seeing he had deeply disturbed her. She excused herself and left the table.

When she returned a few minutes later she had reached a conclusion that enabled her to hide her anger. She would write him a letter, with a copy to Sam, outlining her understanding of the proposed prenuptial agreement. Sam would deal with his father. In the meantime, she forced her lips into a smile and replied, "Indeed you can rely on me to do the right thing, Mr. Meredith. You can be sure of it."

———————

Paul Gregory sat in the Galant as he waited outside the University Club, his hands gripping the steering wheel and his handsome features marred by a fleeting expression of barely restrained anger. Almost at once he visibly relaxed and his face resumed its customary appearance of imperturbability. Self-control was a discipline he'd nurtured over the years. He was impatient with the shortcomings of others and intolerant of his own, weeding them out as quickly as he perceived them.

He flattered himself that he was master of his emotions. When he had been very young, as a nine-year-old boy, he'd sworn he'd never again allow himself to be surprised or hurt by anyone or anything. He'd determined then that he would not be ruled by his feelings and he'd been largely successful in that endeavor.

Suddenly and against his will, memories crowded back in a rush—a quick, unbidden image of Zsuzsa, his mother, as she told him to be a good boy for his grandmother, who was called Nia, short for Apollonia. It had been his birthday, a bright, sunny Saturday, so he was not at school. He'd expected his mother to spend the day with him; he'd thought the three of them would go to the park together, but Zsuzsa had to go to the Hungarian bakery where she worked, just a half-day, she told him. When she returned from her job at the cukrászda, the pastry shop, she would bring rigójancsi, a chocolate mousse cake topped with chocolate glaze, a favorite of his. Then she, Nia and Pál could go to the park.

Only she'd never come home; he'd never seen her again. Gently and through tears she couldn't hold back, Nia had told him that a man in a big car had not stopped for a red light. His car had struck and killed his mother instantly as she left the bakery and was crossing the street. She had been carrying his cake, her last present to him. Although Nia assured him that Zsuzsa had gone to a wonderful place where she was happy, Pál had that day changed from the bright and cheerful child he had been to a somber, pensive boy, increasingly precocious. He was introspective as an adolescent and eventually grew into a sardonic, somewhat cynical man. From time to time he continued to be visited by melancholy, but as he refused to tolerate it, it never became a problem. Nia told him his Hungarian blood was, no doubt, responsible for his occasional moods, but when asked what she meant by this, her replies were unsatisfactory. He felt certain his moods were caused by his failure to avenge his mother.

Apollonia had had a difficult time trying to explain this disaster to the much-loved, sheltered young boy Pál had been and she had done her best ever since to protect him from the harsh world which had treated them so unkindly. The two of them had lived an even more secluded existence since his mother's death, largely because Nia could speak little English and had only the boy to converse with in Hungarian. As she had earlier depended upon her daughter for news of the outside world, she now increasingly relied on Pál.

They'd been poor before Zsuzsa's death, he'd known that. Yet, as he recalled, the three of them had been happy together. Without Zsuzsa's small earnings, however, he and his grandmother suffered greater deprivations. But he didn't mind the loss of what his mother's small salary could buy; he only mourned his loss of her.

When he was eleven and trying to understand more about what had actually happened when Zsuzsa was killed, Pál had searched the microfilm files of old newspapers in the public library until he found mention of the accident. Even though he felt his mother's fate had been discounted as unimportant, the event was made newsworthy because the man who had caused her death was mildly notorious as a member of the underworld, a local thug and suspected dealer in drugs. After he'd killed his mother, the man had kept driving, hadn't even stopped, but witnesses had given the police a description of his car and one of them had managed to note his license plate number. When the police found him, the man said he hadn't realized he'd done anything wrong and he'd laughed. He'd laughed, as though Zsuzsa's life and death meant nothing. And he hadn't even been sent to jail. Pál understood later that the man had probably bought his way out of trouble. In the neighborhood where they lived, it seemed everything, including justice, was for sale.

For months after he'd read the newspaper article, Pál couldn't lose the mental image of the man laughing when confronted with his crime. Such a man must be a brute, a creature incapable of feeling; therefore, he was less than human and didn't deserve to live. That he resided in a large house and drove an expensive car were additional injustices that must be rectified.

Pál pictured himself as he was on his twelfth birthday—as he began to stalk the man, whose name he learned was Louis Ciolino. He learned his daily schedule of activities and grew to anticipate his movements; following him without being seen became an obsession as the boy began to plan how he would end this evil man's life. He learned to recognize the people Ciolino associated with, the places where they would meet, the signals they would use to tell each other things without speaking, how they could disappear when they sensed danger from the police. As he considered the similarities of the city and how he imagined a jungle would be, Paul began to think of himself as a hunter, a hunter of men in the jungle of the city.

During this time, Pál attended school by day and received another kind of education by night; he became shrewd and street-wise. His innate perceptive abilities, already sharp, flourished. Pál was surprised to find he could effectively watch this man even in daylight on weekends and at night by following him on foot or on his bicycle. He rarely left the neighborhood. By then he understood Ciolino wasn't as powerful as he'd originally thought him; he was just a small-time hoodlum, but one of the worst. Pál was now sure he dealt in things that altered men's minds.

In the course of shadowing the man who was responsible for his mother's death and the end of his own happiness, it had come as an unpleasant surprise to Pál when he discovered that the monster actually had a loving family. One day, while watching his house, Pál saw a little girl leave by a gate and run out to the street as the man began to drive away. She waved to him and called, "Daddy, you forgot to kiss my dolly!" The car stopped at once, Ciolino jumped out and, catching the child with her doll in his arms, carried her back to the safety of his walled home, kissing her and the doll as he did so. A smiling woman joined them at the gate, taking the child into her own arms and kissing the man before he turned to leave.

This happening came as an unwelcome revelation to Pál. At first he was angry and felt cheated. This must be a ruse; such a devil couldn't be loved by anyone. But his eyes had told him otherwise and then he knew he'd have to abandon his long-nurtured plan of revenge. The thought of allowing this criminal to get away with what he'd done was intolerable, however, and Pál lay awake night after night, made even more miserable by the loss of his dream of vengeance.

The following Sunday morning Nia had asked him, as she always did, to accompany her to church. How she could still believe in God, how she could continue to practice her religion, was more than Pál could fathom. Usually he refused to go, but on this particular Sunday he felt a new pity for her. He had a great fondness for the old woman and liked to please her, so he'd done as she wished. He recalled again how he'd been kneeling next to her in the ancient and dim coolness of the massive granite building, unaware of his own prayer, when the solution to his dilemma suddenly occurred to him. The enormity of his relief was staggering, almost palpable, as if his soul—and that was how he must describe it—as if his soul had recovered from a long illness. At last the realization came to him that this Louis Ciolino, this wicked man who had killed his mother, had simultaneously robbed him of his own spirit. His soul had been sick for all the years since the man had so carelessly destroyed Pál's family and his happiness.

The next day Pál skipped school, learned where the drug enforcement people worked and went to them with his special knowledge. Not only did he achieve his revenge that day, but also—as a bonus— a long and mutually beneficial relationship between him and the agency was established.

Afterward, his grandmother thanked God that Pál had returned to her in spirit as well as in body and Pál himself was glad he no longer had to leave Nia alone at night, for there was no further need for his nocturnal observations. At least not until he grew old enough to make sleuthing a career.

All these things had happened a long time ago in his youth and he'd been alone ever since his beloved Nia had quietly died in her sleep one night. She'd been fifty-nine, much too young to die, he'd thought. He felt bereft all over again. Now he had no one to speak with him of his mother or of the old days, no one to call him Pál. Since then he'd been known only as Paul Gregory.

He'd been twenty-two at the time, having graduated from a local city college the year before. His school grades had always been good and he'd been fortunate in having received a scholarship to finance his further studies. He'd also worked part-time for a private investigator, who lent him a car for conducting surveillance jobs whenever he was available. The money he earned in this way had helped to support himself and Nia. Consequently, he was accustomed to watching and waiting. This work took his special brand of patience and in the end he was always the victor.

Upon analysis, Paul understood that Lili was the cause of his present, perhaps irrational anger for allowing herself to be involved with the Meredith family in the first place. Now to find her in the company of Stephen himself exasperated him. Paul thought of the senior Meredith as the spider in the center of a large web. *How can she allow herself to be duped by that smarmy character? Surely she should be able to see what a smooth actor he is!* He was disappointed in her; it was as though she had failed a test he'd set for her.

Realizing that perhaps he was being unfair, he shook himself out of his reverie and back to the present as the University Club's door was pushed open, Stephen emerged and held it for Lili. He took her arm, led her to his car, and helped her inside. Purring smoothly, the Cadillac exited the lot, followed at a distance by the Galant. Paul checked the time—it was nearly two-thirty. He was relatively certain he'd learn nothing by following Stephen and Lili, yet he continued to do so. When Stephen dropped her off at her office on Freeman Street, he merely nodded to himself. Picking up his cellular phone, he punched in a number, asked a terse question, listened, spoke a few words and hung up. Abandoning his following effort, he swung the car around and sped off in the opposite direction.

Having parked in a far corner of the roadhouse parking lot, Paul made his way to the gray Toyota and slid in next to Jan. "So our boy Drew is behaving more erratically than usual, is he?"

"Yeah." Jan pointed to Drew's white Taurus parked crookedly taking up two spaces. "He sure looked high when he got here. I was behind him and he was weaving all over the road." She looked disgusted. "That kid is such a bad actor, I don't see how he can be doing what we're sure he is. Talk about risky behavior! He's going to get himself killed one of these days. I don't understand why Gates and his bunch keep doing business with him."

"Jan, he's a Meredith! How can you even ask?"

"You're right; that was stupid of me. But just since I got here, I've seen him in action. There were three guys standing over there, just talking." She pointed. "Drew decided he wanted to park where they're standing, so he reams them out. He's loud, he's belligerent and he's out of control."

"Anything else you don't like about him?"

"He's a bully, he's got a short fuse and he picks fights," she responded immediately as though she'd been waiting to finish her sentence. "I saw all this between the time he got out of his car and went into the bar." She gestured to a long, low building, dark except for the word Harlequin glowing in blue neon script over its door. Occasional shouts issued from inside, accompanied by sounds of scuffling and barks of laughter.

"I don't think he's going to make it back to the house in one piece tonight, Paulie."

"I wish I could care." He scowled in the direction of the bar. "But we need to know what's going down. Do you want me to stick around?" He answered his own question, "I guess I'd better."

"No, Paulie, really. I can handle it. I know you need to get over to Pal's about this time today, don't you?"

"Yeah, I do." He got out of the Toyota and leaned back in before he closed the door. "I'll be back in about an hour and a half, but beep me if he comes out sooner and I'll come right over."

As good as his word, Paul returned in ninety minutes and parked in a far corner where the lights from the bar didn't reach. He walked over to Jan's car and she rolled down her window. He said, "I'll be over there in the corner if you need me. When you see him come out, you take off first and wait down at the crossroads—you know, pull off on the right hand side road and turn around. I'll give him a big lead and follow him out; you pick him up from the side road after he passes. If we're lucky, he'll have a meeting with Gates and we'll film something." He winked as he said, "Don't worry, kid, I'll be right behind you." He closed the door of her car and disappeared into the darkness.

It was another hour before they saw Drew as he lurched out of the bar, accompanied by two men, who followed him to his car, loudly exchanging insults on the way. Paul heard Jan's Toyota start up and saw it leave the parking lot. Drew started his ignition and pulled out, scattering the men as he did so. They lingered a moment, speaking in low tones, then went back into the bar.

Paul's heart sank as he slowly pulled away and turned in the direction Drew had taken. Drew would be lucky if he even got home safely; he looked in no condition to conduct any deals tonight. He saw his tail lights far ahead and a pair of headlights turn from the north side of the crossroads. Paul narrowed the distance when he saw Jan flash her tail lights once. He continued his following effort until, with some surprise, he saw Drew had arrived safely at Meredith Manor and Jan's Toyota had disappeared to the west. She'd taken up her position and would remain until Paul took over in a few hours.

———

Paul didn't trust emotional thinking, so he was skeptical of a vague feeling that told him events might start coming to a head that day. He hoped he wasn't becoming fanciful; he had no hard facts to rely on. He just had a hunch that things were going to start moving fast and he knew the smart thing to do would be to go home and get some rest. He'd been up all night. Deciding not to drive all the way to his house at the lake, he compromised by parking at the end of Lili's street. He could watch the front of her house from there and maybe keep an eye on Sam if he was there. After twenty minutes of watching, however, fatigue overcame him and, in spite of trying to stay awake, he slumped down in his seat and his eyes closed.

———

"Paul?"

His eyelids snapped open and he was fully awake in an instant. He frowned at Lili, who stood at his driver's side window. He lowered the glass. It was daylight; he could now hear early morning bird song through the open window.

"What on earth are you doing here, Paul? Are you spying on me? Do you mind explaining yourself?" A worried frown appeared between her brows and her voice held instant concern. "Did something happen? Are you all right?"

What are *you* doing here, Lili, he wanted to know. Still frowning, embarrassed at being caught asleep, mortified by the fact that he'd obviously failed to keep himself awake on the job, he was gruff, "Get in."

"I have Buff with me; I was just walking him." She shrugged apologetically, adding, "I couldn't sleep." Suddenly disconcerted at catching him in this circumstance, she backed away from the window. Then, apparently reaching a decision, she stepped toward him again and said, "Maybe you'd better come with me to the house. I'll make some coffee."

He nodded, climbed out of his car and locked it. They walked up the sidewalk together, Buffalo trotting ahead. She led the way to her door, pushed it open and entered, Paul close behind. She walked to the kitchen at the rear of the house, her back to him. He followed, head down, hands pushed deeply into his pockets. When she reached the kitchen, she turned to him. "Okay, will you tell me what's going on, Paul?"

He stood in the middle of her kitchen, removed his hands from his pockets and turned them palms up as if demonstrating he had nothing to hide. "I wasn't ready to come forward yet, but since you caught me, I guess it's pretty obvious—I've been watching you."

"Watching me!" She was amused. Why?"

"You're a very attractive woman," he began when she interrupted him.

"C'mon, Paul! You may think I'm dim, but I really wasn't born yesterday. You can't make me swallow that line." She was no longer smiling and raised her chin slightly. "I think you owe me an explanation—of a lot of things." She turned away and ran water into a coffee pot. He watched her in silence for a few minutes, then sighed.

"You're right. I do." He collapsed onto one of the two wooden kitchen chairs situated at each end of the table under the hanging light. The table was covered with a starched white cloth with embroidered flowers and intricate designs at each corner and there was a wooden bowl filled with apples in the center. He experienced an immediate visual memory of his grandmother's kitchen table. It lasted only an instant.

He raised his eyes to her. "I never told you anything that wasn't true, you know, Lili."

"You just haven't told me the whole truth." She turned to face him. "And that's what I'm waiting to hear." She came over, sat in the chair opposite him and looked at him expectantly. The coffee began to perc, emphasizing the strained silence between them.

"Okay." He drew the word out and took a deep breath. "It goes against everything I know and everything I've ever learned, but I'm going to take a chance on you," he said, studying her expression as if it could prove her worthy of his confidence. She remained silent. "Lili, this is really tough. Will you promise me that this will remain between us, only us?"

"If it's that important to you, Paul, of course I will."

He remained silent for several moments longer, as if hoping she'd tell him to forget about it. Finally, he said, "It's important to me and others, many others." When she didn't respond, he said, "Believe me, you don't want to know."

"My God, Paul, who are you? You've got to tell me now."

"Do you promise?" His eyes bored into hers. "Do I have your word?" His voice was low, his tone compelling.

She could see he was in dead earnest. Puzzled, she said, "Yes, I promise."

"My name truly is Pál Gregor, as I told you, but that's not all. I'm Paul Gregory, P.I." He cocked an eyebrow and elaborated. "Private Investigator. A corporate client has hired me to investigate the activities of the Meredith bank's officers and directors. The DEA has also hired me as a subcontractor on a related investigation." He raised his chin, almost belligerently.

"I know I'm being slow, but—DEA?"

"Drug Enforcement Agency."

"And you're watching *me?*"

He hesitated, then said, "Only because you're involved with Sam Meredith."

"Sam? Drugs?" She widened her eyes. "I can't believe you're serious."

He noticed she'd stopped her friendly use of his first name; she pretended to take it lightly and although her lips still held a half smile, she was defensive.

He said, "I told you you didn't want to know, Lili."

Twin spots of red appeared on each of her cheeks and his eyes inadvertently darted to her throat, then the insides of her wrists. He detected no further telltale signs.

"So that's why you were asking me all those questions about Sam and his family. You were pumping me in order to hurt Sam!" Her smile had faded now; she was indignant.

"I've been working this case for almost a year now, waiting for something solid. And Lili, it's coming together and it'll happen soon."

"You've been spying on me for all this time? That's why you were interested in me, because you think Sam is somehow involved in something dreadful?" She was aghast. "Dealing in the drug trade?"

"I know he is. And not just him—his whole family!" He continued before she could interrupt, raising his voice in urgency. "Lili, I'm telling you so you can get out of it before you marry him and get dragged down with them all."

"Don't do me any favors!"

"Ah, Lili..." It was a plea.

As clue followed clue and realization dawned bit by bit, he could follow her indignation as it gave way to dismay. "Sam couldn't do what you're saying, he isn't like that. He's kind and good and honorable." She caught his cynical expression and cried out, "Yes, honorable!" She paused and got up, distractedly running her fingers through her hair as tears sprang to her eyes.

Paul went to her and tried to put his arms around her, but she shook him off with an impatient, "Get away from me."

He heard the edge of hysteria and glanced at her quickly. "It's natural to hate the bearer of bad news," he murmured. "I expected it." He opened three cabinet doors before he found the cups. He poured coffee for them both and handed her a cup. "Come on, sit down and drink this."

"I don't believe you," she said. He held the chair for her as she sank onto it. She carefully picked up her cup, then set it down again.

"I won't try to convince you now, but I think you know it's the truth." He sipped the hot coffee and tried to think of some genuine words of comfort, but none came to mind. He wasn't given to mouthing platitudes. He could only sit there and watch her hurt grow as she recalled Sam's unexplained absences and vague explanations.

"But Sam is always busy with his work." Now her voice begged him to understand. "He's important to the university. He's Chairman of the Department of Forestry! He's often away on speaking engagements, holding seminars, lecturing. He consults. It's all about trees!"

"I guess he does that, too." He offered an apologetic shrug.

She lifted her head in defiance. "I suppose you think Stephen is involved too!"

He was relentless. "Perhaps more than anyone."

"I don't believe you," she said again, but her face told him she did. For a long time she sat very still, trying to stay calm and recompose herself. She felt that to acquiesce in any way would be disloyal, not only to Sam, but to herself and her own soul. She could feel her heart beating in a fluttery sort of rhythm, but she knew her face was now cool and pale. Her hands were like ice and her breathing was shallow. She couldn't remember ever having fainted and fleetingly wondered if she were going to faint now.

Paul reached for her hand, its coldness startling him. He knew he should leave and get on with his job—he should relieve Jan—but he was afraid to abandon Lili. She was so still, so deathly cold. This was a reaction he hadn't anticipated.

"Lili, I..."

She interrupted, "You can go now, Paul."

"I think I'd better stay." He held both her hands now, trying to warm them.

She pulled her hands away. "Don't."

"I'll stay. You can call in sick; you should rest."

She looked at him as if he had lost his mind. "Rest? You must be mad! And what would I accomplish by staying here today—"resting?" How will that help to change the situation?" She paused and shuddered. She dropped her gaze and stared at her untouched cup of coffee without seeing it. She took a deep breath and spoke slowly, putting all her will power into keeping her voice steady. "What you've told me here this morning will change the way I feel about everything and everyone. I don't know what I'll do—I don't know what to think." She raised her eyes to his and spoke even more slowly, pausing between words as if for emphasis. "I only know I wish I'd never met you." She looked at his handsome face without recognition, as if he were a stranger who had intruded inexcusably. "Get out."

Stung by her words, Paul's carefully nurtured self-discipline began to desert him. With an effort, he steeled himself against feeling guilt, an emotion unknown to him. *Why should seeing her like this make me feel like a heartless brute?*, he asked himself as he rose to his feet. *Because you are one,* an inner voice replied; *you're an arrogant, insensitive fool.*

He held out his hand and softly said, "Lili, I'm only trying to help so you can get away in time..."

The words froze on his lips as she cut him off. "I trusted you. You used everything I told you against me. Thank God I didn't know enough to help you much. Now go away and leave me alone."

He let his hand fall to his side. "Not against you," he said, shaking his head slowly. "Never against you." He crossed the floor, turned at the kitchen doorway and looked back. "I'll call you later."

"Don't."

Chagrined, he made his way out of the house and into his car. Unaccustomed to such treatment, he attempted to shake off these wounds to his ego. Early in their acquaintance he'd wondered if Lili were culpable to the extent that she'd marry Sam for security and his ability to provide the good life she'd never had. He tried to see into the future, how his plans might have to change if she tipped Sam off. Then he realized he wasn't really worried about that; he'd decided long ago that he could trust her. Just like Sam, he'd been charmed by her innocence.

When she heard Paul close the front door, Lili ran to lock it. She went to every room and closed all the curtains that she'd already opened for the day. She went into the bathroom, turned on the shower, stripped and stepped under the streaming hot water. She stood there a long time letting it soak into her skin, her bones; she felt chilled to her very core. Then she scrubbed her skin with soap and a loofah until it began to hurt.

Emerging finally, she rubbed herself dry with a large bath towel and stood naked before the mirror while she tugged ruthlessly at her snarled wet hair with a comb. She went to her room, grabbed pantyhose, half-slip and bra from drawers in the lingerie chest and, without bothering to select anything in particular, pulled a long-sleeved blue blouse and a pair of black tailored pants off their hangers, throwing everything onto her unmade bed. Hands behind her, she hooked her bra. She tugged on stockings almost up to her knees, buttoned her blouse, fastened and zipped the slacks at her waist. Barefoot, she held a hair dryer in her left hand and applied makeup with her right, then slipped a watch over her wrist and secured earrings. She tried very hard to think of nothing but each task at hand. She went out to the kitchen, making sure Buff had food and water for the day, then let him into the back yard for a quick trot around while she returned to her room to put on her shoes. She let Buff back into the house, locked the back door, grabbed her handbag, locked the front door behind her and checked the time. All this had taken only twenty minutes. Walking quickly to her car, she backed into the street and drove to her office.

She could hear her desk phone ringing as her key turned in the lock of her office door. When she picked up the receiver and heard Paul's voice she quickly dropped it back into its cradle as though she'd been burned. She could no longer consider Paul a friend; in fact, he'd become her enemy. He was a spy, a barbarian, the vandal who had ravaged her life. She asked the student worker at the reception desk to screen her calls for the remainder of the day. By her count, Paul telephoned five more times.

She wondered how she'd get through that terrible day without going mad. She only knew it was something that had to be done, so she was grateful that it was a busy day; constant demands were made on her from the time she arrived until she left at five-thirty. She didn't go out for lunch, nor did she want to go home; she wasn't yet ready for the dreaded confrontation with Sam. As if she'd ever be. Buffalo, however, had to be cared for, so reluctantly she left the comparative safety of her office.

Driving home, Lili knew she must avoid all contact with Sam and Paul, so she decided to park her car where it wouldn't be seen. Her neighborhood was residential, thus there were no hidden parking areas behind store fronts. Eventually, she found a spot four blocks away from her house. She locked the car securely for the night and hiked home. She let Buff into the back yard and took the phone off the hook. That way she wouldn't have to listen to any messages from the man she wanted to forget. At nine o'clock someone came to her door and knocked, but she stayed hidden in the darkness. She kept the curtains drawn and the lights low. She didn't watch television because she was afraid it could be heard from outside; moreover, she knew she wouldn't be able to pay attention to whatever was being shown. She was afraid to read, as a light could probably be detected through the curtains. Before she turned in, she quietly let Buff into the backyard for a few minutes. When he came in he gave her a look that clearly said he thought she was crazy, almost making her smile. She decided to take a sleeping pill and hoped that longed-for oblivion would soon overcome her. It did.

———

Lili felt happy when she awoke the next morning, heard the birds singing and saw the brightness of sunlight beyond the closed curtains. She'd had ten hours of sleep and smiled as she stretched extravagantly. Then yesterday's memories crowded back, crushing her pleasure in the day. It was as though a black cloud enveloped her, stealing hope, leaving only despair. She told herself she was stronger today, however, and knew she could no longer avoid Sam; the time had come when she must face him. In fairness to him, she must give him a chance.

She went about her morning routine and returned the phone to its place. As if it had been waiting, it rang immediately and she reflexively picked it up.

Paul said, "Lili?"

"Yes."

"Where've you been? I've been going crazy with worry."

"I told you not to call me again. I have nothing to say to you." Her voice was steady and unemotional.

"Are you all right? Can I do anything for you?"

"I think you've done enough. I'm not exactly feeling on top of the world, but don't waste your time worrying about me. I've been in hell before; I know the territory; I can handle it." She hung up.

Yes, I've certainly been in hell before, but a different kind of hell. This one's worse, much worse: I came so close, I almost found the pot of gold at the end of the rainbow. Maybe that's not true, though. Maybe I just had myself convinced I wanted to marry Sam: he represents all I've ever dreamed of. But in my experience, dreams are ephemeral, not real

.

———————

Sitting in his chair by the window, Paul glared at the dead phone in his hand and cursed the day he'd met Liliane Greening. His corporate client could probably recover its money and the job for the Drug Enforcement people could very well be drawing to a successful conclusion, the crowning achievement of his career thus far. He'd successfully performed several investigations for them in the past, but the Meredith operation was beyond doubt the most extensive and the potential for future jobs and remuneration was spectacular. For years he'd carefully created and implemented a false identity as a minor mobster whose past crimes ranged from petty larceny to the rumor of murder. He'd manipulated the truth so that there were those who believed he was a man who was smart and lucky enough to beat the system. People feared him even as they were intrigued by him because he was considered dangerous, possibly lethal. And it had all been going so well; his scheme was beginning to pay off, just as he'd planned. Working under his cover as owner of Pal's, his evidence against the Merediths had been meticulously gathered; no one suspected his true identity.

Until now, that is. He seemed to have misjudged Lili; he hadn't foreseen her reaction. When he asked himself how he'd thought she would have responded to his revelation, he could only admit he hadn't expected the extreme revulsion she directed toward him, her savior and protector, as he considered himself. He'd expected her to be surprised, then to retaliate against Sam, to break their engagement immediately.

In the beginning he'd feared she might be driven by the desire for security, the wealth and power that marriage to a Meredith could provide, but as he came to know her better, he'd found she wasn't the shallow creature he'd originally taken her for. Lili's character was decent, sincere and—he now conceded—honorable. He felt he knew the real Lili now; she valued honor above all.

Perhaps this was the time for him to analyze his feelings for her. He thought well of her; that much was obvious. Although he no longer required proof, she'd proven to his satisfaction that he could trust her. She was modest and unassuming, certainly unlike any woman he'd ever been attracted to, and so he asked himself if someone like Lili could continue to hold his interest. Because he had to admit it—he was interested in her personally, outside the limits of his case against the Merediths. He recognized in a vague sort of way that she now represented a challenge and that pride and vanity demanded he pursue her. He asked himself if there could be another, even more significant, reason behind his increasing interest in Lili. For she was becoming too important to him; he couldn't seem to stop thinking of her. And now—now that she'd learned the truth about Sam and the rest of the Merediths—surely she'd have the courage to break away? Wouldn't she?

The DEA were acting pleased, hinting at his glittering future, and ordinarily he would now begin to feel the soaring exultation of success. But he somehow felt dispirited, aware that he wanted to share his triumph with only one other person—Lili— and to all appearances she now despised him.

He was aware of the familiar vague mood of melancholy once more settling over him and he recalled his grandmother's telling him long ago this was caused by his Hungarian blood. He'd often asked her what she meant by that and her reply had always been that she'd explain it when he got older.

One night she'd finally told him her story. She and her sister lived with their parents in rural Hungary. When she was sixteen, a young man, a stranger to the area, caught her alone. He raped her. She had never been with a man before; indeed, her parents had not even allowed her to be courted because they thought she was too young. Imagine the shame, the catastrophe that befell her family when they learned she was carrying a child. But Nia was happy when her daughter, beautiful Zsuzsa, his mother, was born nine months later. Despite the circumstances of her birth, everyone loved the delightful little Zsuzsa.

Somehow, after the monster Hitler had been defeated, her parents had been successful in sending both Nia and her child to the United States, to a flourishing Hungarian enclave in the city of Chicago's South Side where they were welcomed by old acquaintances. Here they had remained as Zsuzsa grew from a pretty child to a beautiful young woman.

Nia had smiled proudly as she recounted how Sandor, Pál's father, had lost his heart the moment he'd first seen the lovely Zsuzsa. Although Sandor and Zsuzsa had both had strict upbringings, after they'd met, they would give their parents no peace until they were allowed to marry. Pál had been born two years later. By the time two more years had gone by, his father had been killed in a labor incident. Zsuzsa's heart was broken and from that day forward she lived only for her son. Because of her beauty, others had tried to win her, but she would never consider another man.

This somber mood relentlessly plagued and absorbed Paul until he finally submitted to it, no longer trying to shake it off. He continued to sit in his chair by the window, gazing at the dark and serene beauty of the lake, as he thought of Apollonia and Zsuzsa, the only women who had ever meant anything to him—and finally of Lili, who was beginning to mean too much.

Chapter 13

"**D**on't you understand, Drew? We've got to act now in order to keep from losing everything when Sam marries her." Crystal was exasperated, though she tried not to let it show. Drew was being so terribly dim, she thought. He didn't seem to get the drift of what she was attempting to explain to him.

"Just because I don't agree with you, don't think I'm stupid," he said as if reading her mind. "Has it ever occurred to you that you're nothing but a cold-hearted bitch? Granted, I don't always agree with my brother..." At her scornful expression, he amended his sentence. "All right, I hardly ever agree with my brother, but when all's said and done, Sam *is* my brother."

Crystal wondered if that statement was an allusion to the fact that Sam and Drew were full brothers and that she, Crystal, was only their half-sister. Could there be an alliance she was unaware of and, if so, how much had it worked against her throughout the years?

She and Drew were sitting near the pool at the patio table furthest from the house, their usual spot when they didn't want to be overheard. Drew got up and started pacing, head down and hands in his pockets.

Oh, Gawd, Crystal thought. *He's at the stage where he can't sit still; next he'll go slamming into the house and out the front door.* She said, "Surely you can see the practical aspect of my plan, Drew. This way no one gets hurt."

He lifted his head and glared at her. "Except Sam and Lili!"

"Since when have they concerned you?" She stopped and, with an effort, lowered her voice. "I meant none of us would be hurt—financially." *Greed will soon make him see it my way.*

"No," he said. "I'm not going along with your scheme this time, Crystal. There's got to be a better way."

"Come on, Drew, you know you'll come around sooner or later. Why not now? We've got to move on this before Sam ruins us."

He stopped pacing and stared at her. "I said no and I mean no." His voice was beginning to grow louder and Crystal winced as she pointedly glanced around the patio, as if for spies. He approached her chair and stood looking down at her. "Count me out," he said more quietly. "I don't want to hear any more of your crazy ideas. If I find out you're still thinking of hurting Sam—or anyone—I'll make you sorry, Crystal. I mean it." He held his chin in the stubborn position she knew too well.

She hadn't foreseen this reaction. She could usually get Drew to agree to everything she suggested—they were bound, not only by proximity, but by their mutual jealousy of Sam. Crystal had always seen Sam as her adversary and rival for the love of their father. Furthermore, Sam, as firstborn son, prevented her from achieving what she considered to be her rightful place as heir and eventual head of the family. As far as Drew was concerned, he was simply impatient with the way Stephen and Sam were running the business; he was often foolhardy. A true risk-taker, he considered their operations too conservative.

Additionally, of course, Drew was jealous of Sam's position and power, wanting them for himself. Crystal had thought she could read Drew so well, but now he was unaccountably digging his heels in and being stubbornly uncooperative. *Surely his sudden concern for the well-being of his brother was a ruse.*

She changed her tactic. "All right, Drew, maybe you're right. Why don't we sleep on it and see if we can come up with a better idea in the morning?" Seeing him visibly relax and start to leave, she called after him, "Make it an early night, will you? I want you to have your wits about you bright and early. We have no time to waste."

———————

"Lili?" When he heard her voice, Sam breathed a sigh of relief. "Darling, I've been trying to reach you since yesterday. Where've you been?" His voice held concern.

"I . . . I didn't feel well yesterday and it was a busy day at the office, Sam. After work I just came home and turned in early."

"You were ill? Are you all right now?"

"Oh, yes, Sam. I'm fine."

"When I couldn't reach you, I drove by and I didn't see your car. Your lights weren't on, I couldn't get through by phone—I didn't know what to think. I almost called the police to report you missing."

Did you? She took a deep breath. "Sam, we've got to talk. Can you get away for lunch?"

He hesitated. "Sure." His voice held a note of surprise. "Is everything all right, Lili?"

"No, it isn't." *Should she have lied?* "But I'll see you soon and we can talk about it. Shall we meet at that coffee place, Hava Java? It's close."

"I'll pick you up. Twelve o'clock suit you?"

"Fine. I'll be ready."

Sam put the phone down slowly, puzzling over their brief, unsatisfactory conversation. *What could be wrong?*

In her office, Lili hung up and sat staring at her hands clasped in front of her, her diamond ring gleaming in the light from the desk lamp. How wonderful it would be if everything could go back to the way it was before she'd met Paul and he'd told her those awful things. She didn't want to face Sam; she wished she could run away and hide.

Unbidden, a vision from her past marriage assailed her. She stood again in the small bedroom she shared with Steve. It was early morning and they were dressing—she for her job at the university and he was preparing to go on the road again. He was stacking sales literature into the alligator briefcase that was purchased to match his shoes. He looked down at himself and shot his cuffs, a mannerism that had long become familiar to her. He was absorbed in himself and his image and was unprepared when she handed him the divorce papers and a pen.

"Could you sign this before you leave?"

He held them in his hand and frowned at them for a moment. "Been sneaking around to see a lawyer behind my back, have you?" His voice was filled with mockery.

"It's hardly going behind your back when you're never here." She sounded defensive and hated herself for it. "The way things have been between us, it seems the sensible thing to do. If the divorce is uncontested, you won't even have to appear. It won't cost you a cent; I'm paying the lawyer."

"We could see a marriage counselor."

Saying that must have cost him something. "It's too late for that." She tried to picture him listening to a counselor and almost laughed.

"If you say so." He took the pen, signed his name carelessly and dropped the papers on a table. He picked up his attaché case and turned at the door. "Take it easy."

"Goodbye, Steve." *He doesn't think I'll go through with it.*

She quickly glanced around to make sure the coffeepot was turned off and the milk put away, put the documents into her briefcase and closed the front door behind her. She was trying to coax her ancient Fiat into life as she watched her soon-to-be ex-husband pulling away in their new white Coupe de Ville, offering her a negligent wave on his way down the drive.

She wondered if she'd ever see him again and clearly remembered the relief she felt when she realized that she finally didn't really care. Looking back, his taking the new car and leaving her with the old, sick relic was indicative of their relationship and the defining scene of their marriage. Lili squirmed mentally as she recalled how she'd continued to make payments on the Cadillac—the car in Steve's possession—until the very absurdity of her position dawned upon her. She'd always been so responsible in everything she did. Too responsible.

During the many weeks leading to her decision to divorce Steve, she'd anguished over it every day. She'd be driving to the university in the morning or home from work in the evening and tears would stream down her cheeks as she agonized that perhaps she hadn't tried hard enough or made sufficient effort to make their marriage last. Finally, she admitted that she was the one who'd always made every effort; Steve had never cooperated. She'd been naive, a fool.

Although she shuddered to call those scenes to mind, she was nevertheless aware that she'd willingly go through all that torment again if she could only avoid the coming confrontation with her beloved Sam.

———————

Lili and Sam were sitting in the same booth she'd shared with Paul a few weeks ago and she felt somehow perfidious remembering that night. This vague feeling of disloyalty undermined the righteous indignation she'd been experiencing up to this point. The result was that she appeared irresolute. Empty coffee cups and untouched sandwiches were on the table between them.

"Of course I'm in the business of forestry; you know that, Lili." His forehead wrinkled as he added, "Why do you even ask?"

"Sam, perhaps I'm being obtuse, but please bear with me. There are some questions that need answering and I want some explanations for my own..." She paused and seemed to grope for the proper word, then abandoned the attempt. "For example, where do you go on those extended trips of yours? Sometimes you're away for several days at a time. And you never tell me about your business." She bit her lip, then continued before he could reply. "It would seem normal, I think, for a man to speak of his daily problems or successes just in passing if for no other reason."

"I don't get it, Lili. You're acting very strangely. Surely you didn't call this conference to ask me such innocuous stuff. What else is on your mind?" He reached over and ran a finger lightly along the outline of her cheek. "What's troubling you, sweetheart?"

She twisted her hands in her lap and leaned forward in her intensity. "Please answer me, Sam."

"Sure." He feigned long-suffering patience and spoke condescendingly. "Where do I go? To various places—all within the local southern Illinois, Kentucky, Missouri area. You know I consult, try to solve problems nurseries and landholders are having with their trees, meet with other experts. We brainstorm sometimes, try to solve each other's problems. The silviculture industry is a lot more complicated than it sounds." He looked at her, eyebrows raised, as he shrugged. "I never thought it interested you particularly, Lili."

Seeing her look of impatience, he continued. "When I'm not away from campus I oversee the various professors who advise and serve on graduate guidance committees and who are also assigned to the Crab Orchard National Wildlife Refuge and the Forest Science Lab of the North Central Forest Experiment Station."

He itemized. "We're continuously conducting or planning research and demonstration programs on experimental fields and forest plots. The university has about three thousand acres to control." He drew a deep breath and pointedly stopped to sip water.

"We are also allowed the use of forested lands on the forty-three thousand acres of the Crab Orchard Wildlife Refuge, the two hundred fifty thousand acres of the Shawnee National Forest and the four thousand acres of the Trail of Tears State Forest. We additionally conduct basic research on a six hundred forty acre tract representing one of the last central hardwoods remnants of virgin bottomlands and slopes." He emphasized each point by softly thumping the table with his palm.

"I have speaking engagements, offer seminars—but you know that." He narrowed his eyes at her. "Have I lost you? Or shall I continue?"

"I don't need your canned promo speech, Sam, and it's not necessary to talk down to me."

"I'm sorry, sweetheart. It's just that I don't understand what you're looking for."

"The truth, Sam."

He sat back, perplexed. "Do you think I've been lying to you?"

"Of course not. It's just that... ."

"Just what? Exactly what are you getting at?" He didn't smile to soften his words.

Taken aback, Lili nevertheless determined to go on. "It's just that you're so mysterious about your out-of-town trips and you don't talk to me about them." She almost wished she hadn't started all this; maybe ignorance *was* bliss. "If *I'd* been away for days at a time, I'd talk to *you* about it."

"Lili, darling, you wouldn't have any idea what I was talking about—you'd be bored stiff. I've been doing you a favor, you know." He peered at her. "What's behind your questions?"

"I've been thinking, Sam, that I actually know very little about what you do. Everyone says a wife must take an interest in her husband's career if she's to hold his love." This last was added in a feeble attempt at light humor, but her smile was shaky.

"But why are you bringing this up now? What's happened to make you suddenly so interested in my particular field?"

This wasn't going well at all. She wished she weren't bound by her promise to Paul, the Destroyer, as she now thought of him. And, although Paul had to have been lying or at least exaggerating, now that she'd started, she had to go on. If she dropped the subject at this point, she'd never feel justified in bringing it up again. As much as she wanted to stop asking questions, she had to know the truth.

"My interest isn't sudden. I was just reluctant to ask too many questions before." She dropped her gaze. "I didn't want you to think I was prying." *And that's the humiliating truth.*

His heart melted even while danger signals were going off in his brain. "Darling, don't ever be afraid of me. Don't you know I'm crazy about you?" He reached for her hand and held it. "I'd do anything for you."

He has a deceptively easy smile and charm, she suddenly thought; *maybe he's a smooth operator just like his father.* She gave up trying to be subtle. "Oh, Sam, do you promise you're not involved in anything else?"

"Darling Lili, what on earth are you talking about?" *Christ, how much does she know?*

"Nothing in particular, really—I've just been so worried. Do you promise?"

She looked so earnest, so forlorn, so vulnerable. "Of course, I promise." He took her other hand. "Tell me why you're worried. What else do you think I'm 'involved in?'"

"I don't think you're involved in anything, Sam. It's just something I overheard, something about the Meredith family bank business and—you're a director, aren't you?" Her blue eyes were stricken. "It didn't sound nice. Of course I didn't believe it, but I had to give you a chance to deny it." Unconsciously, she pulled one of her hands away.

So the Merediths were being publicly discussed and not very flatteringly, it seemed. Not for the first time he felt doom impending. All his good intentions about getting out had been too long coming. But he merely said, "Lili, I don't even want to think about the implications of what you've just said to me. The very fact that you're willing to give me a chance to deny something contradicts your statement about not believing it." *Do I sound guilty? Am I going to lose her? I love her so much—I need her so badly. But does she need me?*

"Sam..." She was the picture of abject misery.

He knew then what he should do, even though this decision would ensure his future as bleak and hopeless. Lili merited a better life than he was now prepared to provide for her. She was everything that was good and fine and it was up to him to see that she stayed that way. It was his responsibility to protect her and, cruelly hard though it would be, he should resolve that this decision must be irrevocable. But to release Lili would be to relinquish his love forever; he knew he could never love again.

"Darling, please believe me." He sounded too suave, even to himself. He hated lying to her. She was so decent, so good, she deserved better than this. He shouldn't pressure her into marriage, at least not now. It occurred to him that the position he found himself in was absurd. All the women he'd ever known had wanted him, but none of them had ever meant anything to him. The irony of the situation almost made him laugh: it had finally come to this; at last he'd found and fallen wholeheartedly in love with a woman—a woman, however, whom he needed more than she needed him.

Sudden realization slammed into him with the force of physical pain that the depth of his love for her was such that he had to let her go; he must set her free of the Merediths. He released her hand and sat back. His eyes closed in anguish for a moment as full comprehension dawned. He could feel the sting of tears behind his eyes, tears he wouldn't allow himself to shed, even as he set his handsome features into an implacable mask of displeasure.

"Lili, it's obvious you're not happy. You mustn't let me rush you into a marriage you're not prepared for. I think you should take some more time to think about it—and us."

"What? What do you mean by that?"

"I think we should put our plans on hold until you feel you're ready to make a lifetime commitment. Because that's what I want from you—a lifetime."

"Sam, I didn't mean..."

"Whatever you meant doesn't matter. I don't think I want a wife who doesn't trust me."

"Of course I trust you." She was shaken, but not surprised. Nevertheless, she raised her eyebrows. "I know there's a good explanation."

"You want an explanation?" He forced a cynical laugh, sobered and added, "Lili, I think we should break our engagement."

"My God, Sam!"

"It's a small town. We'll be sure to run into each other from time to time—it's not the end of the world." He was trying hard to be offhand.

"Please... don't," was all she could murmur. Tears sprang to her eyes.

His throat hurt and he had to force himself to keep his voice level. "It's probably just as well, after all. When all's said and done, you've just proven to me we really don't suit each other. Our differences would be bound to come back and haunt us after a while." He ventured what he hoped was a reasonable smile. "I hate to admit it, but Crystal may have been right all along."

Tears squeezed out from under her tightly closed lids and coursed down her cheeks. He pulled out his handkerchief and tenderly wiped them away. It was almost too much for him, but he steeled himself and went on, "You'll see I'm right, Lili. It's all for the best."

People at nearby tables were beginning to turn and look at the drama unfolding in their midst. He wished them dead.

She tried, but couldn't seem to control her tears. Finally, with a tremendous effort she lifted her chin and managed to say in a quavering voice, "I'm not crying, Sam, really I'm not. It's just my eyes—they're leaking." She managed a ghastly smile, as if to prove she was untroubled. His heart turned over and he was about to beg her forgiveness when she sniffed audibly, squared her shoulders and sat erect, blindly twisting the ring off her finger. Eyes downcast, she held it out to him wordlessly.

For a moment his will failed him. Having finally found this beautiful and idealistic woman, surely he should be allowed to keep her—she was everything that was fine and good, everything he'd ever hoped for. He wanted to take her into his arms, to cherish and protect her always. He took a deep breath, hoping to stall for time, but knew in his heart that he had to let his angel go for her own sake. His voice was husky as he said, "No, Lili, I can't take that ring back. It's yours—I gave it to you forever."

"No, Sam. Please take it, I can't bear to keep it. Every time I'd see it, I'd remember..." *As if I could ever forget.* Fresh tears stopped her.

"I don't want it, Lili." He cleared his throat and stood to leave. *I never knew about real love until now. And now that I've found it, it's too late. I have to do what's right for her, I have to give her up. Being noble hurts—God, how it hurts.*

"But Sam... ," she whispered brokenly. She looked up at him in mute appeal.

Better she should hate me, he decided, and his heart twisted within him. He dropped some money on the table, turned and walked away.

"Sam?," she called after him, but he'd gone—and she was alone again. She had dared to hope for a happy future and it had been a terrible mistake. Why had she listened to Paul? Why had she confronted Sam? Why couldn't she have left well enough alone? She had only herself to blame. Now her dreams were destroyed and a vast emptiness overwhelmed her; she felt unable to endure such terrible anguish. *This must be how it feels when a heart finally breaks.*

Lili remained sitting there alone, leaning back against the booth, eyes closed, hoping all the people in the coffee house would have the decency to leave, yet knowing she wouldn't be granted that luxury. A tear, and then another, slid from under her lashes, but she no longer took the trouble to wipe them away. She felt exhausted, as though she'd been fighting a war and she was the loser. *But who is the victor?*

"Mind if I join you?" Her eyes opened to witness Paul Gregory sliding into the seat opposite her. He offered her his handkerchief. She waved it away. "Leave me alone."

He continued to hold it out to her. "Take it."

She snatched it, wiped her eyes and blew her nose.

"I saw Meredith leave looking like death. Did you break the engagement?"

"No. He did."

"Sure." He tried to look sincere. "Look, kid, I'm sorry you're feeling down right now, but you did the right thing."

"Oh, well, that makes all the difference, doesn't it? I did the right thing." She tried to work up enough anger to scream at him, or hit him, but all she felt was numb.

"Lili, believe me, it had to be done."

Rather than reply, she took a deep breath, picked up her handbag and, with a great effort, rose to her feet and began to walk away. Craning his neck, he turned and looked after her, stifling a sigh of exasperation as he got up and followed her outside.

I can't even make a good exit, Lili thought, as she neared the corner, suddenly remembering that she and Sam had arrived in his car. And he'd left without her. Forever.

Paul took her by the elbow. "Come on, I'll drive you back to your office." She said nothing as he led her to the Galant and helped her inside. They drove several blocks in silence before he asked, "Did you tell him anything?"

She darted a glance at him, but his face was impassive. "You mean did I keep my promise to protect you?" She sighed, "I did."

I knew it!, he exulted. Aloud, he said, "I've been trying to contact you. Why didn't you take my calls?"

She frowned and turned to look at him. "I thought I'd made it clear I didn't want to talk to you ever again. I distinctly remember saying, 'Paul, don't call me.' We have nothing more to say to one another."

"Come on, Lili, stop pouting. It's not becoming."

She thought how satisfying it would be to hit him, but decided to simply remain silent. She was annoyed to see that by doing so she was lending credence to his accusation. So she said, "What can I do or say to make you understand I loathe you?"

"You'll get over it." He reached across, patted her shoulder and flashed her a look of triumph. She thought she detected the hint of a smile on his lips.

The man was infuriating. She was surprised to feel anything, under the circumstances, but Paul Gregory seemed to have a certain power over her; he was able to infuriate her and, therefore, he made her feel less numb.

He pulled alongside her Chevy in its parking slot, leaned across to push her door open, and said, "I'll call you tonight."

She widened her eyes at him incredulously. "Thanks for the ride, but try to understand: I don't want you to call." She got out. "Goodbye."

She took a few steps and heard the car backing away. She wanted to hit something; she wanted to kick the building. She felt about to explode, so she turned and screamed after the departing car, "Why did you have to tell me?"

She immediately felt foolish, but strangely calm. She entered the building, head bowed, trying to drum up courage to tell everyone her wedding was off. She simply didn't want to think about anything anymore.

———————

She'd known C.J. could be counted on to do and say the right things. In spite of everything else going wrong, she was nevertheless aware she was lucky to have this wonderfully sensitive and sympathetic man in her life. When she'd remarked that she dreaded the task before her of having to explain her broken engagement, he'd told her, "You don't owe anyone an explanation. I'll take care of getting the word out." Then he'd ordered her to go home and get some rest and she'd thanked him and left for the day.

———————

Sam and his father sat in their customary chairs in Stephen's study. As they talked, daylight had given way to twilight—then dusk, in turn, was deepening into darkness before Stephen got up to switch on a lamp as he went to the side table to pour drinks. He pulled the curtains closed. Sam sat motionless.

"I don't want anything, Dad, thanks."

Stephen said, "I think you should," as he splashed a small amount of water into a hefty measure of scotch and handed the heavy crystal glass to Sam. He wondered if Lili had told Sam about his suggestion of a marriage contract.

They wordlessly held their glasses toward each other, then drank. Sam said, "I can't think of anything to toast."

Stephen assumed a suitably solemn attitude, difficult for him under the circumstances, as Sam had just broken the news of his breakup with Lili. Although his heart rejoiced, Stephen gravely asked, "This has hit you hard, my boy, hasn't it?" When Sam didn't respond, Stephen continued, "Are you absolutely sure there's no chance for you and Lili?"

"I love her too much, Dad. I can't let her get involved with us."

"She's a wonderful girl; she'd stick by you."

"I couldn't expect her to—I wouldn't ask it of her." Sam swirled the scotch in his glass as he held it to the light. "I don't know if I can explain it, Dad, but there's this thing about her that I don't want to change. I want her to stay just the way she is. I want to remember her that way." He bent his earnest gaze on his father. "She's not like us, she's—unworldly. I mean, she's sort of untouched by mundane interests." He paused, frowned and hurried on. "Oh, she's totally with it—that's not what I mean. As it is, she's almost too perceptive." He looked at his father in pain. "She's the kind of person who you can always count on to do the right thing. Dad, I don't think I could ever face her again if she found out the truth about us—about me."

"She's one of the world's innocents? Is that what you mean?" Stephen was proud of the way he kept the contempt from his voice.

"Exactly." Sam was relieved to see his father understood. "She's so honorable herself, I'd never want to disappoint her. She'd be too hurt."

"To understate the obvious—you value her good opinion of you so much that you'd rather lose her than lose her respect." It wasn't a question.

Sam nodded and for a few moments neither of them said anything more. Then Stephen stretched and sighed. "I see this as my fault, Samuel. If I'd had the courage of my convictions years ago, you'd never be in this spot now." He looked away while he continued, staring across the room, seeming to study a lovely old print of a fox hunt in a dark wooden frame. "I'd always had others to take care of the work for me, you see; I told myself I wasn't really involved, that my hands were always clean." As if for proof, Stephen put his glass down, examined his well-manicured hands and spread them on his knees.

"Crystal and Drew are different, they like to be directly involved in the day-to-day operation. They both thrive on this business; they live for it, especially Crystal—she loves power and wants more of it. Drew likes the danger, the excitement—and the money, of course. But you're like me." Stephen felt he could now afford to be magnanimous and sent a searching glance at Sam. "Only you're better. You've never liked it and you've never lied to yourself. You made your decision early on that you wanted to quit. Actually, you never even wanted to start, did you?"

"No, I didn't. And now it's too late."

"It may not be too late," Stephen corrected. He rested his head on the high back of the chair and looked through his steepled fingers as he said, "But I'm afraid we need you now, Sam."

Sam exhaled loudly. "I'm not sure how we're going to get through this thing, Dad. I don't even know exactly what we're up against. But if Lili heard something about us, it must be on the street and pretty common knowledge. Or at least common supposition," he amended. "It's obvious we've got to put everything on ice and I mean *everything*. We've got to be above suspicion—all of us. We can't afford to run any risks at all."

"I'll warn Crystal and Drew and have him take care of his contacts."

"Dad, I'd like to send Drew out of town for about a month. Okay with you?"

"Yes, yes. Anything you think best, Samuel."

They stood and Stephen reached up to put an arm around his son's shoulders. "I'm sorry your personal life is suffering because of the sins of the rest of us, son, but we need you now. You have a cool head for planning, which I'm afraid few of the rest of them have." At Sam's look, he hurried on. "Oh, yes, I know, Crystal's a planner, but she's more of a warlord—she's devious and I don't know if I trust her now. With her the end always justifies the means. I know I can depend upon you to help me guide us through a crisis."

"I'll do my best, Dad."

"I'll see to it that you're taken care of when it's over, Samuel."

Sam looked surprised. "You know I don't need to be compensated."

Stephen sank into his burgundy leather chair again. "I meant I'd see you safely out of it. No questions, no recriminations from the others."

Sam got up and stretched. He lightly gripped his father's shoulder as he made his way to the door.

"Thanks, Dad, I'll appreciate it." *But it'll be too late for me,* he added to himself.

When he heard the door click shut behind Sam, Stephen preened himself on his own performance and relaxed, a smile playing around his lips. He meant to see that Sam would come out of this a happier man. All of Sam's present emotional anguish was really for the best; he'd soon be exhausted and tired of it. Although he couldn't see it now, the Greening woman hadn't been right for him. Crystal swore that Cynthia Compton was still wild about Sam and, even though she might be recalcitrant at the moment—she was, after all, a woman scorned— she'd come around sooner or later. Stephen himself would see to it that Sam would be more amenable to a Meredith-Compton alliance now that Liliane Greening was out of the picture.

The next morning when Sam left the Merediths' bank, Paul, a block behind, paused in surprise as he discovered Crystal's Mercedes was already following Sam. Perplexed, Paul let several cars intervene before he swung in behind both of them. He noticed Crystal was smart enough not to be caught tailgating by her brother. Paul pursued the two of them to the Jackson State Bank in a town several miles east of Carbondale. He watched Crystal as she maneuvered to park in the crowded lot behind the bank and, as she did so, he turned at the corner and drew to a stop out of Crystal's vision. He observed Sam as he got out of his car and went inside, where he remained for twenty-five minutes. When he came out again, Paul followed him to the post office, watched him carry a brown envelope inside, and stand in line to have it weighed for the proper postage. Why, he asked himself, would a member of the Meredith family and a director of the Meredith bank travel out of town to do his banking?

Parked behind the bank, Crystal Meredith wondered the same thing. Earlier she'd been in their bank when Sam had come in without seeing her. He'd gone empty-handed into the vault department and had come out with an expansion folder zipped on three sides. He must have carried it in under his coat, she concluded. She'd decided then to follow him. *Could he be liquidating assets in order to run away with Lili?*

Chapter 14

Everyone in the office had been extraordinarily considerate in sparing her feelings and Lili was very grateful. She was sure C.J. was responsible for a large part of the kindness generally being shown her. A few of her co-workers had approached, inviting her to join them for lunch and other activities. She wondered if any of them could even begin to guess just how heartsick and alone she felt. It was comforting to know, however, that she had so many well-meaning friends.

During the afternoon Kathy, the student worker at the reception desk, came to her office with a manila envelope addressed to Liliane Greening and waited while she signed, for it required the signature of the addressee only. When Kathy had gone, Lili, curious, stopped what she was working on and opened it at once. A small white square fell onto her desk. This proved to be an envelope which had been folded over and over, then taped together. Frowning, she then looked inside the manila envelope again and withdrew a single sheet of stationery with both sides filled with handwriting—Sam's writing.

"My Darling Lili," she read, "I have no right, but I'm asking you to do me a great favor. I've enclosed a key to Safety Deposit Box No. 117 at the Jackson State Bank, which I've opened in your name. Everything you will find inside now belongs to you.

It's a gift, it's yours. Don't call attention to it, tell no one and for heaven's sake don't declare it on your tax return. Use it in small amounts as necessary. Perhaps you'll never really need all of it, but I'd like to think you have this shield against misfortune available to you. I want to think of you as free from financial worry, as I understand you well enough to know you'd starve before you'd compromise your principles. I want you to live comfortably and most of all I want you to be happy."

Stupefied, Lili tried to fathom the meaning behind Sam's words. She realized he'd never written to her before and his stilted way with the written word was a far cry from his ease with spoken language. He was simply unaccustomed to expressing himself on paper, so she could take what he'd written as being literally true. Here he had no vocal inflections to help him, nor extravagant language to shade his meaning. She was thoroughly puzzled by now and eagerly turned the page.

"All the foregoing are just words to tell you what I selfishly want you to do to save me from worrying about you. The way I feel, however, can't be put into words. When we parted yesterday—the way I left you—that was the hardest thing I've ever had to do in my life. Never think I stopped loving you—I love you so much I'm consumed by it. You'll always be part of me. I'd do anything for you. That's why, even though it kills me to let you go, I must." The letter was signed with the letter S. Her gaze dropped to the post script: "If you're ever in need of anything—anything at all—get word to me."

Lili swung her chair around to face the window, her eyes shining with tears. Holding Sam's letter against her breast, she was unexpectedly possessed by the incomprehensible idea that she could hold Sam for as long as she kept his letter and obeyed his instructions. Aware she was indulging an illusion, she was nevertheless afraid to tempt fate.

A vivid memory of Sam returned: she could again see the naked longing in his eyes that night at her house when he told her he was afraid of losing her and begged her to marry him at once. Surely he hadn't been pretending then. What could have happened to make him call off the wedding? She knew, of course, that it must have had something to do with Paul's suspicions, yet she felt sure Sam had cut her out of his life not because he wanted to, but in order to protect her in some way. "Oh, Sam," she whispered, aware it was useless, "please come back to me."

Reality and common sense intruded, compelling her to face the fact that, although Sam had indeed broken their engagement, hadn't she been—perhaps subconsciously—trying to force that very result by her questions? There was no use denying that from the moment of Paul's shocking revelation she'd known how this would end and there would be little or no likelihood of her marriage to Sam. He, himself, had said as much and she was forced to accede. When she'd first seen Sam's letter, she'd been indulging the fantasy that there was still hope when, in fact, there was none. She had resolutely pushed Stephen Meredith's suggested marital agreement to the back of her mind, certain Sam had no knowledge of his father's action. If Stephen but knew, she would have signed it willingly, if only to prove she had no designs on the Meredith fortune. She remembered her intention to write to Sam exposing Stephen's secret machinations. But she never had and now there was no point.

She was surprised at her own inner calm. Although she was desperately unhappy, she felt a peculiar sense of relief that the heartwrenching emotional turmoil was ending, that perhaps she could now begin to get on with the business of living her life again, drab and colorless as she may consider her future now to be. It was almost as if this note with those fcw final words from Sam had snapped the chain of emotion and brought her back to reality.

There had been a quality of romantic madness in her feeling for Sam—it was a kind of impossible dream; she'd felt as though she'd been living a fairy tale-come-true. Now it was over and it was time to dry her sentimental tears. She felt as if her heart had hit rock bottom, as though things couldn't get worse for her; therefore, perhaps she could now begin to regain control of her emotions. She had no regrets; her approaching marriage to Sam Meredith had been a beautiful mirage, something that could never be realized, and she now admitted to herself that in her heart she'd probably always known it was nothing more than an exquisite illusion.

Even though intellectually she understood these things, despite everything she told herself, her arms ached to hold Sam, her lips trembled for his kiss and her feeling of loss was overpowering.

Lili pushed herself to her feet and stretched, then shook her head, physically wrenching herself away from further futile introspection. For the remainder of the afternoon she forced her total attention to the work at hand. When she finally rose from her desk she was gratified to see she'd made a serious dent in the accumulated workload of the past few days. That evening, though, before she closed the office and left to go home, almost as an afterthought, she located the small square envelope and dropped it into her jacket pocket.

While Lili was driving home that evening, Drew and Crystal were standing at the far side of the pool engaged in another argument. Although their words couldn't be understood from the house, their angry tone was obvious, as were their gestures. His fury apparent, Drew turned and stalked off, while Crystal turned her back on the house and disappeared into the cavernous garage, appearing again in her white Mercedes convertible as she backed it into the drive, then pulled forward and sped away.

Jan, from her hidden vantage point in the trees across the road, was fascinated with the events as she watched them unfold. Drew had unexpectedly left and, before she could get her car out on the road to follow him, Crystal, whom Jan recognized from photographs, was at last leaving her lair. Jan grimly accelerated, hoping she wouldn't lose sight of the Mercedes as she struggled to keep up in her elderly Toyota.

Half an hour later, Jan was amazed to see Crystal pull into Pal's parking lot. Keeping Paul's basic surveillance instructions in mind, she didn't follow; instead she drove another mile down the road before she could turn around and circle back. She registered further surprise when she saw Drew's Taurus drawn up alongside Paul's car. *This should be interesting,* she said to herself. *In fact, even though it's my night off, it's too interesting for me to miss.* As she left her car, she looked back to be sure she was positioned for a fast getaway should one be required.

When Jan entered she was amused to see Crystal eyeing Paul like a hungry cat and was further interested to observe him feigning indifference.

While Crystal was otherwise engaged in trying to get a waiter's attention, Jan saw Paul pointedly dart his eyes to Drew, who was sitting with a boisterous group of seven young rowdies in the dimly lit end of the lounge. They were well-dressed, but undisciplined; they'd moved two tables together and were loudly engaged in raucous laughter. This was the kind of situation Paul wouldn't tolerate in his club. Jan understood she was to monitor this party, so she immediately crossed the floor and pushed open the door marked "Staff Only." She emerged a few minutes later wearing a low-cut white satin blouse with billowing sleeves buttoned at her wrists and a long straight black velvet skirt. A black grosgrain ribbon circled her neck, meeting and crossing at her throat, secured by a small diamond clip Paul had given her for her twenty-first birthday.

Her appearance at Drew's table silenced the group for a moment as she told them if they'd like to order she'd send a waiter over. She did so, then was kept busy until closing time by her duties as hostess. She was pleased to notice that Drew and his company kept their noise level down for the rest of the evening and she caught several of them ogling her, Drew in particular. This amused her, as she considered these youths nothing more than ill-bred babies.

From time to time she glimpsed Crystal, who had apparently invited Paul to join her and seemed to be doing her best to hold his interest. When they eventually rose from the table, Jan was disturbed to see Paul escort Crystal outside. She breathed a sigh of relief when he returned a few minutes later. She caught up with him, asking, "Where did you go?"

"I walked her to her car."

"Was that necessary?"

"I don't believe you'd be interested in my reasons, Jan." His gaze was direct and cool.

"Paulie, it's just that—you know she's just a spoiled rich brat. Why do you bother with her?"

"I'm more interested in what I'm seeing in you. Jealousy doesn't become you, Jan." His distant manner a warning, he added, "Is there some reason I should be accountable to you?"

She stared at him wordlessly for a moment, then exclaimed, "No, of course not, Mr. Gregory. Why don't you do everybody a favor and go straight to hell!" She turned and stalked away.

I guess I deserved that. Too bad, he reflected, that Jan, who used to be such fun and who was otherwise perfectly suited to their dual lines of enterprise, seemed to be developing an unattractive possessive streak in spite of the fact that he'd recently been trying to maintain an impersonal relationship with her. She'd been indulging in flights of fancy lately, in which jealousy played a large part. It was clear to him that the little romance they'd begun several months ago had died a natural death before it had a chance to become serious. He wondered why she couldn't seem to understand what was so obvious to him.

He crossed to the bar and stood with his back to it, casually leaning on an elbow as he surveyed the room. Everything seemed under control; even Drew and his friends were quiet, their heads together as they conversed in low voices.

He reached across the bar for the phone and dialed Lili's number. When she didn't answer, he narrowed his eyes and frowned.

In the staff changing room, Jan tore her clothes off and pulled on her jeans and sweatshirt in frenzied agitation. She knew she should simply shrug and walk away from Paul forever. She might toss off something casual as she left, something offhand to show he meant nothing to her. But what she really wanted to do was slap his face, hard. That would be satisfying. As it stood now, all the satisfaction was on his side, while she suffered alone. And he knew she was suffering; that was what galled her. Determined not to appear the woman scorned, she opened the door of the dressing room, crossed the lounge, calling out, "'Night, boss," and left by the front door, head held high. If he wanted anything more from her, he'd have to come begging.

Chapter 15

L ili, alone in the narrow viewing room, stood transfixed as she gazed at the contents of the safety deposit box. Stacks of cash were piled neatly one on the other, filling it. Curious to know what all this amounted to, she nevertheless decided to lock it away without touching it, half-fearful that by putting her hands on it she might somehow compromise herself. She would have been unable to explain this fanciful idea, however, if she were asked. She'd leave it for later.

As she left the group of private viewing cubicles and re-entered the main bank lobby, Lili looked about furtively, as if frightened that she might be seen in a setting where she had no right. In spite of her resolution of only a few moments ago, she experienced a feeling of increasing elation. She'd never seen so much money; the top bills on the stacks were in denominations of hundreds, and the stacks themselves were tightly bound and compressed until no more bills could be accommodated. *She was rich!* She couldn't help but wonder just how much wealth was represented in that box, which wasn't one of the smaller ones, but quite a large container. She tried to tell herself it had nothing to do with her and that she wasn't interested. *But it does belong to you; Sam wants you to have it and it's in your name.* It took every ounce of her will power not to turn around and go back to the vault area for a closer look.

Driving back to the office, Lili's thoughts were filled with questions about Sam: Why had he given her this money? And why had he broken up with her? What was the real reason? By the time she pulled into her parking slot at the office she'd come up with no valid answers, only suspicions. Nor had she arrived at any sort of explanation by the time she drove home that evening. She understood that the only person who could explain these things was Sam himself; therefore, they might always remain a mystery. She wished she had someone to discuss it with, although she knew she couldn't tell anyone about her strange gift from him. She herself was unable to fathom his feelings and knew instinctively that she had to keep his magnanimous gesture a secret. *If only I could confide in someone.*

As if on cue, Angela Hoenig called, opening the conversation with, "Lili? Why didn't you tell me?"

"About Sam and me?"

"Yes. I just heard." Her voice was subdued.

"Sorry, Angie, I simply haven't wanted to discuss it."

"I understand." After a pause, she went on, "That's not the truth; I don't understand. But it's none of my business, except insofar as you're my friend. I'm sure you had your reasons."

Lili chuckled in spite of herself. "It's obvious you're an English teacher—or maybe you should be a lawyer. "'Except insofar as... '" She sobered as she added, "I didn't break up with Sam, Angie. He broke up with me."

"That bastard! How does he get off jilting you?"

"He's not a bastard. It was very hard for him; I could tell."

"Do you think there's someone else?"

"No, I'm sure there isn't. Maybe there will be sooner or later, of course, but at the moment I really don't feel that was his reason." Lili's tone changed and her voice grew stronger. "And it's pointless to dwell on it. 'Qué será, será,' and all that. It's over."

"Right! That's how I want to hear you talk. Shall we have dinner soon? I've just got past my deadline, so I'm more or less free for a few weeks until the next one."

"Yes, that sounds like a good idea. I'd love to."

"What about tomorrow night? My treat."

"Angela, I'm embarrassed to admit that I don't even know what day it is. What's today?"

"Boy, you are in a bad way, aren't you? This is Wednesday, making tomorrow Thursday. Where do you want to go?" Without waiting for a reply, she hurried on. "How about Pal's? It seems to be the place to go these days, so I've heard. I've only been there once, but it was a long time ago."

Lili drew her breath in sharply, then in an effort to appear unruffled, quickly added, "Fine. Six o'clock okay with you?"

"Six it is. I'll meet you there then. And Lili?"

"Yeah?"

"Chin up, kiddo. Remember my motto: 'And this, too, shall pass away.'"

"I know. 'Bye."

Angela and Lili met in the parking lot as they were getting out of their respective cars and they walked into Pal's together. As they stood trying to adjust their eyes to the dimness, Jan approached.

"Good evening, ladies. Two for dinner?"

Both answered, "Yes, please."

Jan led them to a table at the far end of the lounge, where she inquired, "Is this table all right? Or would you rather sit in the other room?" Lili wondered where she'd seen the pretty blonde before. Her face and her hair style looked familiar. All at once it dawned on her—she'd been the singer at her own engagement party.

"This is fine," Lili said and they sat down, wondering if Jan had recognized her, too. "It's okay with you, isn't it Angie?"

"Sure. There's probably more going on in here anyway." She looked up as a waiter appeared to take their drink order. They each ordered a rosé wine spritzer and were halfway through their drinks fifteen minutes later when Lili glanced in the direction of the bar and saw Paul making his way to their table. She had to run into him sooner or later, so this was as good a time as any and she might as well get it over with. She only had time to swallow nervously and then he was there, waiting to be introduced.

"Angela Hoenig, this is Paul Gregory."

"I'm pleased to meet you, Ms. Hoenig. Welcome to Pal's." Then, looking from one to the other, he continued, "May I join you?" He was already pulling out a chair.

"Yes, of course." Angela darted a swift glance at Lili, who would not meet her eyes. She continued, "I believe we have you to thank for some wine you sent to our table at Cosmo's one evening a while back?"

"It was my pleasure." He held a glass in his hand and took a swallow, then looked from one to the other. "Are you planning to have dinner?"

"Yes," they chorused, then giggled, much to Lili's dismay.

"Let me recommend the Steak Diane tonight. I'm told it's very good."

"We haven't seen the menu yet," Lili ventured.

Angela broke in with, "Actually, I'd like to start with some onion rings."

"I'm sorry, but we don't do any deep frying. It's too much to clean up on a daily basis. We try to keep it simple by limiting the menu."

Angela raised her eyebrows. "Do you work here, Mr. Gregory?"

"Please call me Paul." He smiled, adding, "Yes, I do."

"Angie, it's his place; he owns it."

Looking distinctly uncomfortable, Angela said, "Leave it to me to put my foot in it." Turning to Lili, she hissed, "Why didn't you tell me?"

Paul and Lili laughed, then he said, "Whatever you two decide to have is on me tonight." As they began to demur, he hastily added, "As long as you'll allow me to join you again before you leave. At the moment, please excuse me; duty calls."

He rose and went to the door where a large group had entered. He greeted people by name, as Jan called to a busboy to help draw some tables together in the adjoining room. The flurry of activity dispersed, Paul could be seen pushing through the door on the far side of the bar.

"Lili, why on earth didn't you stop me making a fool of myself?"

"I couldn't very well warn you in front of him, Ange. And it was a natural mistake anyone could make."

"Oh, well, what's done is done, I guess." She grinned. "His recommendation does sound good, doesn't it?"

Lili smiled and agreed as a waiter, bearing two more wine spritzers, came to take their order.

When they'd finished eating, the same waiter brought two small glasses of liqueur, presenting them with compliments of Mr. Gregory. Lili involuntarily glanced toward the bar where Paul was holding an identical glass raised in salute. She lifted hers in response, then let her eyes dart to Angie, who was smiling knowingly.

Lili squirmed uncomfortably in her chair. Paul was staring as if he couldn't take his eyes off her. Disconcerted, she was sure Angie was getting the wrong idea and shrugged her shoulders the slightest bit to indicate her ignorance of whatever game he was playing. Angie simply smiled back and winked significantly.

Lili told herself to stop acting like a schoolgirl and gave herself a mental shake. Lifting her eyes, she returned Paul's gaze as she recalled the personal agony he'd so recently caused her. Once she'd thought his intent look meant that she appealed to him, but she'd since decided he was too self-absorbed to share himself with anyone. She was now convinced that his meaningful glances weren't the usual masculine demands for attention preceding a love affair. Lili concluded that Paul was a loner, intent on achieving his goals for his own personal glory, and she intended to waste no time on him. She considered him cold and heartless, a man who wouldn't hesitate to use her to achieve his own ends; she'd already had proof enough of that.

And so she was pleased that with her newly found self-confidence she was able to lift her glass in a toast to him and while her lips smiled, her heart felt like ice.

Encouraged by a smiling Lili, Paul crossed the room to their table. Angela gestured to a chair and he sat, this time directing his questions to her. Flattered, her responses were enthusiastic and the three of them laughed often. When Lili eventually pushed her chair back and announced it was time to leave, Angie directed a reproachful look towards her.

"Don't let me rush you—you can stay, Angie. We drove here in separate cars, remember?"

"Oh, you're right, I know, Lili. We should go. Tomorrow's a work day for both of us. It's just that it's been so much fun."

Paul rose, saying, "I should get back to work myself." His gaze rested on each of them in turn. "Please come back soon."

"We will," they chorused laughingly and thanked him for the wonderful meal and company.

Outside, Lili said, "Angie, I'm sorry if you wanted to stay. I'm just tired. Please don't think you have to leave because of me."

"No problem. Don't worry about it." Then she grinned and added, "Actually, it's a good thing you brought me back down to earth. I was enjoying myself too much. That man is so attractive, he's dangerous!"

Lili agreed, but didn't reply. She gave her a quick hug, wished her good night, and got into her car. As she drove home, she realized she hadn't had a chance to discuss her windfall from Sam. Not that she was ready to disclose any details; she'd simply wanted Angie's reaction to a hypothetical situation. Paul had spent so much time at their table, however, that she'd not really had the opportunity to bring the subject up. It was just as well, she decided. Sam had asked her to keep it secret; this was something she would have to mull over alone.

Later that night, lying in bed, Lili dropped her arm over the side and called Buff. He came pattering over at once and settled down as she stroked him. *Dogs are surely one of God's most wonderful gifts to us.* She felt at peace then and so was able to sleep the whole night through.

Behind the bar at Pal's, Paul Gregory was vainly trying to reach Jan by telephone. Earlier that evening, after Lili and Angie had come into the club and been seated, he'd told Jan she could go home and to wait there for his call. He was now pacing up and down the length of the bar, a cordless phone held to his ear. As he'd walk one length, he'd hit the redial button and grimace as he heard the repetitive busy signal. Then he'd repeat the process. *She must have left it off the hook—it's been busy too long.* Finally, he exploded: *I told her to be ready for this call!*

Thinking dark thoughts, he pushed open the swinging door to the kitchen and beckoned to Johnny Hughes, who was busy at the sink.

"John, could you see to locking up tonight? I've got to be someplace and can't get back until later. Get Joey to clean up for you and you take care of the bar."

Johnny was already loosening the strings that tied the apron around his waist. "What do you want me to do about the cash register, boss?"

"You know where we keep the receipts. Balance the register and lock the checks and cash in the safe."

Paul was almost at the door. He paused, then returned. "If you can't balance it the first time, don't stay late. Just lock everything up and I'll take care of it in the morning." He clapped him on the shoulder. "Thanks, man."

He strode to the door and jogged to his car, jumped into it, turned the lights on and pulled away.

As he approached Meredith Manor, Paul slowed in order to execute the sharp turn necessary to reach his vantage point in the trees. As he turned, he glimpsed a white car leaving the Meredith driveway and decided to come back out and follow. All the

Merediths had white cars, so he couldn't be sure whom he would find himself shadowing. Crystal's white Mercedes convertible flashed past. He glanced at his dashboard clock; it indicated nine-thirty-four. Where was Ms. Crystal Meredith going at this hour and in such a tearing hurry, he wondered. He tailed her all the way into Carbondale, careful to keep well behind to avoid compromising his following effort. When he guessed she was on her way to Pal's, he took a shortcut, parked behind the building and let himself in by the kitchen door. Johnny Hughes, behind the bar, raised his eyebrows in question. Paul held his finger to his lips and whispered, "Continue with what you're doing. Pretend I'm not here—ignore me."

When Crystal walked in the front door, Paul was sitting at the bar and ready to greet her.

She smiled as she neared him. He realized again that she was truly an extraordinarily beautiful woman. Her abundant hair was long and voluminous and so dark it appeared black. Her eyes were large and dark, too, with lashes so profuse and long he thought they must be artificial. She was dressed in white—a white sweater with a cowl neck, white crêpe pants, a small white leather purse suspended from her shoulder by a slender strap, and on her feet were gold leather penny loafers. A golden sunburst ornament was suspended from a massive gold chain she wore around her neck. It looked heavy and very expensive.

She stopped when she reached the bar. Her full scarlet lips parted to greet him. "Hello, Paul."

"Will you have something to drink, Ms. Meredith?"

"Crystal." She looked meaningfully at him as she asked, "Whatever you're having. Or are you?"

"Yes, I think I will—now. How about a martini? Vodka."

"Perfect. Rocks."

He mixed and poured them, then impaled two giant olives with extra-long plastic spears and dropped them into the heavy rocks glasses. He handed one to her and raised his glass to his lips, his eyes seeking hers. She met his gaze and drank.

Paul came out from behind the bar and, taking her arm, led her to a corner table. Crystal was tall—the top of her head came even with his eyes. About half the tables in the room were full, several people sat at the bar, and almost every eye followed the movements of the handsome couple. Paul could see Crystal was aware of this and that she reveled in the adulation. He had to admit it was good for the ego—but bad for the spy business.

"Ms. Meredith, are you here to meet someone or should I flatter myself you've come to see me?"

"As it happens, I have." She dazzled him with a smile. "Come to see you, that is." He didn't respond, so she continued. "I thought that we could dine...," she paused for effect. "Then perhaps go for a drive."

Paul decided to be blunt. "The purpose of the drive being?"

"There's something I'd like to discuss with you."

"You have my interest, Ms. Meredith."

"Can't you call me Crystal?"

"I don't think so—maybe when we know each other better. But at the moment Ms. Meredith seems more appropriate somehow."

"Shall I call you Mr. Gregory?"

"My name is Paul." Before she could respond, he hurried on. "Let me get us another drink and bring back a menu."

"Paul." She looked down at her glass, then glanced up at him provocatively. "Don't bother with a menu. I know I'll be happy with whatever you suggest."

As he turned away, he thought, *Christ! She's going to be a handful. Where am I going to find all the time I have the feeling she's going to demand?* By the time he'd mixed new drinks and was carrying them back to their table, however, he'd already decided any time spent with Crystal Meredith would not be wasted; it would put him just that much ahead in the game.

———

Jan Janiczewski, looking even younger than her companion in her navy blue silk blouse and new white skirt, was thinking identical thoughts about Crystal's brother as he sat across the table from her in the Harlequin. *What a dump this place is,* she thought. But at least sitting at a table is a step up from leaning on the bar in the next room. If she could just play her cards right, she reasoned, spending time with Drew Meredith could pay dividends as well as save countless hours of perhaps fruitless surveillance. She realized she'd have to play it very cool with this character—she knew that he was easily apt to take offense at some imagined insult and fly off the handle. She could also see that it wouldn't take very much encouragement on her part to make him throw caution to the winds, not that he was the least bit restrained in the first place. At the moment he was touching her knee with his and she automatically moved away.

She began to question the wisdom of what had seemed like a good idea as she was driving home a short time ago. Her thoughts flew back to early evening at Pal's. Those two pretty brunettes had come into the cocktail lounge, she'd seated them, and then she'd seen Paul go over to their table and sit down. The smaller one with the pageboy hair style certainly looked familiar. She could very well have been the one with Sam Meredith when she and Paul tailed them to the Cave-in-Rock picnic area that Saturday a few weeks ago. *Of course she was!* And she herself had sung at their engagement party! She wondered where Sam Meredith was at that moment.

After Paul had spoken to the two women, he'd sent her home with instructions to wait for his call later in the evening. She was still smarting from his rebuff earlier in the week and was feeling rebellious, so why, she'd asked herself, should she blindly obey him? She knew that when he'd finally get around to calling he'd only tell her to watch the comings and goings at Meredith Manor and probably follow Drew if he went out. So why shouldn't she use some initiative and take some independent action on her own? Why shouldn't she simply call Drew Meredith, identify herself as the hostess at Pal's, and meet him somewhere for a drink? He'd been open in his admiration of her that evening recently when he was there with his rowdy friends; he'd remember who she was.

So that's what she'd done and it had worked— only too well. Now she was beginning to realize she'd need all her past experience plus a lot of imagination to keep him at bay. She sighed inwardly: he was so young and he had all this tremendous energy. If she could pull off this coup, however, she would certainly get Paul's attention and he'd be forced to admire her for it. It did look as if she were going to have to earn his praise the hard way, though.

"Let's have another drink, Drew." She picked up her glass, drained it and set it down on the table with some force.

He grinned at her lasciviously. "I know from the minute I saw you, Jan—can I call you Jan?—I could tell you were my kind of woman. Sure, let's have another drink, then let's drive around for a while, right?"

She groaned inwardly. It was going to be tough going trying to get information out of this jerk. "Drew, we only just met. I want to get to know you— the real you. Tonight let's just stay here and talk." Jan gave him what she hoped was a sincere smile.

"My life's an open book." He made a flourish with his hands. "You have but to ask and I'll tell all." Doubt momentarily marred his all-American blond good looks, lending the lie to his statement.

Don't I wish. "Tell me about your family, Drew." She rummaged in her bag for a pack of cigarettes. "May I smoke?"

"No." Consternation fleetingly crossed his face. "I mean, no, I don't mind. Go ahead. I don't think they care here." He looked around the room and shrugged, as if deciding that management's wishes weren't important. He spied a small metal ashtray at the next table and got up to get it. He set it in front of Jan, sat down again, and asked, "Why do you want to know about my family?"

"What I mean is, if I'm going to get to know you, I want to know all about you. And that includes your home, your family, what kind of things you like to do—and what you do to earn a living." She paused, then hurried to add, "I guess you don't have to earn a living, do you? I mean, you're a Meredith and all." She was flicking cigarette ashes into the ashtray too frequently, a sure sign of strained nerves. She made herself stop, then found herself playing with a matchbook cover instead.

"Yeah, well, all of us work—we all do something. Dad's probably beginning to think about retiring, but Sam works at the university, you know. He's head of Forestry." He was speaking hurriedly, as though his lines were memorized. "Crystal, she mostly works for the family—I mean—that is, she's always on call to arrange parties and entertain Dad's friends and lately she's been busy with Sam's engagement and wedding and all..." His voice trailed off.

"I'd like to meet Crystal and Sam sometime. Do you think I will, Drew? And what about you? What is it that *you* do?" Jan looked at him, her sparkling blue eyes wide in inquiry.

God, she's pretty, Drew thought. *For an older woman, she's damn good looking. And what a figure! But I wish she wouldn't ask so many damn questions. Does she know we're connected or are these just innocent questions?* "Me? I—uh, I try to help out as much as I can, you know." In a desperate attempt to change the subject, he asked, "What about you, Jan?" He felt daring, using her first name. "I've seen you at Pal's. You're the hostess or something?"

"That's me, I'm the hostess. Actually, that's my usual job, but I can sub for anyone there." She grinned, her dimples deepening. "Except the cook, of course."

A thought seemed to occur to him: "Hey, I recognize you now! You sang at my brother's party, didn't you? You're terrific!"

"Yes, I did. Thank you." He went up a notch in her estimation.

"Jan, I've got to tell you now. I think you're the prettiest woman I've ever been out with. Will you go out with me again?"

"Why, Drew! Of course I will, silly." She felt like a pathetic imitation of Scarlett O'Hara, but couldn't seem to stop herself. *In a minute I'll be calling for Mammy!*

"All *right!*" He sat back, pleased. He drained his glass and called for two more drinks.

It was a little after one-thirty when they left the Harlequin. Drew stumbled as he stepped across the threshold and Jan grabbed his arm to keep him from falling.

"Let me drive you home, Drew."

"Not on your life!" Suddenly cross, his strident voice rang out in the otherwise silent parking lot.

"I don't think you should be driving now, Drew. I'll take you home in your car and call a cab from your house to bring me back here for my car."

"There's nothing wrong with me. I usually drink much more than this and nothing's ever happened yet. Come on, let's get to know each other better." He began to pull her toward the white Taurus.

This is turning ugly. How can I stop him? "Let me go, Drew, or I'll call for help!"

Taking hold of her wrist, he jerked her to him while she flailed ineffectually with her free arm. She tried to slap him, but he took hold of both her arms. He faced her, pressing against her while his arms held hers behind her back. Pulling her to him, he kissed her fiercely, forcing her head back while she struggled to keep her balance. Twisting her neck, she wrenched her head back and made a sound of disgust.

She staggered back a few steps as he abruptly released her. "All right, Miss High and Mighty. I don't need you. I don't need anyone."

As he turned away, Drew's face was a mask of despair. He stood immobile, his brow furrowed. *Why do I always screw up? Why can't I ever do or say the right thing?* He turned and took a few steps toward Jan, who was already walking away, and called to her to wait. She either didn't hear him or pretended she didn't, for she kept walking. His shoulders slumped in defeat as he breathed, "Oh, Jan, come back!" He looked after her a moment longer, his arm outstretched, then straightened. *I guess I don't blame you. I've had enough of me, too.* He stumbled to the

Taurus, brought it to roaring life, and sped away, gravel flying.

Hearing the squeal of tires, Jan threw a glance over her shoulder in time to see the Taurus's tail lights turn out of the parking lot and disappear in the curve of the highway. "He'll never grow up," she muttered under her breath. "Just don't get too far away before the police can catch up with you, Drew." She hurried to the public phone on the wall, fumbled some coins into the slot, and dialed the number of the state police. At that moment, she heard screeching brakes and the unmistakable sound of metal being mangled, which seemed to go on endlessly as Jan shouted directions into the phone, ran to her Toyota and swung it mercilessly out onto the highway in the direction Drew had taken.

———

Crystal's mouth opened under the pressure of Paul's lips. He kissed her with bruising force as he held her crushed against the passenger door of her Mercedes convertible. *The door handle is probably gouging her back,* he thought with a mental shrug.

To his astonishment, she had casually flipped her car keys to him as they left Pal's. He assumed it was a signal she wanted him to take charge, so he'd driven to a quiet parking area overlooking Devil's Kitchen Lake where he knew they'd be alone. Although Crystal had been gazing at him in open admiration, Paul didn't delude himself that she was smitten with his masculine charms; he was certain she was softening him up for something. Now her sighs were giving way to gasps of desire, her hands moving down to his zipper as he kissed her closed eyes, then her mouth again, thrusting deeply with his tongue.

Suddenly he stopped. With an effort, he pulled away from her. He sat back and studied her as first she opened her eyes, then touched her lips with her fingertips as though they burned. He cleared his throat as she struggled to an upright position. "May I help you with something, Ms. Meredith? Why don't you tell me what it is? Then perhaps we can avoid this playacting."

She gave a throaty chuckle. "You're a cool one, aren't you?" He noticed she was no longer breathing heavily and was looking at him with frank approval. She went on, "You know, I like the way you look and the way you talk." She chuckled again, seductively. "And, of course, I like the way you kiss." Sobering, she leaned forward, maintaining eye contact. "I feel I can be honest with you, Paul. I've always preferred having men friends. For the most part, I despise women—they're generally so petty, so frivolous. And their interests are unfailingly mundane."

"What is it you want from me?"

"Perhaps nothing. First I have to decide if I can trust you." Her eyes bored into his. On close observation he noticed her impossibly long, thick lashes were real. He remained silent, studying her candidly. She didn't flinch from his scrutiny.

"Tell me, Paul, is there any truth to the rumors about you?"

"Are you referring to my reputation as a killer?"

She laughed. "I like that—you get right to the point. You're not a bit conventional, are you?" She smoothed her long hair away from her face as she leaned back against the door and continued to scrutinize him in return. "Yes, that's exactly what I mean."

Unperturbed, he responded, "I don't like discussing the subject; someone might get the idea it sounds like an admission." He raised an eyebrow.

"May I ask why you want to know? Or is it just idle curiosity?"

"You do look satanic when you do that, Paul. And terribly, terribly attractive." As she spoke, she arched one of her own eyebrows. "But back to business. I've been told—on good authority, I hope— that you are a thoroughly wicked man and it's on the strength of that sort of statement that I'm here."

"You want me to be wicked?"

"As wicked as possible."

"I don't suppose we're talking about sex here, are we?"

"No, darling. Although I do find you fascinating. And very, very sexy."

"Tell me what you have in mind."

"I want you to arrange an accident."

"From which no one walks away?"

"From which no one walks away."

"Single or group?"

"What do you think I am, a monster? Single, of course." She appeared to be unaware of any irony.

"I'd have to hear a lot more." He paused for effect, silently cursing himself for not wearing a wire, but on reflection realized she'd probably have discovered it by now. "And I make no promises."

"Of course." She pushed herself away from the seat back and leaned forward. "But before we discuss any details, let's talk about money."

"Let's not. Not yet. I need to know more before I decide if I'm interested." He turned away to peer through the windshield, then gave her a sideways glance. "What makes you think I need money?"

"Everyone needs money, some more than others."

"With me money is of little importance. I have everything I want."

"I don't believe that. You're not the kind of man to be satisfied with the status quo." She pulled a silver compact from her small white leather bag, and casually flipped it open as she applied her trademark scarlet lipstick. She looked at herself in the tiny mirror for a moment longer, then smiled as if satisfied with proof of her beauty, and snapped it shut. "Tell me if I'm right. I think you're the type who's always looking for something different, some new challenge, aren't you?" She turned wide, inquiring eyes to him and he knew she was measuring him.

"If I weren't, I'd be stagnant. Stagnation is fatal." *She understands me too well.*

Crystal was busy with her own thoughts: *His price is low; he simply doesn't want to be bored. With very little effort, the beautiful and clever Ms. Meredith can arrange to keep his interest level high. This is almost too easy.*

She smiled dazzlingly at him. "Paul, what I have in mind won't take much of your time. There's this female person who's getting in my way and she won't take a hint. She could be dangerous to me and my plans. I want her taken out." Her look was a challenge which he returned. She extended the silence between them for a moment before she continued. "I think we can make a deal—to our mutual benefit."

He said nothing, but made a movement with his hand, urging her to continue.

———————

Jan sat cross-legged in the road with Drew's head in her lap. His eyes were closed; he appeared to be resting and, although the skin was scraped along the left side of his face, his features were relaxed and his lips held the hint of a curious smile. A heap of twisted metal, the remains of the white Taurus, smoldered brokenly at the side of the road against the concrete abutment. The insistent repetitive scream of a faraway ambulance klaxon announced its arrival minutes before it appeared, but she remained motionless, afraid to move. When eventually the ambulance appeared, its massive energy slowing to a stop dangerously near her, still she sat looking down at the boy who had died in her arms.

For the next half hour while the ambulance technicians vainly tried to revive Drew's lifeless body, Jan remained sitting motionless in the road, her usually lively features a dull mask.

Two medics checked Drew's vital signs and, finding none, carefully placed his body on a stretcher which they put into the ambulance.

"Miss, we'll need you to come with us." A tall, thin young medic strode toward her, his arms extended to help her to her feet. Jan raised her head and, recognizing pity in his earnest gaze, allowed his arms to support her as she struggled to rise. "Can you follow us to the hospital? Will you be all right to drive?," he asked.

She nodded, then tried to speak. "Yes, I'll come."

She was surprised to find her throat felt raw, her voice little more than a croak. Idly, she wondered why, then memory returned with a rush. She'd been screaming, screaming from the moment she saw the fiery ruins of Drew's Taurus, screaming as she saw his unconscious body caught halfway outside the sprung door, screaming as she dragged him clear of the wreck, screaming until she became hoarse and her voice failed her. Tears had dried on her cheeks and, looking down, she could see enormous blood stains on her new white skirt. Though it had been only a few hours since she'd taken it from her closet, it seemed a lifetime ago in another world.

Chapter 16

The persistent ringing of the telephone endlessly echoed throughout Meredith Manor. Although answered promptly each time a telephone call came through, the calls, by their sheer number, were countless. Martin's appropriately subdued tones assured callers not only that their thoughtfulness was appreciated, but that unfortunately the family was presently in seclusion. He hoped they would understand. Invariably, they did.

When she heard of Drew's accident, Crystal had grown pale and would have collapsed had Sam not caught her before she fell. She was helped to her rooms, where she'd remained despite everyone's best efforts to communicate with her. First the servants, then Stephen, then finally Sam had tried in vain to coax her out. Although meals were regularly sent up, Crystal's door remained locked and, while the coffee and tea had been disappearing, her food for the most part remained untouched on the trays left outside her door.

Stephen and Sam spent countless hours in Stephen's study, while Martin kept the household staff busily grooming the mansion in the somber hues appropriate for a family bereavement. The kitchen crew prepared sufficient fare for an onslaught by the public.

"Dad, I want you to be aware of what I've done today." Sam looked at his father expectantly, hoping for his attention, yet afraid that Stephen might have again lapsed into melancholic musing, which tendency had recently become more frequent.

"What? Oh, yes, Samuel." Stephen's latest attempt to appear attentive failed. "Of course," he finished lamely.

"I've been in touch with Gates."

"Gates?" Stephen's brow furrowed.

"You know, Dad. Frank Gates—uh—Drew's customer." Sam spoke in simple, direct sentences. "I've explained to him that now, since Drew's accident, all deals are off."

"Yes, ah, Sam. Did he agree to that?"

"What do you mean, did he agree, Dad? What choice does he have? He has to agree. That's the way it is." Sam felt impatient, but tried not to show it. "What can he do about it? Report us to the narcs?" Sam made a movement with his hands, as if washing them. "I won't touch his money."

"Ah, yes, of course." Stephen again lapsed into silence, apparently abandoning any further attempt to appear alert. Staring into space, his head resting on the back of his chair, his hands folded in his lap, he reflected that he and Drew had never had a traditional father/son relationship. He now regretted they hadn't been closer. Perhaps if they had, he could have been spared this unfamiliar and unwelcome feeling of remorse he was now experiencing. Drew had been such a difficult individual, however. First he'd been an incorrigible child, then a trouble-prone adolescent and, finally, a demanding young man. *Finally.*

Suddenly he and Sam were jarred from their respective contemplations by the clatter of rapid footsteps descending the stairs, muted momentarily by heavy carpeting in the hallway as they neared, then the door to Stephen's study was flung open and Crystal burst into the room. Her hair was in disarray and seemed to float about her head like a dark cloud; her clothes were crumpled as if she'd slept in them, but she was most remarkable for the wild look in her eyes as she stood facing them, feet spread and hands on her hips in a classic position of challenge.

"Father, I just tried to call Frank Gates and he hung up on me!"

"Gates?" Abruptly returning to the present, Stephen frowned, perplexed.

Sam glanced at Stephen, explaining again, "Drew's customer."

"Well, Sam? What do you know about this?" Crystal was seething.

"I told Gates he has to find another laundry."

"What in God's name are you talking about?"

Sam rose to his feet, taking a step toward her, his hand outstretched, perhaps in supplication as much as in an effort to appease her. "The writing's been on the wall a long time—can't you see it? With Drew gone, now's our best chance to get out of it."

Crystal reacted as though she'd been struck. "You want to get out of it? Fine, get out!" She turned her fury on her father. "But you? You want to get out, too? Or do you just let Sam make all your decisions for you these days?"

Sam drew his hand back as he stepped between his father and Crystal. "That money's dirty, Crystal. It's narco dollars—it's black!"

"You're getting terribly sanctimonious, brother dear. You've been as eager as any of us to accept a share. What's happened to you?" Her voice dripped sarcasm. "Or should I even ask?"

"You don't have to worry about Lili anymore."

"As it happens, I'm not worried about her anymore." Her lips held a twisted smile that a part of his mind recognized as a threat.

"Look, Crystal, we talked it over before Drew... died. It's way past time the family got out of the business—we should never have been involved in the first place." He kept his voice lowered to a reasonable level, as if hoping to influence her to respond in kind. "It's vital that we drop Gates now."

"But what about me? Drew would want me to take over for him," she said with growing desperation. "You didn't even discuss it with me!"

"How could we?," Sam asked reasonably. "You were locked in your rooms." He walked to the window and pulled the heavy draperies aside to peer out. Crystal seemed to waver. Then she choked back a sob and started for the door. When she reached it she turned and glared at Sam, hatred burning in her eyes.

"It's all your fault, you know. You and that holier-than-thou little bitch. The two of you have ruined everything and I'll never forgive you." She opened the door, yet stood there for another moment as she lowered her voice and continued. "I'll get you for this, Sam. You'll be sorry." Then she was gone.

In the silence that followed, Sam said to his father. "I think I liked it better when she was screaming."

"I'll go up and talk to her, Samuel."

"I'd wait a while, Dad, if I were you. I don't think she'd be very congenial at the moment. Have a drink with me and then you'll be better able to face her if you still want to. By that time maybe she'll have calmed down. Although I don't hold out much hope that she'll ever see reason." He walked to the side table and poured two stiff whiskeys.

As he accepted one, Stephen said, "It must take a lot of energy to keep up that level of anger. Perhaps she'll exhaust herself." He turned and looked at Sam as he continued, "You know, she's very like her mother."

"Is she really? You've never told me that before. No wonder you..." Sam shook his head. "Poor Dad."

"Yes, that's why our marriage didn't last very long. Nora was the most completely self-absorbed person I've ever known." Stephen didn't seem to find his words ironic as he continued, "She had a filthy temper and it never took much to set her off. She could become quite physical when she was angry, too." Stephen rubbed the back of his neck, ruminating. "You know, I don't even know if Nora's still living. After our divorce, she simply disappeared and we've never heard from her again." He slowly moved his head from side to side and frowned. "I must admit I didn't try very hard to find her. She didn't need money; that was never a consideration. I'd offered it, but it was unimportant to her. Her family was wealthy." He looked up at Sam, perplexed, as he went on. "Nora left me and she left Crystal, her baby—never came back, never inquired about her—she just disappeared from our lives. I've always suspected it was another man—her ego demanded constant attention and by the time I'd discovered what she was really like, I'd lost interest in giving her that attention." He smiled again, as if in apology. "I suppose that's why I've always tolerated Crystal's behavior, perhaps more than I should have."

"You felt sorry for her."

"You could say that, I guess. Her mother left her; mothers aren't supposed to leave their babies, are they? If nothing else, a child should be able to count on its mother." He sighed. "Nora was quite unnatural."

Sam, remembering his own mother, couldn't help but agree. Death had taken her from him, but he was secure in the certainty she would never have left him otherwise.

As if reading his mind, Stephen smiled and said, "You're right, your mother was another story. Pam was a wonderful mother, as she was a remarkable wife. I've always rather felt that by my terrible experience with Nora, I earned my happiness with Pam." He managed to look unutterably sad. "It just wasn't long enough."

Stephen wasn't normally given to such self-revelations. Sam hoped to encourage the atmosphere of shared confidences as he fell silent for a few moments, sipping his drink.

"Too bad Drew couldn't have had more years with Mother. I've always kind of felt he would've turned out differently if she'd still been around."

"You were several years older than Andrew." Stephen paused, then nodded his head once. "But I see your point, Samuel. Those extra years you had with your mother were very beneficial to you, while the loss of them was devastating to your brother."

Sam rose from the comfort of the leather chair, stretched and looked at his father as he nodded agreement. "Yeah, Dad, that's what I figure. I'm no psychologist, of course, but I've always thought that since Mother's death, Drew has been looking for attention of one kind or another and that's why he kept getting into trouble. I'm probably being simplistic, but I think he missed his mother more than he'd ever admit and he's always been looking for—sorry, Dad, this is just my call: he needed love and guidance. He needed somebody to say no to him when he pushed his limits. When we were young I tried to help him out, but as he got older—probably when he needed me most—I deserted him. He'd get so obnoxious that I'd just take off."

Sam had been pacing about the room and now stopped to rub the back of his neck meditatively in a gesture similar to his father's. "But I think in the long run, Dad, Drew would have turned out okay. If he had to choose between you and me and the other side, I think he would have made the right choice."

"Do you really think so, Sam?" Stephen looked at him anxiously.

Sam was touched and hurried to assure him. "Yes, Dad, I really think so." He paused, trying to find the right words. "We fought a lot—brothers often do. But it was surface fighting. Deep down, we were allies." He came over and put his hand on his father's shoulder.

"His heart was in the right place, wasn't it, Sam." It was not a question.

"Yes, Dad, I'm sure of it."

Upstairs in her suite, Crystal frantically tried to reach Paul. She'd been calling him at Pal's for hours with no response, but at last someone other than the machine responded and she was politely advised that Mr. Gregory wasn't expected until noon that day and that no, the voice didn't know his private number. She wanted to scream at the imbecile, but forced herself to civilly ask if she could leave a message for him. When the voice told her he was kitchen crew, Crystal hung up without another word.

Now she quickly showered and dressed in a black silk blouse and a linen pants suit of dove grey, then made up her face and brushed her long hair until it crackled. She ran lightly down the back staircase, then out onto the patio. From there she entered the garage and a moment later backed her Mercedes convertible into the drive.

From her vantage point across the road, Jan dialed Paul's private number on her cell phone. When he answered, she simply said, "White lady bird just flew, heading your way." She listened to his response, nodded her head once and replied. "Okay, I'll stay." She hung up and slouched down in her seat again, watching Meredith Manor. She recalled sitting in this very position only a few short weeks ago as she watched a very alive, very vital Drew Meredith arrive in his white Taurus. After her emotional upheaval on the night he died, now what she felt was numbness and an inability to believe she'd never see him again. His had been such a forceful personality, whether you liked him or not–and many people didn't–you had to admit he seemed somehow larger than life. She was troubled by the thought that if she'd had more time to influence him, that if she'd played it differently, the story might have turned out otherwise and Drew Meredith might still be alive. She shook her head, trying to clear the image of his fiery death.

Paul frowned as he put his phone down. He started to pace, then he picked it up again and punched in a single speed-dialed number. When he heard a male voice, probably one of the kitchen crew, answer, "Pal's," he immediately said, "This is Paul Gregory. Who is this, please?" He began to pace again as he continued. "Are you alone there, Joey? Is anyone else in the restaurant who answers the phone? No? Well—did you take any messages for me?" He looked surprised at the response. There was a short silence, then Paul said, "I'm on my way in now. If anyone asks for me, say I'm on my way and to wait. Do you have that? Thanks." He slammed out of his house and ran to his car.

Forty-five minutes later Paul Gregory and Crystal Meredith were sitting at a table in a dark corner of Pal's lounge with their heads close together, as Crystal, her eyes huge and dark under raised brows, questioned Paul. At his reply, she exclaimed loudly, "What?" When he repeated his answer, she sat back in her chair, stunned.

He leaned forward, his elbows on the table. "What's wrong? Didn't you know Drew was still alive when Jan pulled him from his car?"

"No!" Her face was a mask of shock. "They said... I'd assumed he'd been killed instantly."

"No, Jan said he was conscious and able to speak, but he died soon afterwards." Paul added softly, "In her arms."

"Did she—did Jan tell you what he said?"

She looked tired and had obviously lost weight since he'd last seen her. Paul eyed her carefully, wondering how far to push the lie. "No, she was pretty shaken up, so I didn't want to force her to talk about it. The police brought her in to the station to question her, though."

"Why? What did they want?" Crystal began to chew the inside corner of her mouth nervously.

"Oh, probably routine. They have to go through all the motions, you know." His answer was purposely vague.

"Of course. Formalities." She was now trying to appear unconcerned, but he could see she was near her breaking point. "But I wonder—do you know if he... ?"

"If he mentioned your name? I can ask Jan if you want." Paul kept his expression bland.

"Maybe I can talk to her, Paul. Where is she now?"

"I told her to take a few nights off. She needs rest, so she may be sleeping—she's been pretty upset the last few days."

"I want to see her now," she insisted. "Could I talk to her tonight?"

"I don't know, Ms. Meredith. It's pretty short notice."

"Can't you ever call me Crystal?" Her voice was shrill, the familiar suggestion of teasing gone.

He didn't reply to her question. Instead, he said, "I'll see what I can arrange." He stood. "Excuse me, please. I'll be right back." She remained at the table, her face a pensive mask.

A few minutes later Paul returned, sat down and bent toward Crystal, holding her with his gaze. "She doesn't want to come into the club, but she says she'll meet you in the parking lot in twenty minutes." Her change of posture indicated a release of tension, as she relaxed against the back of her seat. He, too, leaned back in his chair. "Now, can I interest you in another drink or maybe something to eat?"

Crystal didn't answer for a moment and, when she finally did, it was clear her thoughts were elsewhere, so he politely excused himself and returned to the bar to greet new arrivals. A few minutes later he glimpsed her as she rose from the table and walked out the front door. Paul spoke to the barman for a moment, then slipped away to his darkened office where he stood at the window looking out over the parking area, secure in the knowledge the window's tinted glass kept him hidden. He saw Crystal approach her white Mercedes and get in. She'd only been waiting a few minutes when Jan parked in a far corner, got out of her car and walked over to Crystal's Mercedes.

He was tiring as he stood at the window, tension obvious in his posture, his every nerve strained. He found himself wishing the two women would wind it up and leave. He trusted Jan to handle herself discreetly, but was well aware Crystal had a quick intelligence that could not only scent danger, but deception as well.

He made an abrupt movement of surprise as Crystal got back into her car and slammed its door. He realized he'd allowed his attention to wander. He peered through the glass, straining to see Jan's expression as she remained standing next to the Mercedes. Curiously, Crystal lingered inside her car and he could see it moving as she seemed to rummage beneath the front seat. Then she lowered her window and motioned Jan nearer. Crystal handed something to her, then put the car in gear and sped away. He could see her headlights turn west as she swung out onto the highway.

Jan returned to the building, came directly to Paul's office, closed the door and stood leaning against it, a look of amazed satisfaction on her face.

"Well, boss, I think we've done it."

"What did she give you?"

"This." She covered the distance between them swiftly and handed him a pack of currency held together with a rubber band, which he quickly removed and shuffled the bills expertly through his fingers.

"There's ten thousand dollars here."

"That's what she gave me so I won't talk to the police. She promised me another ten later."

Paul raised an eyebrow.

"I told her I'd already talked to them." Jan smiled. "She asked me what I'd said, so I repeated what you told me to—that he mumbled something about his brother's girlfriend being in danger, that I must warn her to be careful of someone. I didn't say who, I just looked at her sort of meaningfully and let my voice trail off. Then she told me to call the cops tomorrow and tell them I was upset when they took my original statement. That I'd made a mistake. I'm to get the other ten thou in three months' time."

He gave her a quick one-armed hug, then dropped his arm as he said, "I guess she thinks three months should be enough time for the D.A. to bring her in if he was going to. Now we've got to find out what she's afraid Drew told you." He walked to his desk and positioned himself on a corner. "Are you up for continuing this?"

"Sure, Paulie. What do you want me to do?"

"Get in touch with her before she's had time to think much about it. Soon, real soon. You want to discuss something with her. Ask her if she'll meet you again."

"She'll smell a rat. What more could I have to discuss?"

He got up and walked toward her, placed a hand on each of her shoulders, looked into her eyes and saw the expression in them soften in response. "We need to know what else she thinks Drew said. Since we don't know for a fact what that could be, we have to fake it somehow..."

"Paulie, I really don't know! I don't even know what direction to come from. What am I looking for?"

"I think I have a pretty good idea." He drew back, frowning, as he gazed past her for a moment. Then he took her hand and led her to a sofa in the corner, skirting the low table in front of it, releasing her hand as they each sat down.

"Jan, we've got to have her on tape. Will you be willing to wear a wire for the meeting?"

She flinched, then quickly covered her reaction by consciously willing her body to relax. She adopted an expression of worldly sophistication, her brave words ringing false as she laughingly replied, "For you, Paulie, anything."

He pretended to be fooled by her forced optimism. "I knew you would." He told her about Crystal's approaching him to buy a hit for Liliane Greening and confessed his carelessness in not taping their conversation. He then told her his plan to nail the Meredith bank. "She's close to panic now, but she's still angry with her brother Sam for taking over—she holds him responsible for pulling the family's horns in. He took both her hands in his and smiled into her eyes, experiencing a twinge of guilt as he saw her begin to glow with pleasure. "Here's the way I want you to play it."

Chapter 17

Stephen Meredith sat at his desk, his head in his hands, darkness shrouding cloaklike about him. With great effort he raised his eyes and reached to switch the desk lamp on. He lifted the single sheet of paper and read it again.

"Lili," he spoke the words aloud as if to a living person in the room with him, "I wish you could have been my daughter-in-law for Sam's sake. He's so unhappy. But you simply wouldn't fit in with the way we do things. You'd have made a wonderful daughter, though. I've missed having one." He brushed the back of his hand across his eyes in a gesture that betrayed the extent of his fatigue, then picked up a small white box and tipped its contents out. Diamonds glittered as they fell to the surface of the desk.

"Very touching, father dear." Crystal's brittle voice penetrated the stillness of the room and he started from his chair, mood broken.

"You startled me. I didn't hear the door open." Then he frowned as he said, "How long have you been standing there?"

She didn't answer. Instead she said, "What was in the box? Are those diamonds?"

"Yes, Lili sent them back."

"You gave her diamonds? What about me? I'm your real daughter."

"What are you talking about, Crystal? These earrings belonged to Sam's mother. You've plenty of your own jewelry. How can you want more?"

"As your daughter, I'm entitled." Crystal had remained standing just inside the door, which she'd left open behind her. She was wearing a burgundy colored full-skirted dress with long sleeves and a high neck. Ebony and diamonds glinted at her ears and on her fingers. She was a handsome woman—regal in appearance, he thought irrelevantly.

Stephen rose from his chair and stood at his desk, leaning forward on his hands, looking at her incredulously as if seeing her for the first time. "Crystal, come to your senses. You're acting like a spoiled child." He took a breath and continued. "I gave them to Lili as an engagement present the night of the party."

"How can you give something of value—obvious value—to some mealy-mouthed stranger?" She took a step into the room, her skirt swirling about her as she stood with her legs apart, braced as if for combat. "Actually, she shouldn't have accepted them in the first place. They should have been mine." She broke off and frowned. "Why did she return them?"

"If you weren't so self-absorbed, you'd know that Sam's engagement is broken."

"The wedding's off?" She was incredulous. "Are you sure?"

"Yes."

"Oh, this is rich!" *I've arranged this complicated scheme to get rid of the Greening woman—I've tipped Paul off trying to hire a hit—and it's all for nothing!* She threw back her head and hooted with laughter. At Stephen's enquiring expression, she only managed, "You wouldn't understand," before being convulsed again.

When she brought herself under control, the smile faded and she resumed her bitter harangue.

"You shouldn't have given valuable stones to that Greening woman. They should have been mine."

His self-control deserted him. He snapped, "You're entitled to nothing unless I say so." He straightened, stepped behind his desk chair as if to protect himself. "I'm ashamed of you, Crystal. You're greedy and vicious. Sam says you..."

Her eyes wild, her voice rose as she shrilled, "Sam says, Sam says! Perfect Sam, Sam the Good, Sam the Firstborn Son, Sam Who Can Do No Wrong!"

"What's come over you, Crystal?" Stephen was amazed to realize he was afraid of her; there was madness in her laughter and glinting from her eyes. She seemed driven to the point of hysteria. *Had he overplayed his hand?* "This isn't about diamond earrings, is it? You're jealous of Sam."

She flung her head back and laughed. "Oh, really, father, you are a fool! I've always been able to do everything better than Sam, yet you think I'm jealous of him." She stopped, all trace of laughter vanished from her expression as she strode toward Stephen, her skirt swirling about her disguising the movement of her hand to a pocket as she withdrew a pearl-handled revolver and pointed its blue-black barrel at him.

"You and Sam robbed me of everything that's important. How dare you treat me as though I don't matter." She waved the gun for emphasis. "Tell me the truth, father, are you afraid of me? I count for something now, don't I? Remember, your sixty-sixth birthday looms ever nearer. There's nothing in the legend that says how you're supposed to die, just that you will die."

Stephen involuntarily clutched the high back of the chair, gripping it tightly as if it were a shield. "You're mad, Crystal!"

She laughed. "We're alike, father, you and I. You won't beg, will you?" She laughed again. "And I'd never beg either, not for your affection, not for my rightful place in the family." Mother-of-pearl gleamed in the light of the desk lamp as she waved the pistol at him again. "Aren't you afraid of dying, Father? Beg for your life."

Aghast, Stephen stared at her, then past her as a movement in the darkness caught his eye. Crystal spun around and fired as Sam raised his arm to knock the gun from her hand. She watched him as his knees buckled and he fell backward and crumpled to the floor, his face a mask of surprise, his remarkable green eyes wide and questioning, as the light slowly faded from them. Stephen bolted from behind his desk to kneel at Sam's side. In the sudden silence the acrid stench of cordite filled the air.

"Sam? I didn't mean..." Shocked, she swayed, yet remained standing looking down at her brother's body and her father kneeling over him. Footsteps muffled by heavy carpeting could be heard rapidly approaching the study, then Martin stood in the open doorway instantly taking in the scene. Crystal maintained the stillness of a statue, the only movement in the room provided by the pistol dangling from the fingers of her right hand.

Chapter 18

P aul Gregory held a cell phone to his ear with his left hand, while with his right he worked his hair out of the knot that held it together, then shook his head and raked his fingers through his loosened hair. He allowed himself this show of emotion only because he was alone in the privacy of his house at the lake.

"But Jan and I were about to close in. We had her thinking Drew—that's her brother who was killed in an car accident recently—had talked before he died. She'd already bribed Jan to change her statement to the police..."

Paul listened for a moment, then interjected, "She was about to break and we could have had them all." He paused, listening, then replied in a dead voice, "Yes, I guess she did break." Paul was silent as he listened, then uttered a single, "Understood," and broke the connection.

He wandered from his bedroom to the living room, crossed to his chair by the window and sank into it. He gazed disconsolately into the green serenity of the morning. He listlessly bent, lifted the newspaper he'd dropped earlier and peered at it again. The headline screamed "Second Meredith Manor Tragedy." Although he'd read the entire story in detail, he scanned it again as it related the sensational story of Crystal Meredith shooting her brother, Professor Samuel Chasen Meredith, who died before the very eyes of his father, banker and philanthropist Stephen Meredith. The elder Meredith had been incommunicado since witnessing the event and continued to be in seclusion in the privacy of his home. The family retainer, Edward Martin, had come upon the scene and observed the literal smoking gun in the hand of Crystal Meredith. Mr. Martin reported Miss Meredith herself had begun laughing hysterically as he telephoned the police. She was taken into custody and her attorney, J. Warren Hamilton, of the firm O'Brien, Roemig and Hamilton, had no comment for the press at this time.

Once more Paul let the paper drop to the floor, while he remained sitting in the chair by the window. His telephone rang, but he made no move to answer it, allowing the machine to pick up the call. He could hear Jan's voice, raised in agitation, announcing that she'd been trying to get him for hours and telling him again to call her as soon as he could. The phone began to ring again and, sighing, he got up and walked outside, taking the familiar path down to the water.

Standing in her kitchen, Liliane Greening stopped in mid-motion, her arm extended to a top shelf as the voice on her radio announced the death of Dr. Samuel Chasen Meredith. She turned toward the radio as if to better understand the news. Like Paul, she, too, walked outside, took only a few steps and stooped to reach the newspaper that had been thrown under a bush. She found her hands were shaking as she held the paper to read the lead story.

An hour later she returned to her coffee-making, her movements mechanical and slow. She discovered her mind wasn't functioning normally; its commands to her body seemed to be somehow short-circuited.

She was capable of only one recurrent thought: she would never see Sam again, would never hear his voice, would never feel the touch of his lips. She'd never again see the love in his green eyes as he smiled at her. She consciously comprehended, but was unable to believe he was gone forever. Not her Sam. Her eyes burned with tears that stung and her throat ached as she slowly proceeded to her bedroom and lay on her back upon the bed, her eyes open but unfocused. In the kitchen the coffee finished brewing, but she was unaware of it and, even had she known, she wouldn't have cared.

Although her lawyer pleaded temporary insanity on her behalf, Crystal Meredith was formally charged with involuntary manslaughter at the inquest following the autopsy. People found it curious that Stephen Meredith—her father, after all—said not a word in her defense. She herself spoke only when directly questioned, and then in monosyllables. Members of the press were not permitted to attend the inquest, but word was leaked that when asked if she shot and killed her brother, Samuel, she responded that she had; she hadn't meant to, but it didn't matter anymore. To the consternation and dismay of Attorney Hamilton, Crystal would say nothing further in her own defense, appearing content to remain in custody. When members of the press eventually caught a glimpse of Crystal Meredith, the famous beauty, they were appalled at her unkempt appearance and her dismal prison attire. Through the years they had been led to expect otherwise.

Sam Meredith's funeral was held three days later at St. Michael's on Main Street. The curious from all walks of life crowded into the church and later followed the cortege to the family's private cemetery atop a hill amidst the magnificent Meredith holdings where only a short time earlier Andrew Meredith had been buried.

Clad in black, wearing a hat with heavy black veiling to hide her face, Lili walked quickly to catch up with Stephen Meredith as he followed the casket to the grave site. She touched his arm and he turned, surprised; she was relieved when he offered his arm. She was also relieved to note that Crystal wasn't present, at least she hadn't had a glimpse of her either at the church or at the cemetery so far. She'd probably be under guard, she realized.

Stephen took her hand, saying, "Stay with me, Lili, will you?" Although he was perfectly attired and groomed as usual, he no longer looked sleek and self-satisfied.

"Of course I will."

"He loved you, you know. More than anything in the world."

At his words, Lili's careful control deserted her. She could feel the stinging behind her eyes and the familiar ache in her throat and she prayed she wouldn't burst into tears. *What could be worse than this unnecessary tragedy?* All the weeks of telling herself she and Sam weren't meant for each other, rationalizing their break-up—they were just empty words. *Why had this good man to die—and his brother before him? For what reason did their father have to become a shell of his former self, his future denied? Why? Who could profit from all this misery?* The minister continued to speak, but Lili wasn't listening. Her ears heard only the howl of despair and her heart was filled with anguish.

From the edge of the group gathered around the grave, Paul Gregory watched Lili as she stood with Stephen. When he'd first spotted her in the crowd, she'd held her head high and, although the veil prevented him from seeing her eyes, he'd known they were dry. But suddenly she appeared to crumple; her knees gave way and he could see Stephen's arm tighten around her to prevent her from falling. She was the picture of heartbroken despair and he experienced a feeling long unfamiliar to him—one of loss, dreadful and irrevocable.

Chapter 19

H er expression one of determination, Lili's hands gripped the steering wheel tightly and she frowned in concentration. Then, as if willing herself to relax, she took a deep breath, changed her driving position and forced a smile. She turned to look at Buffalo, who was curled up in the seat next to her and whose eyes were closing in the warmth of the day as they sped east along Highway 13 on their way out of town. A wicker picnic basket was nestled in a loosely folded blanket in the back seat, a book next to it.

As they were passing Pal's on their left, a midnight blue Mitsubishi stopped at the edge of the parking lot before pulling out. Paul Gregory twisted his head around, squinting to better examine the Corsica as it sped past, then spun the wheel to change direction as he accelerated across traffic to follow. *Maybe this will be my lucky day and I'll have a chance to talk to Lili–at last!* Even as he was experiencing the excitement that this opportunity might bring, he wondered absently why neither he nor Lili had changed automobiles. They were both driving the same cars they were driving all those months ago. It wasn't a question of money, in his case at least. Pal's had been doing very well; he'd even been thinking of extending the building to increase its capacity.

As she continued driving east, Lili soon found herself alone on the road except for a dark car a quarter mile behind her and so was able to leisurely view the panorama of burgeoning vegetation as she continued eastward. Impossible as it seemed, time had not stood still, seasons had moved easily from summer to autumn, to winter, to spring and then repeated themselves. She cast brief glances into her rear view mirror from time to time, eventually becoming accustomed to the lingering presence of the car maintaining its distance behind her. When she reached the exit ramp to Cave-in-Rock, however, she was mildly surprised to observe its driver following suit. As she reached the road at the foot of the ramp, she turned left and was relieved to see her follower turn in the opposite direction. She continued on this route until she found the turn-off for the secluded glen where she and Sam had picnicked on that lovely day when life was still good.

She parked the car, let Buff out and allowed him to run ahead while she retrieved the basket, blanket and book from the back seat. As she came upon the clearing under the tree with the water's edge a short distance away, she was suddenly aware of just how little everything had changed. Surely the undergrowth should have encroached on the little glade since she and Sam had last been here. The coming and going of the seasons should have altered it as well. But, she reasoned, it's open to the public; others would have picnicked here, placed their blankets where theirs had been, walked about, maybe danced to music they'd brought with them. She set her things upon the ground and shook out the blanket, allowing it to rest where it had lain when she and Sam had been here long ago.

It seemed only yesterday. Lili stretched her arms skyward and, sighing, sank to her knees, then positioned herself to sit with her back against the trunk of the oak tree she remembered, just as she had sat that time before. She opened the basket, lifting out a sandwich wrapped in foil, a bottle of fumé blanc and a stemmed wine glass. She unwrapped the sandwich, opened the bottle and poured the wine. She took a long swallow before she set the glass down. She picked up the sandwich and bit into it.

"May I join you?"

Lili drew her breath in sharply, spun around and began to cough. Tears of distress streamed from her eyes as her face grew red. She dropped the sandwich and pulled herself to a kneeling position.

Paul stood at the edge of the clearing, hands on his hips, and began to grin. The grin changed to a chuckle and finally he threw back his head and indulged in a full-throated laugh, before he eventually managed to sober. "I seem to cause this reaction in you whenever we meet."

Lili shook her head in dismay and rummaged in the basket for a napkin to wipe her flowing tears. Paul quickly reached into his pocket, withdrew a handkerchief and handed it to her.

"Use this."

She took it gratefully, wiped her eyes and blew her nose, then tucked it into the back pocket of her jeans.

"I'm sorry, really. I shouldn't have startled you."

She didn't respond, but gazed at him questioningly.

"I'll ask again: May I join you?"

"Why do you want to?" As she regained her composure, Lili resumed her position against the tree.

"You wouldn't answer any of my calls. Then you had your number changed and unlisted. You've avoided me for a long time now." Although she still hadn't invited him to join her, he came over and knelt before her on the blanket. Dressed in faded jeans and a gray sweatshirt, he should have looked typically American. Instead, she couldn't help but notice his choice of clothing had the opposite effect. He seemed more foreign, less ordinary than ever.

"The last time I saw you, Paul—that is, the last time we spoke—I told you then not to call me. After all that had happened—what I mean is..." She paused, trying to find the right words to explain.

"What you mean is, I was a part of your life at a time you don't want to think about. Maybe you even hold me responsible in a way. Am I right?"

"Yes."

"I was the harbinger of doom?"

She nodded.

"And so you resent me because you think I was the cause of your pain."

She nodded imperceptibly.

He sank back on his heels and studied her. "Then, if it's so painful, why are you here now? At the same spot where you and Meredith came that day and you picnicked here? I could hardly believe it when I saw you turn off the highway and drive to this place."

"That was you following me all the way from Carbondale? But you turned the other way at the junction."

"I saw you as you passed my place. I was just pulling out and thought maybe today would be the day I'd get to talk to you again."

"You just said Sam and I were here in this same place before. How did you know that?"

His gaze didn't waver; he compressed his lips and said nothing.

Her eyes narrowed thoughtfully. "You were following me then, too?"

"Not you."

"Oh." She looked down at her hands.

He stopped and eyed her quizzically. "But to get back to the subject, is it some sort of anniversary? Is that it?"

"It is."

"Don't you think you're being a little morbid, Lili?"

"Actually, no. But who are you to question if I'm being morbid or not? It's not as though it were any of your business." She saw the rapid shift in his expression, a sudden return to the remembered arrogance. This verbal sparring wasn't necessary; she felt nothing for this man, so had no need to hurt him. The breeze had picked up and she shivered involuntarily, frowned and again groped for words of explanation.

"This obviously isn't one of my more articulate days. You asked if this was an anniversary, Paul. The answer is no, it's not an anniversary by the calendar. It's just that it's the first time I could force myself to come back here. And it's a beautiful day, just like that time we were here before. When Sam and I came here I was very happy that day. So today I figured if I could stand it—if I could live through coming here, sitting in the same place, eating the same food, drinking the same wine—then maybe there's hope that I might get better. Not get over it—him—that will never happen. But I might get stronger. I'm trying to—I guess what I'm trying to do is..."

"Exorcise his ghost?"

She caught her breath at his words. "I think so."

"Are you ready to come out of mourning? Does this mean you're getting ready to live again?"

"I hope so." She was frowning at her index finger where she'd been avoiding his gaze by creating a hangnail. She took a deep breath, squared her shoulders and faced him. It was her turn to make him squirm. "Paul, long ago I asked you a question and you've never answered me."

He knew what was coming. "And what was that?"

"Is the rumor true? Have you ever killed a man?"

"This is important to you?"

"In a way I don't want to know, but I think I need to know for sure."

"Would you believe me if I tell you no?"

"I must believe you."

"I'm teasing, Lili. I'm sorry." He reached for her hand, but she drew back and he let his hand drop. "No, I've never killed anyone. I started that rumor myself because I thought it would help my cover identity as a bad guy." He shrugged, adding: "I don't even carry a gun."

She tried to hide her relief. "I think you've done a very good job convincing people you're a shady character."

"I must have, because a while back someone asked me to take somebody out for a hefty fee."

"You mean kill someone? How did you get out of it?"

"Circumstances took it out of my hands before I had to answer."

"Why didn't you tell me this years ago when I asked?"

"You were still tight with Meredith and..."

"You didn't trust me enough to tell me the truth."

"I was ninety-nine percent sure of you, but..."

"I could have ruined everything for you and your case."

"You could have. But that's not the whole reason. I guess I wanted you to like me and trust me enough not to believe what you'd heard about me."

She was wearing a long sleeved cotton shirt tucked into her jeans and as she looked up at him so earnestly he thought her charming. Charming and still vulnerable. She still had that same inadvertent seductiveness he'd found so provocative. She seemed much the same as he remembered her, yet he knew she was different. He tried to put a name to it and finally it came to him. Her spirit was weary, he decided, and wondered if he were becoming overly imaginative.

"It's been hard for you, hasn't it, Lili?" Even as he asked, he knew his question was stupid, inadequate.

She frowned and nodded, then tilted her head, forced a smile and changed the subject. "Paul, the invitation is belated, but please join me. Sorry I don't have another glass, so you'll have to share mine. But we do have a whole bottle of wine, and I'll give you half my sandwich." She pulled the basket toward her, lifting out a bunch of grapes. "And here, have some of these; they're wonderfully sweet."

Warmed by her apparent change of heart, he smiled, too, accepted the glass of wine and drank appreciatively. He edged closer and observed her carefully. He detected fine lines etched at the corners of her eyes and her cheekbones seemed slightly more prominent. She appeared older than he remembered her, but no wonder—it had almost been two heartbreakingly long years since he'd had more than a distant glimpse of her. But she still looked so lovely, so innocent and unspoiled that the shield of cynicism he'd wrapped around himself since childhood began to dissolve, and he felt unexpectedly lonely and hollow. He set the glass down and drew even closer, his eyes never leaving her parted lips, as he reached out, cradled her face in his hands and bent his head toward her. He saw alarm in her eyes as she reflexively drew back, leaving his outstretched hands empty, touching nothing.

This was the second time she'd thought he might kiss her, but instead his lips formed a meager smile as he said, "Don't be afraid; I won't overstep my boundaries."

She knew she'd over-reacted and, to cover her embarrassment, chattered about whatever came to mind. Then, on impulse, she asked, "Paul, do you know what really happened to Stephen?"

"Why are you asking me?"

"You're the detective, after all."

He sighed deeply. "Am I? You wouldn't think so for the amount of work I've been doing for the last couple of years. Lucky I kept my regular job."

Lili watched him closely. "I hear Pal's does wonderful business. It's always crowded."

"We've been lucky." He cleared his throat. "So you want to know about Stephen Meredith. Well, it seems he broke the legacy of the legend."

"You mean about dying at sixty-six? He's still alive?"

"Yes, he's still alive and probably conning someone somewhere in Brazil. They say that's where he is."

"You know, that's the rumor I heard, too, but it's hard to believe." She paused and feigned an air of nonchalance. "And Crystal? She didn't stay in prison very long, did she?"

"I don't think you'd like to be where she is."

"And where is that?"

"In her own particular ring of hell. Money comes from somewhere—probably from Stephen—to keep her in a very posh, very private and very secure home."

"Mental?"

"So I'm told."

"It's a kind of poetic justice, isn't it?"

"Uh huh. Like when the state confiscated Meredith Manor for back taxes and the university bought it."

Lili looked down at her clasped hands. "Yes, all those beautiful acres—and that mansion—all public property now."

For a moment they fell silent, each apparently lost in private thoughts. Then, seemingly on impulse, she asked, "Are you still working for those people, Paul?"

He was amused. "Those people?"

"You know who I mean, the government agency that had you investigating the Merediths."

"No." His amusement vanished.

"Why not? You seemed so earnest about your work." It was obvious he didn't want to discuss it, but she plowed ahead, thinking she might as well continue. She felt she was being gauche, but struggled on; she'd feel even more awkward if she abruptly dropped the subject.

He set his mouth in a grim line and changed his position to lie on his side, leaning back on his elbow and supporting his head with his hand. He frowned and looked up at her intently, as if recalling an unpleasant memory. "They began to give me little jobs, Lili. Small jobs any baby could do. I was past that—I'd done those things years ago when I first started out. And I was good, I deserved better. So I refused." He turned and positioned himself on his back, his hands locked behind his head and gazed at the clouds racing across the sky.

"You were insulted and your feelings were hurt."

"I guess you could say that. At the same time, I could understand where they were coming from. They thought I'd bungled the Meredith job because I held off too long. They lost confidence in me; it's as simple as that." He frowned again and went on,

"Maybe they were trying to discipline me, teach me a lesson."

"You wouldn't take well to being disciplined, would you?"

"How would you know that? You don't know me at all."

She laughed, "Oh, Paul, you're more transparent than you think." She darted a look at him. "Now you're taking offense. I've hurt your pride." She stopped laughing. "I'm sorry." A gust of wind made her shiver.

"Are you cold? I've got a jacket in my car." *Damn the woman. She zeroed right in on my weakness, yet she has me wanting to protect her.*

"No, I'm all right." She looked at him intently. "Did you hold off too long on that job because of me, Paul?" She couldn't seem to bring herself to refer to it as the Meredith case; she'd never been able to think of Sam in that context.

"I told you then that I was taking a chance on telling you. That was unprofessional of me; it was something they'd never forgive. And I should have gone in sooner." He grimaced. "It was my own fault; I've never forgiven myself either. I've played it over and over in my mind, though, and I can't see—with you involved—how I could have handled it any differently." His eyes asked her to understand. "I had to give you a chance to get out, to get away from it."

"To distance myself from the family?"

"Yes."

"Sam put the distance between us for me, Paul. I gave him the opportunity. He could tell I suspected something. He didn't want me to be hurt—if it all came out, if there was a scandal—and so he broke our engagement." She raised her chin and looked at him defiantly. "I didn't want us to break up. I pleaded with him, but he wouldn't listen to me and he left."

"That day in the coffee shop."

"Yes, that terrible day." She bowed her head and asked quietly, "May we change the subject?"

"Sure. You're the one who opened it, though."

Her head snapped up and her eyes challenged him. "All right then, let's continue. Why *did* you hold off? Exactly why did you want to give me a chance to get away?"

He returned her gaze. "Because I thought you were caught up in something you didn't understand. I thought you deserved a break."

She continued to regard him, waiting for him to continue.

"What more do you want me to say, Lili?"

"Is there more?"

He unwound himself from his position on the ground and rose to stand before her, causing her to look up at him as she sat at the base of the tree. He held out his hands. She took them and he pulled her slowly to her feet. When she stood before him, he put his hands on her shoulders, drawing her to him. He wrapped his arms around her, bent his head and kissed her gently on the lips, then slowly released her. "Didn't you know? Hadn't you guessed?" His voice was low and husky.

"Paul..."

"I never wanted to admit it, but I think I've always loved you. Ever since I first laid eyes on you." He pulled her into his embrace again, but didn't kiss her, and she rested her head on his chest. She could feel the strong rhythm of his heartbeat and marveled at how right it felt to be in this man's arms.

"How could you love me before you ever knew me?"

"You were the girl I'd always dreamed of, but never really thought existed. It was very strange; I was almost totally preoccupied with you; I couldn't stop thinking about you. I even dreamed about you—literally. And this was before we'd even met. I knew it must be love or something very like it."

He continued, as if by starting to confess he somehow couldn't stop himself until he'd revealed all. "When I began investigating you when you started going with Meredith I thought you were probably no different from the others I'd seen him with." She stirred in his arms as if in protest. "But as I got to know you, Lili, I could see you were different, even while I was telling myself not to be a fool."

She pulled her head back to look up at him, her blue eyes serious. "When you were investigating me, as you say. Was that why I kept catching you watching me?"

"Uh huh. Although a good P.I. wouldn't have let you notice him. In your case, Lili, I did it on purpose. I wanted you to see me."

"Why?"

"I guess I sort of wanted you to prefer me to Meredith and eventually break away on your own."

"You were pretty sure of yourself, weren't you?"

"I was until I met you. Do you remember the night we first met, when we first spoke to each other? At Cosmo's? Your friend was with you, then she left and I came over and we talked. And laughed? Remember how we laughed?" Before she could reply, he hurried on. "I almost kissed you then, that night, when we were standing by your car."

"I know," she said softly. "I think I kind of wanted you to." *How much time we've wasted, and all because we were afraid to trust each other.*

He kissed her again, more thoroughly this time, and felt himself go weak with wanting her. He held her to him as closely as he dared without hurting her. When he finally released her, they stood, breathless, looking deeply into each other's eyes.

With an effort, she broke the spell. "Paul, let's sit down and have some wine." She gave a shaky little laugh. "And finish the sandwich. And eat the grapes."

"If you want to." In one fluid movement he sank cross-legged to the blanket.

She handed him half the sandwich and took the half she'd earlier begun for herself. Then she broke off a cluster of grapes for him and poured another glass of wine, offering him the first sip.

He drank, then asked, "What's wrong, Lili? Are you afraid? Is this happening too fast for you?"

She nodded and nibbled abstractedly at some grapes, then seemed to reach a decision. "Paul, you have to remember it's been a long time since we've seen each other and then it wasn't in the best of circumstances. You know all about me; I've told you my life's story. And you probably know that my life hasn't changed in any significant way since we last met. You're a detective, after all—it's your job. But I know almost nothing about you—your personal life, that is. I assume you're not married, but I don't know it for a fact. I remember seeing you with a pretty blonde several times. Is she still in your life?"

"Jan? No, she got smart and married a guy who came to the club and fell for her." His eyes took on a faraway look as he remembered. "She was singing at Pal's one night and he was just passing through. But he came back the next night and the night after that and the rest is history." He smiled. "He was a lawyer, of all things."

"She just went off with him?"

"Practically. She told me all about him, that he was a nice guy, that she had a chance for happiness and asked me if she should take it." The expression in his eyes was soft as he said, "I told her she'd be a fool not to. She left that night."

"Have you ever heard from her again?"

"No. But he came in a month or so ago and we had a few drinks." He took a long swallow of wine as he remembered. "He'd driven over from St. Louis where he'd gone to take a deposition. Want to hear some irony? His firm was working on the case for the Merediths' bank and he knew I'd been involved with the investigation." At the stricken look in Lili's eyes, he broke off. "Sorry, Lili, but facts are facts. To get back to the subject of Jan, I wasn't taking any more sleuthing jobs and she wanted..." He raised an eyebrow. "Did you think that Jan and I... ?"

"You two looked pretty significant to me whenever I saw you together."

"That's what you were supposed to think. Jan worked with me, both at Pal's where she was my hostess, and on jobs in the field." He saw no need to try to explain their complex relationship; it was all ancient history.

"And there's been no one else?"

"Never. Oh, superficial relationships, sure. But no one real until I met you—and certainly no one after." He fixed her with a steady gaze. "And what about you, Lili? Are you... ."

"Involved with someone?"

"Uh, yes."

"If you've been keeping track of me, Paul, you'd know the answer to that question is . . ."

"No?"

"Yes. That is, I mean no, there's no one else."

He fell silent for a few moments, sipping his wine. Then he cleared his throat and spoke her name. "Lili?"

"Yes?"

"Do you think there's a chance for us?"

"By *us,* do you mean... ?"

"Yes. You and I." He turned to face her and grinned. "Let's go steady, okay?"

"Well, I'll have to think about it." Then she asked meekly, "Do you think we're too young?"

"That's what they'll say; they'll try to tell us we're too young."

"Too young to really be in love?"

"They'll say that love's a word, a word we've only heard..." He smiled, despite trying not to.

She was giggling, but managed to respond, "And can't begin to know the meaning of."

"And yet we're not too young to know..."

"Never mind," she was laughing hard now, her eyes shut tightly in glee as she took sobbing gulps of air. "No more!"

When her breathing became regular again, he pushed her gently down onto the blanket and as she looked up at him he could almost swear there were stars in her eyes. "I'll give you my high school ring."

"And I'll wear it with adhesive tape to make it fit."

"You're *my* girl now. Remember that." He kissed her again and again. They were alone together in the glade and time ceased to matter. Daylight began to fade.

Buff returned from an adventure with a squirrel and trotted back and forth at the edge of the blanket until they presently became aware of him. Lili propped herself on her elbows and looked around. "Paul, I think it's time to go." She got to her feet, running her fingers ineffectually through her hair.

"Leave it alone. You look beautiful."

She felt her heart melt again as she gazed at him, remembering the night long ago when she'd originally become aware of him. She found herself thinking her first impression of him had been half-right—he was astonishingly good looking—but she'd been wrong in judging him arrogant and egocentric. Although there had always been a quiet assurance in his manner, she knew now it was borne of a subtle strength and intelligence that few men possessed.

They drove back in their respective cars, hers in the lead. When they reached her house, he saw her safely inside, kissed her and gave her a quick hug.

"See you tomorrow?" His breath on her cheek felt good.

"Of course."

"I'll pick you up at seven. We'll eat at Pal's, all right?"

She nodded happily.

"Until then." He returned to his car and, as he drove off, he felt as though a weight had been lifted from his shoulders. At last he was free to laugh, to enjoy life—free now that he had this beautiful innocent woman for his own. His heart sang.

Inside, Lili locked the door, turned and leaned against it with her eyes closed and a beatific smile on her lips.

Over the next few weeks, her growing interest in Paul produced a subtle change in Lili. It was as if events were edging her toward a greater maturity; she felt confident and secure; her life seemed to have some direction and purpose at last. More important still, she was happy; she actually looked forward to the days ahead.

With Sam she'd felt as if she were powerless, a bystander being swept along by his forceful magnetism. Perhaps she would never love another man as she had loved the idea of Sam. She knew she would never lose the memory of the depth of her feeling for him. But there was already a growing distance between herself and Sam as she began to realize, little by little, that he represented the past and, no matter how much she might miss him, she would be a fool to hold too tightly to his memory, as he had no place in the present or the future. The quixotic notion occurred to her that she and Sam had dwelt in the house of yesterday; he could not join her in the house of today.

Her relief was almost palpable as she slowly began to comprehend she had the strength to control her memories now.

———————

A sign spanning the double front doors of Pal's announced it was closed for the evening. The supper club, however, was dimly lit and two figures sat at a secluded corner table. Darkly handsome, he raised his glass to her, manifestly absorbed. Not a word was spoken as she raised her glass in response. They were drinking *egri bikavér,* a strong, dark Hungarian wine Paul had produced from behind the bar. He had placed a deep blue velvet ring box on the table between them. Lili couldn't help but remember the night when Sam had presented her with his magnificent diamond ring while they drank champagne. That ring was now in the safety deposit box along with the stacks of untouched cash.

Paul said, "You're thinking of the night Meredith gave you that flashy ring, aren't you?"

She shook her head, yet couldn't help looking sheepish. *It's uncanny how he can see right through me.*

"And you're going to be sad and sentimental."

"No, Paul, really I'm not." She looked about, self-consciously.

"Then why don't you open it? Do you want me to do it for you?"

She nodded.

He shot her a desperate look and suffered a moment of indecision, realizing that a situation like this where he could feel so ill at ease could never have happened in his professional life. But this love business was something else again. In the past, he'd armored himself against such feelings with a show of detachment and professional skepticism. Without such protection his job would have been more painful, less bearable. So now, even as he was about to irrevocably commit himself emotionally, he rebuked himself for his sentimental lapse. He'd been a fool to have allowed himself to be drawn toward Lili's obvious innocence and warmth. He inexplicably felt as if he were standing at the brink of an immense chasm, that if he went forward he'd be making a great mistake.

It was her turn to read his mind. "Paul? Are you having second thoughts?"

"No lies between us, right, Lili?"

His words chilled her. "No lies, Paul."

"I think you're not ready to make a commitment—to me or to anyone. I think Sam Meredith is still between us."

Her eyes appeared to darken with the intensity of her feeling. "He's not between us, Paul, I promise." She hesitated and frowned. "I'm not sure if I can explain it, but I'll try." She took a deep breath. "I loved Sam very, very much. Rather, I loved the idea of who I thought he was." She paused, caught her lower lip between her teeth and looked up at him, but when he didn't respond, she went on. "My idealized Sam represented something I thought I'd never have, never be able to attain, and when I found he loved me—*me*—I was in heaven. That period in my life is something I'll never forget." She shrugged and shook her head in denial. "I can't forget it."

She'd been glancing at the glass of wine in her right hand, at her left index finger tracing circles on the tablecloth, at the flame of the candle. She looked up at him again, peering through the candlelight to see if he understood, but his expression was unreadable. "When Sam broke up with me I thought my life might be over. When he was killed, I was sure of it." She looked away, then back again. "I don't know how I would have survived the constant thoughts of his death, the pointlessness of it all, if I didn't have the other part of my dream to lose myself in."

"The other part of your dream?" He frowned. "What is that?"

"I've been working on a novel I started before we'd even met."

"Sorry if I'm a little slow, but I... wait a minute! That night we ate at Rosewood Inn... you did tell me you were working on a book. I'd forgotten about that. Sorry." He paused a couple of beats. "What's it about?"

She hoped she didn't appear coy. "I don't think you'd be interested."

"C'mon, Lili," he teased. "Now you've got to tell me."

"It's a romance."

"Oh." He looked pained, trying to think of something agreeable to say.

She was amused. "I told you you wouldn't be interested. It's not your kind of thing at all. You, the man of action, reading a book about relationships?" She couldn't hide a smile. "Anyway, I wrote almost every night after work and on every weekend." She chuckled again, remembering. "I can't tell you how many times I rewrote it." She sobered and looked up, as if making an admission. "Actually, Paul, that day you came to my solitary picnic?"

He nodded, motioning her to continue.

"I'd completed the final rewrite the night before. 'No more rewrites,' I told myself. 'If it's not finished now, it never will be.'" She looked at him in perplexity. "You know, I could spend the rest of my life rewriting and always find something else to change. It was then that the idea of the picnic came to me."

"I'm glad it did." He put his hand on hers.

"The point I've been trying to make is this: Working on my dream, acting on it, saved me from dwelling on the past, on what might have been *if only*—you know the 'if onlies?'"

He nodded grimly. "I do indeed."

"They can drive you mad." She shuddered. "I stayed so busy working days at the office and writing at night that it kept me sane—reasonably." She paused before continuing. "I think I might have been stalling so as to never really finish it. I needed to be writing about my characters' problems so I wouldn't think about my own. Because I couldn't solve what had happened to me."

"But you say now you've finished it."

"Yes. And now you're in my life." Quiet settled between them as they gazed at each other.

Lili broke the silence. "Getting back to the Meredith family, I think you should know it wasn't all happiness and light while Sam and I were going together. His sister was impossibly cruel and his brother, Drew... well, I've never been sure of him and his loyalties. On the surface he was civil."

Paul spoke at last. "He was a hothead, but I think, if he'd lived, he might eventually have... stabilized."

"Maybe so." She sighed again. "Anyway, what I'm trying to explain is this: I can't believe Sam was what you said he was." She rushed on before he could interrupt. "No matter how sure you are of your own opinion, I know in my heart he was a good man."

"What makes you so sure?"

"He had a particular kind of integrity, scruples— no, let me finish. I can't explain how I know; I just know. And he was so kind to me. He loved me."

He searched her face for traces of self-deception and could find none. She really did believe Sam was an innocent victim. Now he could see at last that she needed to believe this or she'd be forced to relinquish her romantic dreams of days gone by. To admit she'd been fooled would be the same as confessing their love had never been, for the person Lili *was* could never have loved Sam, the criminal Paul knew him to be.

At that moment he knew his instinct had been right, that he'd finally found the only woman who could make him happy—her idealism, loyalty and her own strong sense of honor matched his own. She was unique and he resolved to keep her unchanged. And so, paradoxically, he decided to protect her by telling a lie.

"Lili, I have something to confess: I'm ashamed to say I've been jealous of Meredith, so I never did get around to telling you the final results of my investigation." He clasped his hands before him on the table and rubbed his thumbs together. "The Meredith bank was laundering money from many sources—funds from embezzlement, extortion, drugs, theft, prostitution, you name it. Stephen, Crystal and Drew were all in it up to their eyebrows. Sam was cleared, though. As a director of the bank, he wasn't hands-on; he only learned about it near the end. And when Crystal was waving that gun around, Sam sacrificed himself to save his father. She finally admitted as much."

Lili's sudden, dazzling smile spoke volumes. "I knew it, Paul, I knew he was innocent." She reached across the table and took his hand. "Thank you, my darling."

She sat back, quick tears glistening in her eyes. She gazed at him, loving him—his smooth olive skin, his brilliant dark eyes, his flashing smile. His every movement and expression were familiar and dear to her now. Moreover, she realized she'd love him no matter how he looked. She loved him because she knew finally and irrevocably that she could trust him completely. Although the life he'd led until now represented a past filled with intrigue and danger, she understood he was the man he'd become because of these things. She felt secure in his love; he had the power to make her feel cherished.

He didn't want to talk about the Merediths anymore. "What will happen to your book now?"

"Oh," she shrugged, "I suppose I'm as ready as I'll ever be to send it on its way and hope for the best."

"Your book was your dream?"

She shook her head. "First I thought my dream was Sam—but he turned out to be an illusion. Then I thought my dream was my novel." She looked deeply into his eyes. "I don't know why I didn't realize it long ago, Paul. But all the time my dream was you."

He was immediately ashamed for ever having doubted her. He searched for something to say, but before he could reply, she reached for the velvet box.

"May I have this now?"

"No, give it to me, please."

She wordlessly handed it to him and he opened it. She had a fleeting impression of a sparkling flower. He removed a ring where a brilliant central diamond was encircled by garnets cut to resemble flower petals, the stones intricately worked into a delicate raised gold setting. Taking her left hand, he slid it onto her third finger.

She gasped at its beauty.

"I love you, Lili."

"And I love you, Paul."

"Are you happy?"

"Terribly, wonderfully, beautifully happy."

"Will you marry me?"

"Of course I will."

He leaned forward and raised her hand so that the ring gleamed in the candlelight. "How long will you love me, Lili?"

"For the rest of my life. And Paul—" she paused to take a breath. "How long will you love me?"

He whispered a few words in Hungarian.

Puzzled, Lili smiled and frowned a question.

"You asked how long will I love you. I replied, 'only forever.'" His eyes continued to hold hers. "And I don't care what Gibran or any other philosopher says. You and I shall dwell together—and happily —in the House of Tomorrow."

Epilogue

"C'mon, Lili, have a heart," Angela Hoenig's voice on the telephone coaxed. "It's only for a few hours. What do you have to do instead?"

Aware that she didn't have a valid reason for refusing other than that she simply didn't want to go, Lili relented, sighing inwardly. "All right, you win, Angie. What time do I have to be there?"

"Cheer up, kiddo. You're not being tried in the Star Chamber, you know. It's only a reception where you'll be fed pastries and tea or sherry. All you've got to do is wax eloquent about our current luminary author's latest published work. I'll get a copy over to you."

"Do I have to read the whole thing?" Lili knew she should make an effort to be more gracious. *But I'd really rather be with Paul.*

"Skim it. You're a researcher, after all—you'll be able to pull out the main points. Then try to sound enthusiastic."

Lili didn't reply, so Angie continued, "How long have you and Paul been married?"

"A year next Sunday. Why?"

"You always used to like coming to our English Department receptions."

"I know, Ange, and I'm sorry. It's just that..."

"You'd rather be with Paul."

"Am I that obvious?"

"You are." She paused. "If this is going to work a hardship on you," she cajoled, "then don't..."

Chagrined, Lili broke in, "Of course I'll come! How soon can I see the book?"

"It's on its way—I've already put it in inter-office mail. And Lili?"

"I'm still here."

"You told me once that Paul was interested in Kahlil Gibran's philosophy."

"That's putting it a bit strongly. He was intrigued by one of his ideas—that we can only live in the house of today. Only our children can live in the house of tomorrow; we can't even visit." Lili laughed. "Now, you know Paul, he doesn't like to be told what he can't do."

"Well, here's another of Gibran's thoughts for you. In his treatise *On Marriage,* he also wrote, 'Let there be spaces in your togetherness.'"

Lili hooted. "Have you been waiting to tell me this? You are, are you not, implying that I'm smothering my husband? I love him too much?"

Angie's voice dropped. "Of course not. I'm only teasing." Lili could hear the smile in her voice as she continued, "And I'm probably a little envious, too. You and Paul were meant for each other."

"Don't say that, Ange."

"Why ever not? It's true."

"I don't know—it's sort of like tempting fate."

"Why, Liliane Greening, uh, Gregory—don't tell me you're superstitious!"

"I try not to be. It's just that—it's hard to explain—and I don't even know if I can. But Paul and I..." A silence fell and lengthened.

"Paul and you what?"

"You'll laugh."

"Now you've got to tell me."

"We're almost too good to be true. I'm afraid—I'm honestly a little afraid something will happen to separate us."

"Like one of the gods will look down from Mount Olympus and be jealous of your happiness and send an imp to spoil it?"

"I knew you'd laugh!"

Angela sobered and explained, "I'm not laughing at you, silly. But I never cease to be amused at human nature. See, in your case, you feel you somehow don't deserve to be happy with Paul—don't ask me why. And so, it must be wrong. Therefore, since this happiness is wrong, it must be punished. And what could be the worst punishment? Losing him."

She paused, not for effect, but to choose her words thoughtfully. "Be careful, my dear Lili, that you don't make this a self-fulfilling prophecy."

As if... Lili forced a laugh and changed the subject. "So—I'll see you Sunday. Let me know what time."

When Lili replaced the receiver in its cradle, she stood looking down at it as she thought about what Angie had said. As if she'd ever do anything to lose Paul. Nothing could ever separate them—she loved him so.

Printed in the United States
1535100002B/56